JOEL AUSTIN

REGIME CHANGE

VINCI
BOOKS

Vinci Books

vinci-books.com

Published by Vinci Books Ltd in 2026

1

A CIP catalogue record for this book is available from the British Library.
Paperback ISBN: 9781036705374
The EU GPSR authorised representative is Logos Europe, 9 rue Nicolas
Poussion, 17000 La Rochelle, France contact@logoseurope.eu

By Joel Austin

Frank Sherman Thrillers

Happenstance

Reckoning

Perpetua

Nomad

The Last One Out

Regime Change

A Long Violent History

The Old War

To all the wonderful and colorful characters in my life that make writing enjoyable.

Chapter One

Equatorial Guinea, West Africa

The room jittered into focus like a kaleidoscope, with each piece slowly fitting into the next. First came the ceiling, dirty and stained. Then came the fan, squeaking and vibrating with each languid rotation. Sergeant Raylan Gournsey's eyes slid painfully across the spackled surface. His head hurt —no, throbbed—with the blows of thousands of tiny hammers. A hangover of epic proportions. Not since high school had he felt so terribly useless the next day… assuming it was morning. Sunlight streamed through the blinds, which meant daytime, although he did not know the exact time. The thin plastic slats also showed a more salient fact. This was not his hotel room. His had curtains and no fan, nor a water-stained ceiling.

Not my room, he thought.

The strangeness did not bother Gournsey. He'd woken up in many mysterious places over the years. During his junior year of high school, it was a coal mine in his home state of Kentucky after too much bourbon. Then a jail cell in Lexington right before he enlisted. He'd even woken up in a flattened kiddie pool two houses down from the Base Commander's house in Japan.

Despite his checkered history, Gournsey had not blacked out in years. This meant one of two things—he had a great night and would suffer the consequences, or he had already suffered some indignities, and more were coming.

Gournsey searched his memory for any sliver of the previous night but came up empty. Nothing. A dark hole of hours. But how many? He raised his arm, took a painful glance at his watch, and couldn't recall anything in the last… twelve hours.

Not great, he thought.

Despite the piercing pain in his skull, he chanced a glance around the room.

The walls were off-white in color and smudged with dirt, but not disgusting. A lone picture hung on a wall above a plain pine dresser. The image looked stock, like it came with the frame and no one bothered to change it.

Tilting his head further, Gournsey discovered a wooden chair in the corner and a nightstand next to the bed, on top of which were an alarm clock and a set of keys.

Keys to what?

Attached to the keyring was a tag—a big green plastic diamond like dozens of cheap motels used. The realization brought him some comfort. He'd had the foresight to sleep off his bender away from his unit and the other Americans.

Assuming he was still in Africa. Still in Equatorial Guinea. Still on the main island.

A lot can happen in twelve hours, he thought.

The sounds of movement outside the door gave Gournsey reason to sit up. He didn't want to, nor did the hammering pain make it easy, but he realized there wasn't a stitch of clothing on his body. Anyone coming into the room would be in for an awkward sight.

Elevating his torso took a good deal of effort and two waves of nausea, but he managed. His mind ached. His body shook.

Worse hangover ever, he thought.

The scuffling outside grew louder, then came a knock at the door. Gournsey rolled to his right and looked for his pants. Finding none, he rolled to the left.

What he found on the floor was not any form of clothing, but a naked young woman face-down on the brown tile floor. Gournsey knew death intimately, and it didn't take him more than a glance to know the woman was dead.

Crap, he thought.

The knocking grew louder, but Gournsey couldn't take his eyes off the woman. She was painfully young and exquisite—a local to the country if not the region. Her beauty and youth only made the tragedy even more powerful. Life snuffed out before it could shine brightest.

The knocking stopped, and Gournsey looked up in time to see the door frame splinter apart as four men charged into the room.

"*Policía!*" they shouted.

Their dark blue uniforms were a blur of movement in Gournsey's eyes. He pointed down toward the woman as if to say, 'get help,' but the words caught in the dryness of his mouth.

He raised his arms in the face of the armed officers as they encircled him. A fifth man stepped inside the cramped motel room. He was thicker than an oil drum, wore a shiny polo shirt, and smelled of aftershave.

"*Estas bajo arresto,*" said the shiny man.

Gournsey's Spanish was rusty, but he didn't need a translation. Those twelve missing hours loomed large in his mind. He looked at his hands and then down at the woman on the floor.

I didn't, did I? he wondered.

Chapter Two

On the other side of Malabo, in a much nicer hotel, Captain Frank Sherman enjoyed a cup of coffee under the shade of a banana tree. The coffee contained plenty of cream, and Sherman contented himself with watching the hotel guests.

At the closest table, a Spanish couple on holiday bickered passionately over a plate of cured meats. Beyond them, a businesswoman read a German newspaper, no doubt several days old. She ignored the loud couple and took notes in a small journal. Further out, with his back to the wall, sat a wiry man in athletic clothes. Sherman guessed he was a shade over fifty, but fit and deeply tan. Not the kind you got in a store, but the sort burned into your very soul by sheer toil under its rays. The man's eyes skittered around, and he spoke accented English the way only Afrikaans speakers could.

None of the guests surprised Sherman or seemed out of place. West Africa drew all sorts. Equatorial Guinea was no exception. The capital, Malabo, had a quiet majesty that

Sherman couldn't shake. Something about the air or the light made the world sing.

A Saturday morning with no agenda only buoyed his contentment. Sherman's team had landed a week before at the behest of some Equatoguinean general who'd gone to school with a senior leader at the State Department. They called it a *Joint Combined Exchange Training*. Sherman called it a vacation.

State put them up in the fancy hotel around the corner from the embassy, and in return, they trained a small Equatoguinean army unit in counterterrorism. The soldiers were motivated but not exactly skilled, and Sherman had spent most of the last week covering the basics.

Behind the scenes, in private rooms and dark booths, people in suits gushed about economic ties and negotiated mineral rights. Sherman tried not to listen, lest their sleaze spoil the beauty of Bioko Island. A vacation was a vacation, and he was intent on enjoying it.

The waiter, a man named Diego, approached and smiled. He and Sherman liked to play a game of linguistic 'guess who' each morning. Diego spoke at least a dozen languages and enjoyed Sherman's unusual background.

"*Bonjour Monsieur,*" said Diego with a low bow.

"*Bonjour. Comment allez-vous?*" asked Sherman, whose French remained sharper than his Spanish.

Diego smiled and didn't miss a beat while switching to German. "*Sehr gut. Wie geht es dir?*"

The businesswoman glanced in their direction upon hearing her native tongue, but quickly returned to note-taking.

"*Gut. Mehr Kaffee, bitte,*" replied Sherman. The exchange exhausted his German skills, save for swapping coffee for beer or schnitzel.

Diego nodded and left to retrieve a fresh pot of coffee.

The morning smelled of hibiscus and jasmine with just the faintest hint of unregulated car exhaust and raw sewage. Even in the early hour, Sherman's shirt clung to him like plastic wrap, and clouds loomed heavy in the distance.

When the waiter returned, he had the pot of coffee and a visitor. One of the embassy staff trailed behind Diego. The American looked flushed and out of breath as if he'd run the quarter-mile to the hotel. Sherman recognized the thin, pale face, but couldn't recall the name.

Something British sounding, he thought.

"You have a visitor," Diego announced. The switch to English only highlighted the urgency.

"Captain Sherman, my name is Edward Rake. I'm the political officer at the embassy." Edward raised his badge as if to prove his validity.

"Good morning, Edward. Do you want some coffee?" asked Sherman, curious why the embassy would intrude upon his Saturday off.

"Uh, um… no, thanks. I'm afraid this is an official visit."

"I hope you don't run around in a collared shirt for fun," said Sherman.

Edward glanced down at his sweat-stained shirt and rail-thin frame. A moment of embarrassment washed across his face before he plowed on.

"I'm afraid there's been an incident, Captain."

Sherman didn't like the tone of their developing conversation. "Care to elaborate?" he asked.

Edward looked around at the other guests suspiciously before leaning in closer. He whispered, "One of your team is in police custody."

Sherman suppressed a laugh. "Who drank too much?"

"Sergeant Raylan Gournsey."

The answer did not surprise Sherman. The sergeant had a penchant for mischief and the bulk for serious violence.

"Can you bail him out?"

"No," said Edward. "They're charging him with murder."

The news caught Sherman off-guard. Drunk and disorderly made sense if that was even a crime in Equatorial Guinea. Judging from the average Friday night, it was not. Murder... well, that was something else entirely.

"Bar fight?" asked Sherman, naming the most logical of scenarios in which Gournsey might inadvertently kill someone. He was a mountain of a man.

Edward leaned ever closer, his voice barely audible. "They aren't saying much, but a source said he killed a woman. A sex worker. The police found him in bed next to the body."

Sherman finished his cup of coffee and stood up. He didn't need a fancy degree to know the optics were terrible. *Crazy American kills local.* The newspapers would be all over the story, which would make serious waves in the international community. Any goodwill they'd built would burn up quicker than a cheap barroom matchstick.

"Lead the way," said Sherman.

"Uh, where?" asked Edward, suddenly taken aback.

"Wherever they're holding my man."

"Right, he's downtown, but the police will not turn him over."

"Look, he didn't do this. We need to poke enough holes in their case, apply enough pressure, and they'll let him out."

"Sorry to be blunt, Captain, but what if he's guilty?"

Sherman motioned toward the exit and explained, "Two things you should know about Raylan Gournsey. First, he abhors violence against women. Saying he killed a sex worker is like saying Santa ran over the Easter Bunny. Second, the man is the size of a couch. He can drink a gallon of beer and walk straighter than a nun's ruler."

They exited the hotel and hurried along the recently paved road towards the embassy. The dense morning air swirled with a mix of charcoal cooking fires and flowers.

"Captain," said Edward, a little breathless from Sherman's pace. "I don't think you understand the situation."

"And you do?"

Edward gestured towards the embassy, just visible above the hedges. "I'm the Chief Political Officer."

"Okay, then politic my man out of this mess."

"I'm afraid the situation is not so simple, Captain. Factions within the Equatoguinean government view America rather poorly, and the Chinese—not to mention Russians—are gaining favor in this part of the world. These ministers don't approve of our joint training exercise, and they certainly won't let this opportunity pass by."

Sherman frowned. He didn't like politics. "You're saying Gournsey is the scapegoat."

"Simplistically, yes."

They stopped near the front gate, and Sherman locked Edward in his gaze.

"I'm a simplistic sort of man. Three plus three is six. Six thousand pounds of force to break a man's femur. Thirty rounds in my rifle magazine. Simple math, I think you get my point. So, why don't you tell me how I'm going to get my guy out of a Malabo jail before we're all kicked out of the country."

Edwards's eyes remained narrowed, as if lost in concentration. "Does it really take six thousand pounds of force to break a femur?"

"Yes! But that's not the point. Focus, Edward."

"Right, getting the sergeant out is tricky. Innocence doesn't usually matter in cases like this. A big enough bribe will make many crimes disappear."

"Great, tell State to fork over some shoe money."

"Well… things are proportional here. You can't extort a poor merchant the way you would a business mogul. The police take an equitable share, and Uncle Sam won't pay what they'll ask."

Sherman ushered them through the ramshackle embassy security as they spoke, with a look of utter indignation.

"This faction that doesn't like us… what do they want?" he asked.

"Well—" Edward began.

"Never mind, I don't care. How do I get Gournsey out?"

Edward stopped as they crossed the manicured lawn. "That's what I've been trying to say, Captain. I don't think you can."

Dead ends did not sit well with Sherman. His mind didn't work that way. It whittled and twisted and turned until an option appeared. Often, those options weren't palatable to the civilized bureaucrat, but the army didn't train him to act like one. They taught him to survive at all costs.

"Bullshit," Sherman retorted. "We just need to apply enough pressure on the right person."

"Captain! We can't just go around beating people up."

Sherman took a deep breath before speaking. "Edward, you look like a smart guy. Nice college, good internship, impressive track record. All that shit. But you misunderstand me and my methods. I don't beat people up. My unit is surgical. We disappear terrorists from their homes in the night. We are the boogeymen. What I need you to do is point me in the right direction. You're the political officer, think politically. I need to know who wants America out of the country. Where do I start?"

Edward sat down on a nearby bench, looking out of his element. Events such as this were not in the State Department handbook, and the Chief Political Officer wanted time to think it over.

"No," commanded Sherman. "You can think in the car. Come on. We're burning daylight."

Chapter Three

The tea kettle expelled a harsh lament into the stuffy apartment air. Miguel Ondo reached across the table and switched off the small electric burner. It was the only appliance he owned and the only one he needed.

Miguel was on his third cup of Nescafe. The morning chaos of his crowded building still echoed as people left for their jobs—if they were lucky—while others sat outside on plastic chairs facing the street and talked. For some, there was nothing else to do. Lots of people in Malabo wanted to work, but jobs were scarce.

Others, like Mrs. Obiang, were too old for anything but the gossip afforded to those who paid attention. She sat in a white plastic chair outside of Miguel's apartment.

"How are you?" she asked in Spanish, through the open slatted window. Mrs. Obiang insisted on speaking the colonial tongue.

Miguel finished making his coffee and sighed.

"Good. And you?"

"*Mr. Edu lost another chicken,*" she replied as if that summed up the entire existential crisis of the country. Forget about poverty or inequality. Mr. Edu's chicken made up all the conveyable news.

"*Is that two or three for the week?*" asked Miguel.

"*Three,*" answered Mrs. Obiang enthusiastically.

Miguel rubbed his forehead. He wanted a bigger place, not because he needed more space, but because privacy didn't exist in his building. Everyone knew intimate details about their neighbors they never wished to know, save for the gossipers.

"*Shouldn't you be at work?*" added Mrs. Obiang.

"*The police don't work normal hours,*" he replied.

"*Join the Gendarme,*" she offered.

Miguel didn't care for the militarized police. They were new and flashy and full of themselves. Besides, it went against his family tradition. He was the third generation of police in his family, stretching back to his grandfather. Trading that in for a new uniform and a fancy gun didn't sit well with his sense of convention.

"*You've said that already, Mrs. Obiang.*"

"*What, can't I tell you again? Don't hold age against an old woman.*"

Miguel sighed again. "*Yes, Mrs. Obiang.*"

"*Are you going to work or not?*" asked the woman.

Had Miguel not been up late watching smugglers by the dock, he would have gone in already, but the three cups of instant coffee weren't doing much good, and he was tired. "*I'm going,*" he replied and grabbed his gun and badge.

From his door to the paved road took only a few minutes' walk, but Miguel trudged slowly. He waited outside the petrol station with a dozen other commuters until a minibus arrived with enough room for everyone to fit inside. Miguel handed the boy manning the sliding door a few francs for the ride downtown.

Lost in thought, Miguel almost missed the shout for his stop. The boy slid open the door, releasing him into the subdued chaos of a Malabo morning. Horns honked. Vendors called out to pedestrians. People yelled at each other across the street. None of this bothered Miguel... he found the activity comforting, like a familiar dish or a favorite drink.

The woman who made omelets in a small stand on the corner called out. "*Hey, skinny!*"

Miguel waved. "*Good morning.*"

"*When you gonna get a wife to fatten you up?*"

"*No need,*" he retorted. "*I've got you.*"

She waved him off with a good-natured flick of her wrist and Miguel continued inside the police headquarters. The building was old—a remnant of colonial rule masquerading as history. Chunks of faded blue paint littered the dirt outside. The windows were more wood than glass. Nothing like the new Gendarme building down the street.

"Good morning, Lieutenant," said the officer at the front desk. His voice rose with each word.

The strangeness of his greeting did not escape Miguel. "What am I walking into?"

"They arrested an American. The chief is asking for you."

Practically speaking, Americans didn't get arrested often. Miguel recalled a handful of drunken tourists over the years, but someone from the embassy staff usually came by to pick them up in the morning. Americans meant paperwork and lost revenue. Tug at the purse strings and even the stodgiest bureaucracies budged.

Walking into the chief's office, Miguel hoped it wouldn't be his paperwork mess.

"Close the door," said the chief no sooner than Miguel had opened it. He obliged and the chief motioned toward a battered wooden chair that once belonged to the Spanish colonists. The chief took a perverse pleasure in knowing dozens of Equatoguineans suffered terrible fates in that very chair.

Miguel sat.

"We have a situation. A delicate situation that needs our upmost discretion."

"The American?" asked Miguel.

"Shhh," hissed the chief as if the walls had ears. "Where did you hear that?"

"The sergeant at the front desk."

"Eesh, if he knows, the damn building will know. What did he say?"

"Nothing… other than you arrested an American."

"Shhh," repeated the chief, waving his hands about to dispel the words.

Baffled, Miguel leaned closer. "Care to tell me what happened?"

"I need your eyes on this, Lieutenant. Be careful, be thorough. We can't afford to mishandle the case. Do you understand me?"

Miguel didn't. The chief made no sense. Drunk Americans were tiresome, but not dangerous. "What happened?" he asked.

"Go here and then report back to me. No one else. No stops. Straight back here," said the chief.

Miguel glanced at the paper his boss had slid across the desk. He knew the spot. A middle-tier hotel that mostly catered to Indian or Chinese workers. Not the typical place for an American, at least not one traveling on the government's dime. Those stayed near the embassy. The oil company suits stayed downtown in an opulent place dripping with luxury.

Maybe a backpacker, thought Miguel. *Someone out from an adventure. Or worse… a sex tourist.*

From the police station, Miguel took an unmarked police sedan and headed east then south. It didn't take over ten minutes with traffic. He parked his car across the street from the hotel. The modest three-story building looked like most others in the area. A brown concrete brick façade with glass walls on the first floor. A thick metal fence and gate protected the facility.

Miguel crossed the street and held up his badge to another officer on the other side. The woman nodded and creaked open the gate.

"Second floor," she said solemnly, and Miguel realized he wasn't getting any more details.

Not great, he thought and ascended the stairs to the second floor. The desk manager hadn't said a word either, which only gave Miguel worse vibes.

He opened the door to the second-floor hallway and quickly spotted an officer guarding a door halfway down. Bright fluorescent lights flickered across the brown tile floor reminding Miguel of a dingy hospital in which he'd spent a long week recovering from malaria.

The guard stepped aside without a word and Miguel entered the musty hotel room that smelled faintly of mildew and… death.

On the floor, draped over with a white sheet, was a

body. Bare feet with painted nails protruded. Miguel leaned down and gingerly peeled back the covering. Bile rose ever so slightly in his throat. Even after fifteen years as a policeman, death did not sit well with him.

Anger closely followed. The woman looked a year or two younger than his niece, which made her seventeen or eighteen.

Too young, thought Miguel.

A thin bruise wrapped around her neck. Ligature marks from a wire or cord. Strangulation.

There was no blood on the tile floor. No sign of a struggle. The room appeared orderly but sparse. Not much to break.

Miguel turned, poked his head out the door, and spoke to the officer in the hall.

"Do we know who she is?"

"No, Lieutenant."

"Any ID or purse?" he asked. She seemed like the type to have a purse.

"No."

"A phone?"

"Nothing else, sir."

Miguel turned back. The woman was naked. "Where are her clothes?"

The officer shrugged. "We didn't find any."

Miguel scanned the room. He went to the dresser and searched but found nothing. The nightstand contained a bible, but no clothes. Nothing under the bed either.

Odd, he thought.

"Did you make the arrest?" Miguel asked the officer.

"No, we came after."

"Who did?"

"The Gendarme."

Miguel whipped around from the drawer he'd been searching through. "What did you say?"

The officer looked quite nervous. "Well, technically, we made the arrest, but the Gendarme did the initial questioning."

"Who?"

"I don't... know."

Miguel didn't like the meddling of another group in his investigation—assuming it was still his investigation. If the case ballooned in size and turned against the American, the Gendarme could take the credit. If it went badly, like such cases often did, then the blame would fall solely on the underfunded police. Park the blame and steal the credit. A classic solution.

"Did you question the manager?"

"Yes," replied the officer. "He saw the American and the woman come in together."

"Video surveillance?"

The officer swallowed hard. "We didn't ask."

Miguel furrowed his brow but said nothing. He headed down the two flights of stairs and up to the front desk. The manager, who was not keen to have the hotel closed for any reason, smiled as Miguel approached.

"Are you done, Lieutenant?"

Miguel ignored the question. "Do you have surveillance cameras?"

"Yes. The front gate and front desk."

"Good, I'd like to see them."

The manager didn't move. "We have very discerning customers that won't appreciate my sharing."

"I'm sure you do, but I imagine a police blockade of your front gate would not help them or your bottom line."

The manager sniffed and cracked a patently false smile.

"This way," he replied and ushered Miguel into a small office that smelled of sweat and curry. A desktop computer sat on a metal table and the manager clicked through a few screens until finally pulling up the footage.

"When did the couple in question arrive?" asked Miguel.

"Around one this morning."

"Show me."

The video sped backward in a flurry of frames until it arrived at the allotted time. At first, there was nothing, only the stillness of night. The exterior camera caught their arrival on foot from the north. Miguel took note. The woman rang the buzzer. They appeared a bit intoxicated, but not stumbling. Drunk and happy.

"The inside video too," said Miguel.

The manager obliged and a second video appeared, which showed two people entering through the front door. Maybe it was the high angle of the first camera, but Miguel had missed the sheer size of the American. The man was a mountain, both in width and height.

"That's a big guy," he mused out loud.

The manager nodded. "Got a little worried when he walked in. Although he seemed nice enough."

"You talked?"

"Briefly. He apologized for his bad Spanish and asked for a room."

"And why did you call us?" asked Miguel.

"One of the guests heard something like a scream."

"Which guest?"

"Uh, I don't recall. A woman called into the desk phone and said something terrible was going on in their room."

"But you don't know who called."

The man looked embarrassed, as if details were his business and he'd missed an important fact.

"I'm afraid not."

"Can you tell which room called?" asked Miguel.

"Not for certain. We had several calls around that time."

"About the screaming?"

"No, sir. Mostly breakfast."

Miguel glanced around. "You serve breakfast?"

"No, sir, but it's mentioned in one of the old brochures."

"That no one bothered to update?"

The manager shrugged innocently.

"Can you write the room numbers that called in around that time?"

The man did and slid across a piece of paper with five numbers.

"And do you have names?"

Based on the snide look, Miguel knew the answer was a resounding 'no'.

"Okay," said Miguel. "Thanks for your help."

Begrudgingly, he walked back up the stairs and knocked on the doors listed. Three rooms were recently vacated. The fourth held a rather angry Cantonese businessman who shooed Miguel away. The fifth room was empty and not recently occupied or cleaned. Miguel made another note.

He returned to the crime scene and the tragically young woman with the thin bruise around her neck, took one last look, then returned to his car.

For a murder case, this one was straightforward. Guy meets girl. Things get heated. Guy kills girl. A crime of passion or premeditation, it didn't matter. He got caught red-handed. An open and shut case, if the legal system worked, which was not always true. It tilted toward the highest bidder and America had deep pockets.

Still, Miguel couldn't complete his report without questioning the accused, so he drove back towards the police headquarters.

Traffic clogged the streets. Throngs of people milled about. Several vendors hawked red, white, and blue striped flags.

Not French, thought Miguel. *The other one.*

An electric charge rippled through the crowd as if they were all watching the World Cup. People jostled and jumped. They sang and chanted, but Miguel couldn't quite hear what.

Circling the roundabout that led to the police station, Miguel had to weave between groups spilling onto the street. He exited at the top of the circle and stopped in front of the flimsy metal gate protecting the police parking lot. The officer in charge pulled it open by hand as rusty hinges squeaked in protest.

"What's all this about?" asked Miguel.

The young officer looked toward the growing crowd and shrugged. "Unemployment?" he offered.

Miguel parked and headed toward a side door but observed the growing crowd.

Not unemployment, he thought. *Wrong building.*

The government buildings were one roundabout up the road. His block held the police station and courthouse—nothing directly related to job creation or economic policy.

Miguel shrugged at this incongruence and headed inside. He didn't have the luxury of time to ponder such questions.

He went straight to the chief's office, who acknowledged his return by leading Miguel to a small holding cell removed from the others. This VIP section was reserved for the rich and famous, who occasionally got caught doing something a bribe cleared up, but only after they sweated in the cell for an hour. It was discreet and the chief wanted discretion.

"What did you learn?" asked the chief in a low whisper.

"The killer strangled her, probably with a thin rope or wire."

"The American?"

"The perpetrator."

The chief frowned at Miguel's indirect assertion of innocence until proven guilty. "Witnesses?"

"A guest called to report screams, but I couldn't find them to ask what they heard."

The chief nodded. "How strong is the case?"

"They found him in the room with a dead woman. The video shows them checking in together, likely drunk or drinking. I'd say it's an easy prosecution."

"I'm sensing a 'but'," added the chief.

"There are some incongruities in that narrative."

"For instance?"

Miguel pointed toward the American, whose size up close baffled the policeman. He didn't think men came that big.

"Look at him. Does he seem the type to use anything but his bare hands? Also, the purported call reporting screams came from an unoccupied room."

"Circumstantial," said the chief, but he seemed interested in Miguel's line of reasoning.

"Did you know the Gendarme questioned him already?"

The chief said nothing but rubbed his wide bald head with both hands.

"What's going on here?" asked Miguel. Secrets practically dripped from the walls, but he didn't understand their meaning.

"Something feels off," said the chief.

"The entire city feels off. People are running around outside with Russian flags like they're supporting Manchester United or Chelsea."

The chief grunted something Miguel didn't hear and then said, "Go and question your suspect. I don't want this case to linger any longer than necessary."

Chapter Four

Raylan Gournsey kept one eye on the two men talking while he examined his temporary accommodations. The cell appeared ad hoc, like an afterthought, converted from an old storage room. The walls were concrete but exterior, meaning there was fresh air on the other side. It was also close to the back exit and stood to reason they were keeping his arrest on the down low. The steel bars were old and poorly set into the wall. They rattled when he applied modest pressure.

Escape swelled to the top of his mind. The twelve missing hours and corpse in his room elevated the idea. *In deep shit*, didn't fully describe his predicament but came close.

The younger of the two men stepped forward. He was in his mid-forties, taller than most, but skinny in that genetically can't gain a pound sort of way.

"*¿Habla Español?*"

"*Un poquito*," replied Gournsey, stretching the truth. He

understood much more than a little but preferred to keep that a secret.

"English then," said the man.

"Better."

The cop pulled up a battered metal chair and took a seat outside the cell. Gournsey peered through the bars at him.

"My name is Lieutenant Miguel Ondo. I'm investigating the murder that occurred in your hotel room. Can you tell me your name?"

Gournsey considered sticking with name, rank, and serial number, but the US government was not at war with Equatorial Guinea. He was a prisoner but not a prisoner of war.

"Sergeant Raylan Gournsey, United States Army."

The man's brow furrowed ever so briefly, but it revealed his surprise and consternation.

"But I already told that to the other guy in the shiny shirt," Gournsey continued, curious to see how the cop reacted.

Miguel gave a conceited half-smile and gestured around. "Bureaucracy works... how do you say it? Slow as syrup."

"Molasses," said Gournsey. There was an honest competency about the lieutenant that he appreciated and Gournsey considered himself an excellent judge of character. That didn't prevent him from making poor choices, but he made them with knowledge of the shortcomings of those involved.

"Right, molasses. We don't grow sugar cane here. Did you know that?"

Gournsey did indeed know. He'd memorized the CIA factbook as he had with every deployment in a new country. Equatorial Guinea, by most economic measures, was a rich nation. It had lots of petroleum reserves. Lots of oil money. None of that mattered for the average citizen. The president for life that had ruled since 1982 made sure his cronies siphoned up all that wealth. He knew a man such as Miguel statistically wouldn't live much past sixty. Seventeen years less than the average American. Of course, none of those facts mattered if they convicted him of murder.

"I go where they tell me," he replied.

"And where did you go with the young woman last night?"

Good question, thought Gournsey.

"Would you believe me if I told you I don't remember anything from last night? In fact, I'm missing the twelve hours before your lot kicked down my hotel door."

Miguel Ondo barely blinked as Gournsey relayed the truth.

"You don't remember killing her?" he replied.

"And therein lies my predicament," said Gournsey. The lieutenant had laid out the case against him in a single iron-clad sentence. He didn't know. They didn't know. And the dead didn't speak. "I don't remember not killing her either."

The cop sighed and stood to leave. He looked beyond tired. Almost weary.

"I'll have them take a sample of your blood to test for any foreign substance, but our lab shut down last year and the nearest one is in Nigeria, so don't expect a result for a few weeks. But even if it comes back positive for something, I'm afraid it won't help your cause much."

Gournsey nodded but appreciated Miguel's willingness to look beyond the obvious. "I don't remember where I started the night but that doesn't mean I don't know."

Miguel gave a half-smile. "You're a creature of habit."

"Of that, I am guilty. I always start the night at Antonio's. Do you know it?" Gournsey guessed he did. It was the only place to get a decent bourbon on the island. A good cop would know that.

"I know it."

"Good. Now, I don't think I'm able to ask for favors, but when my friend arrives, could you please let us chat?"

"Who's your friend?"

"He'll be the scary-looking guy with a beard who insists vehemently that we need to talk."

Miguel laughed quietly to himself. "You're accused of murder. I doubt the chief will let him in the building."

"Oh, he's quite persuasive."

Miguel nodded at the statement like one might acknowledge a passing word of advice on the street. A trivial exchange of limited value. But Gournsey knew better. Frank Sherman did not leave men behind. Not at any cost. Proportional responses did not apply.

"I'll run down where you started, maybe even where you went afterwards, but I might find something you don't want to hear."

Incriminating evidence was a risk Gournsey happily accepted. Nothing could beat what they already had, and he was almost certain he hadn't killed the woman. Yet there remained a small, dark corner of his brain that understood his potential guilt—that sliver of violence ingrained in all humans, the one holding our misdeeds like a library holds books, just waiting for them to be checked out and unleashed upon the world.

I didn't, did I? he wondered.

Chapter Five

Measured in miles, the distance from the embassy to the police headquarters was in single digits. Getting there, however, took far longer than expected.

Edward drove like a new father taking his child home from the hospital. He slowed at every intersection and yielded to every pedestrian who stepped near the street.

"They'll move," said Sherman, annoyed at the delay.

"And if they don't, we'll have an even bigger mess on our hands," said Edward.

Conceding the point didn't bother Sherman, but time was not an abundant commodity. He didn't know the next steps in Gournsey's journey but getting him out of the police station was exponentially easier than an African prison.

On one rather narrow street, vendors vied for customers. Each small, ramshackle booth made of timbers and corrugated tin overflowed with clothes and fabrics. Sherman craned to see through the growing crowd awash in red, white, and blue.

"Are they selling Russian flags?" he asked.

Edward glanced over. "This happens when US foreign policy shifts its attention elsewhere."

"Filling the void," added Sherman.

Edward swerved into a roundabout like his life depended on it. "Precisely," he replied.

They exited at the top of the circle and parked in the first open spot some distance up the street. People milled about on the streets. The atmosphere surged with positive energy like a football match about to start.

Edward led the way around the dilapidated building and through the front door. The officer at the front desk, which blocked entry to the station, looked up from his newspaper and assessed the situation. A frown quickly formed on his face.

"*Can I help you?*" he asked in slow enunciated Spanish.

"*I'm with the United States embassy. You're holding an American citizen, and we'd like to talk with him,*" replied Edward. His Spanish was crisp, precise, and bland.

The officer appeared unmoved, but a lone bead of sweat formed on his forehead. "*Are you a lawyer?*"

"*Yes,*" said Sherman. "*And his accountant, dentist, and priest.*"

The man gingerly tapped a half-filled piece of paper attached to a clipboard. "*Please sign in and state your business.*"

Edward leaned over and scribbled down the details. "*Now, please escort us back to speak with him.*"

"You can wait there or outside," replied the officer.

Sherman moved closer and the man eyed him wearily.

"*Now,*" said Sherman.

"*Wait,*" replied the officer as another bead of sweat formed.

Sherman placed both hands on the man's desk and leaned forward so their noses almost touched—a trick he'd learned from his father who hated waiting at the DMV office almost as much as he hated Communists.

"*I'm going to ask you nicely, once more, to let us speak with my friend. If you say 'wait', I'll cut out your tongue with a rusty razor and feed it to the dogs waiting outside. Am I clear?*"

The cop slid back his chair and pointed at Sherman, who guessed the gist of his remark came across even if he wasn't sure of the Spanish word for rusty.

"*Calm down*," said a voice from up the stairs.

Sherman turned to see a plainclothes cop descend to meet them. He was in his mid-forties, tall, and deceptively thin.

"You must be the scary one with a beard," said the man in unaccented English.

"Captain Frank Sherman, United States Army."

The man smiled and extended his hand, whose long, slender fingers belied a wiry strength.

"I'm Lieutenant Miguel Ondo. Please follow me."

Sherman and Edward followed. Edward talked fast and nervously about releasing the prisoner at once. Miguel politely ignored him. Sherman, meanwhile, memorized the floorplan and the number of personnel. He noted all the entrances, exits, and weaknesses—everything.

They came to a halt near the opposite end of the police station. Miguel pointed toward a cell that resembled a closet with bars.

"You have ten minutes. Not more," he said and then retreated a respectable distance.

Gournsey sat on a cot, but his bulk made it look like a toddler's bed.

"I told the lieutenant you were persuasive," he said as they approached.

"And scary," said Sherman.

"He threatened to cut out a man's tongue," added Edward, clearly shaken by the idea.

"A classic," replied the sergeant.

Sherman leaned against the wall and looked through the bars. "What happened?" he asked.

Gournsey shrugged. "I ain't sure. Last thing I remember is leaving the base yesterday. I woke up buck naked in some cheap hotel with a dead teenager on the floor and the cops kicking down the door."

"Not good," said Sherman.

"No, Captain, it ain't."

"Completely blank?" asked Sherman.

"For twelve hours."

"Maybe Rohypnol or something similar," said Sherman. "Were you carrying any ID or keys? Something worth taking."

"I don't think so. You know I take security seriously."

Edward interrupted in a hoarse whisper. "Why are you asking that?"

"Who's he?" asked Gournsey.

"The Chief Political Officer," answered Sherman before turning back to Edward. "I'm asking because the sergeant here has access to highly classified material that foreign agents could get into if they had his ID along with other pieces of information that he cannot remember sharing or not sharing."

Gournsey nodded. "Better check my hotel room. You know where to look. Everything else should be in the embassy."

"I'll tidy things up," said Sherman. "And Edward here will start making calls. I'm sure someone around here wants a new stadium or port we could pay for as a bribe."

"I saw her, Cap," said Gournsey with a heavy sigh,

sinking down onto the cot. "She was young, so much life left."

There wasn't much Sherman could say about that. Gournsey's sister suffered some unspeakable trauma around that age. The rage still boiled under the sergeant's calm exterior.

"I'll save whoever did this for you, if I find them first," said Sherman.

Gournsey nodded in appreciation.

Edward leaned back in and whispered, "Aren't you going to ask if he did it?"

"That's a stupid question. Gournsey could float on a sea of empty bourbon bottles and never hurt that woman."

"You can't say for sure, Cap. And neither can I," said Gournsey.

"Semantics," replied Sherman. "I can't say for certain the sky will stay blue while we're inside, but I know it will. You didn't do this because I know the man you are."

"Thanks for the vote of confidence."

"Any time. Now, hang tight while we figure out our next move."

"Not like I have anywhere else to go," replied Gournsey with a laugh.

Sherman gave him a wink and wandered toward Lieutenant Ondo, who was reading the same newspaper.

"Can you tell me how this woman died?" asked Sherman.

Miguel looked up slowly from the paper. "Definitively? No. My gut says strangulation with a thin rope or cord."

"Does my man strike you as the type to use a cord?" asked Sherman.

"No."

"Did you find a cord or rope?"

32

"No. We found him lying next to a dead woman. I'm afraid that's more than enough for a conviction."

"Is that what you believe?" asked Edward, who'd followed Sherman.

Miguel shrugged. "It has nothing to do with what I believe and everything to do with what I can convince a judge to believe."

"How long until you move him out of here?" asked Sherman.

"A day or two."

"Can you ask for two?"

Miguel nodded. "I suppose so, but why should I help you or him?"

"Because he didn't kill that woman, but you already know that."

A grin flashed across Miguel's face, showing his white teeth. "Why would you think that?"

"Because I can see a dozen holes in your case. I'm guessing that there are even more problems."

The cop shrugged. Life moved differently in the tropics. Slower. More deliberate.

"The case is the case. I can't change the facts," said Miguel.

"This man is an American citizen and deserves due process—" Edward began in a scholarly tone that sounded awfully like scolding to Sherman, who cut him off.

"Lieutenant Ondo already knows that. I think the best thing for us to do is get out of his way."

Miguel smiled and gestured toward the stairs.

"We'll be in touch tomorrow," said Sherman.

"Of that, I have no doubt," replied Miguel, who returned to his newspaper.

Sherman ushered Edward through the old colonial

building with its high ceilings, grand arches, and crumbling brickwork. The Chief Political Officer hemmed and hawed about potential trades and the ramifications of a high-profile trial. Trade didn't concern Sherman, neither did mineral rights or drilling leases.

The stench of trouble followed them out the door, through the still gathering crowd and to Edward's car. Sherman sensed it from word one. Raylan Gournsey was a killer, and a damn fine one, but he was not a murderer. Violence of that nature just wasn't in his bones.

Edward slid into the driver's seat and guided them back toward the embassy, still grumbling over economic outcomes.

"This is bad," he said.

"Agreed. Gournsey didn't kill that woman. So, who did?"

"You got any enemies, Captain?" asked Edward.

"Hundreds, but most of them are dead."

"Then the question is not who, but why?"

"That's your area of expertise," said Sherman.

"Could be an attempt to scuttle our mineral rights deal. The Chinese or Russians would love for that to fall apart."

There goes my vacation, thought Sherman.

Chapter Six

On the ranking of US embassies, the Equatoguinean one sat near the bottom on multiple fronts. The building dated back to the 1960s and needed repair. A tall, beige, single-story affair with a flat roof, it had a dozen dilapidated satellite dishes sticking off at odd angles like warts. The front door was glass and steel and protruded from the façade—a security afterthought during some remodel. Taken as a whole, the building did not inspire awe or project power abroad as many embassies did. In fact, with the architectural addition of tall columns out front, it had the look of an Antebellum plantation house. Not a great look for West Africa.

Tactically, the place was no better than an oversized gingerbread house. The fence lacked strength and the gate wouldn't stop a Toyota sedan from punching through. While the local guards did fine with keeping the riffraff away, they weren't armed, lest they turn on the Americans. Most importantly, there weren't any Marines inside, just one

DSS agent who'd rotated through twice in the week since Sherman's arrival.

Scott was the current gatekeeper's name. He was young and drew the obvious short straw to be shipped off to a dead-end post like Malabo. Sherman didn't dislike the man, but Scott, with his wraparound shades that looked like ski goggles, didn't inspire confidence. He checked the box of an armed American but not much more.

"What brings you in on Saturday, Captain?" asked the agent as he buzzed them through the main door.

"It ain't for a backyard barbeque," answered Sherman as he breezed past and headed toward an unused conference room they'd commandeered once the joint exercise began.

Corporal Raul Lopez was already there when Sherman walked into the room. The sniper, dressed in shorts and flip-flops, was meticulously cleaning his rifle. He looked up quizzically at the new arrivals.

"Did you miss the memo, Cap? It's Saturday."

Sherman wanted to give a glib reply, but Lopez always cleaned his weapon on the weekend. While some found solace in gardening or fishing, Lopez's Zen involved gun oil and terry cloth—church and religion wrapped up in one.

"Gournsey's in trouble," said Sherman.

"Like he smashed the commander's pool, gonna get shipped to Antarctica, kind of trouble?"

"Worse. The police arrested him for murder."

"Who'd he kill?"

"The police found him in a bed next to a dead woman this morning. They say he strangled her, and he can't remember the last twelve hours."

Lopez stopped cleaning and squinted in confusion.

"Well, that's a steaming truckful of BS. Did he piss someone off or sleep with a general's wife?"

"Not sure yet," answered Sherman.

"They found him in a room next to a corpse," said Edward. "But neither of you seem to acknowledge that fact."

Lopez looked at Edward and then back at Sherman.

"He's the Chief Political Officer," said Sherman.

Lopez grunted and went back to cleaning. Responding to stupid questions was not worth his energy. Edward threw out his hands in mock surrender and took a seat next to the fancy office phone.

Sherman followed suit, picked up the receiver of another line, and dialed a number he knew by heart. On the other side of the world, Major Sanders answered, despite the seven-hour time difference.

"Captain, how goes the joint training?"

"Fine, sir, but that's not why I'm calling."

"As it is four in the morning, I expect not."

"I wanted you to hear it from me before you get an earful in the morning briefing. The local police arrested Sergeant Gournsey this morning. They found him in a hotel with a dead woman and they're going to charge him with murder. But here's the problem, sir. He doesn't remember the twelve hours leading up to his arrest."

The silence that followed would have unnerved most, but Sherman waited patiently.

"Have you secured his gear?" asked Sanders.

"Working on that now. His ID cards and laptop are still in the embassy," answered Sherman, then remembering something he should have asked, covered the receiver and shouted down the hall to Scott. "Did Sergeant Gournsey enter within the last sixteen hours?"

A clipboard clattered loudly in the distance before Scott replied, "No. He checked out at six yesterday evening. Nothing since then. Why?"

Sherman ignored the question and spoke to Sanders. "He checked out yesterday evening and didn't come back. I don't think we've been compromised but you should have IT double-check."

"Already working on it," replied Sanders. "Is someone working the local angles?"

"Edward, the political officer is making calls. He suggested possible Russian or Chinese involvement to scuttle a mining deal."

"Lithium," said Edward from across the table.

"Lithium mining rights," added Sherman.

"I've heard," said Sanders. "Sit tight for now and work the local side. I'll loop in State and the CIA. Things will get weird and people will question the sergeant's innocence. Don't take the bait."

"Understood," said Sherman.

"In the meantime, you know what to do."

"Prep for an extraction."

"Good man, I'll be in touch."

Sherman placed the phone back in the cradle and leaned back. He didn't enjoy sitting still. It went against his nature.

"Extraction for who?" asked Edward. He was leaning forward and looking rather confused.

"Everyone," said Sherman.

"Why?"

"Because wars have started over less, Edward."

The answer didn't sit well with the Chief Political Officer, but Sherman didn't care. He started pulling out gear and prepping bags. Not five minutes into the exercise, the phone rang.

Major Sanders spoke first. "I don't think this will make the front page, but it's certainly stirring up some bees in Washington. Expect someone from the agency this afternoon."

"Quick turnaround," said Sherman.

"They were in the region."

"Understood."

Miguel Ondo spent his afternoon working through a heavy stack of paperwork—forms upon forms whose only explanation for existence was to keep bureaucrats employed. Everything came in triplicate. No computers or centralized database, just carbon copies that disappeared into hundreds of cabinets lining the walls. A holdover from the colonial system and a general lack of funding.

The sun was setting, and his stomach was rumbling by the time Miguel finished. He stood stiffly and unfurled his thin frame to its full height. Stretching his arms high, Miguel twisted and cracked his back.

He looked over at the VIP cell and its inhabitant. The giant American lay on the cot, his arms behind his head. The man's eyes were closed but Miguel couldn't tell if he was awake or not.

Guilty men sleep, he thought. *And soldiers.*

"Can you at least leave me the newspaper?" asked the man in the cell in Spanish, his voice deep.

Not sleeping.

"I thought your Spanish wasn't good," said Miguel as he picked up the paper.

"Kids shows and newspapers are the best way to learn."

Miguel tossed the paper through the bars. He didn't want to get any closer.

"Where'd you learn English?" asked the American.

"Baywatch," replied Miguel.

The answer caused a deep thunder of laughter from within the cell. Miguel left to the echoes of mirth and the shouts of a local drunk, now sober and mad.

He exited through the back door and walked towards the leafy enclave of wealth closer to the shore. The Spanish favored the area, where ocean breezes kept the mosquitos at bay.

The sun edged closer to the horizon before plunging towards the sea, a great fiery orange ball sinking into the shimmering expanse. Miguel walked slowly. He loved dusk. The city came alive at night, when the torpid heat of day subsided. The air buzzed with anticipation and insects.

When he arrived at Antonio's bar, the doors had just opened. A few expats sat at the bar, drinking cold beer and watching European football reruns. British, maybe German. The fans were too pasty to be Spanish and too quiet to be American.

After filling out all those reams of paperwork, the case against the sergeant looked stronger than ever. Video footage showed them entering together. The police found him next to her dead body. Whatever happened in the intervening timeframe didn't matter much to the prosecutor or judge.

Despite those undeniable facts, Miguel couldn't help but feel doubts rumble inside, insidious little second guesses. Why didn't the American leave? Why risk staying in the room for so long? Where was the cord that caused those ligature marks? And what of the twelve missing hours? Criminals lied all the time. That was their nature. But the

American gained nothing by telling him that. It only made the case against him stronger.

Insidious second guesses.

Miguel ordered a whiskey and sipped slowly, letting it burn down his throat and warm his stomach. He ordered a second and, when the bartender stopped, he asked him about the American.

"Did a big American come in here last night?"

"We get all sorts," said the bartender. He was youngish and smartly dressed, with thin lines expertly shaved on the sides of his head.

"You'd remember this guy. Built like a mountain."

The bartender stopped pouring. "Señor Raylan."

Miguel nodded, *"Yes, him."*

"Sure, he was here."

"Alone?"

The bartender picked up a glass to clean. *"It was a busy night."*

Miguel placed his badge on the counter,

The bartender shrugged off his authority.

Miguel slid over a dozen beers' worth of cash.

"I suppose I noticed a few things," replied the man and tapped on the wad of bills.

Miguel put his pistol on the table. The stick to his carrot.

"Right, yes, I saw him. He had his usual, two fingers of bourbon, and watched the game."

"Alone or not?" asked Miguel, his hand still resting on the gun.

"Not really my business what a man like that does."

"You ignored the badge and took the money. Don't make any more silly mistakes."

The bartender tentatively eyed the pistol like he was deciding the odds.

How much did this American tip? wondered Miguel.

"There was a woman. She joined him after the game."

"Describe this woman."

"Young. Hot."

"Had you seen her before?"

"Once. She's not the type to come this far west."

Miguel understood what he meant. He'd seen plenty of women coming and going from fancy hotels. The police turned a blind eye to most. *"More of a high-rise and suits type?"*

The bartender nodded uneasily.

"Did the American know she was working?"

"I couldn't say."

"Did they leave together?"

Another nod.

Miguel put away the gun and took out his notepad. *"What time was that?"*

"I didn't keep tabs on him. It really was a busy night."

"Do you know where they went?" asked Miguel.

"No, man. I don't."

"Fine. Last question... did you see anyone else unusual?"

"Yeah, you. Two days in a row of flashing badges at me as if that shit means anything around here."

"Me?" asked Miguel, confused. *"The police were here last night?"*

"No, the other ones," answered the bartender with a wave of his rag.

"The Gendarme?"

"Yeah, no offence, but your badge looks weak. They have real metal ones, not some laminated crap."

Miguel ignored the insult and the truth underlying it. *"What did they ask?"*

"If we had surveillance cameras."

"And do you?" asked Miguel.

"Of course not. This isn't a bank."

"Did you catch a name?"

"No, he flashed the badge quickly and wasn't wearing a nametag."

Miguel frowned as he scribbled down the note. *"What did he look like?"*

"So much for one more question. I've got thirsty customers."

Miguel stood to his full height, which had the intended effect. Something about looking up made people talk.

"Okay. He was average-looking. Shaved head. Sharpish smile and much nicer clothes than you."

"Thanks for your cooperation."

The bartender waved him off and went to get more beers for the pasty Europeans.

Miguel stepped outside into the still cooling night. He paused just past the front door and looked down the street in either direction. There wasn't another bar in sight. A few restaurants but nothing worth stopping at. Not for a drunk American and possibly an expensive—perhaps on-the-clock —prostitute. Assuming she was working, and he was paying.

Seeds of doubt sank their roots into his skeptical mind. Miguel didn't like incongruencies and the case overflowed with them. The corpse alone would convict the American, but Miguel wasn't the type to leave a loose thread dangling. He liked to tug until everything unraveled.

He wondered, *How did you get from here to that hotel?*

The night was young, and Miguel had no family or obligations. Work consumed his waking hours, and he was awake with an itch that needed scratching. He turned right, heading south towards the cheap hotel. Intermittent light pooled along the street and Miguel nimbly dodged potholes and uncovered sewage gutters.

Smoke rose behind fences and with it came laughter, conversation, and the longing for more than just work. Miguel was so consumed with the moment that he almost missed the shadows slithering around him. By then, it was too late.

The shadow took form and speed, colliding with a painful crash of bulk against Miguel's thin frame. Force equals mass times acceleration, and the right side of the equation had substantial mass. The sum sent Miguel skidding across the pavement along with his service pistol, which slid out of sight.

Another outline appeared with the first. They advanced upon him with methodical precision.

Miguel tried to run, but his body didn't follow his mind. Something hot and slick stuck to his shirt. His head hurt. His legs felt weak.

The gun, he thought. *Find the gun.*

But he couldn't. The darkness, outside of those small patches of streetlight, was absolute.

A boot cast out of that inky soup and caught him in the ribs. Pain shot through his body, radiating up and down. He felt it in his teeth and toes.

"No," he moaned.

Another kick came. This time, Miguel was ready and rolled clear of its arc. He crawled toward a yellow cone of light. Maybe someone would see him or at least he could see his shadowy attackers.

He managed a few good steps before something hard hit him square in the back, sending him sprawling again to the broken pavement.

When Miguel turned, he saw a third outline appear in the haze of night. The shadow moved quickly and quietly, with none of the heavy breathing of his assailants.

Before Miguel quite understood, there was the loud crack of bone, but not his bone, and then a soft gurgling sound like a thin stew simmering down.

Two shadows dripped to the ground with hollow thumps and the third stepped closer. Miguel slid back into the light. He felt the blood running down his arm and head.

Bracing for the worse, Miguel raised his good arm up, hoping to block whatever pain was coming. Instead, he heard a voice. A vaguely familiar voice.

"Lieutenant Ondo, you look like hell."

A tan, bearded face emerged in the light. The other American soldier.

"Captain Sherman?"

"You looked like you needed a hand."

Miguel struggled to his feet, found his phone, and turned on the flashlight. Beyond the American, face-down in the road, two men lay motionless.

"Are they dead?" he asked.

"If they aren't, call an ambulance," answered the American.

Miguel poked one man with his shoe. A moan followed. Miguel recognized the figure. A local thug, happy to steal or harass for his supper.

Same as the other. But the second body didn't move, and Miguel's shoe came back smudged with blood.

"Friends of yours?" asked the captain, who stood watching with utter detachment.

"Local troublemakers," replied Miguel, still dazed by the entire encounter.

"And they just found you here by happenstance?"

As the adrenaline wore off, his brain started connecting the rather scattered dots of the last few minutes. Muggings were common enough, but not so much in that part of town. The strangest part, the bit Miguel realized could not be coincidence, was the American army captain's arrival.

"You were following me," he said.

"Guilty, but so were they."

"What?"

"These two followed you from the bar and I followed them."

"Why were you following me?" asked Miguel, who suddenly felt the need to sit down. The dissipating adrenaline helped him think clearly, but it no longer masked his injuries and the pain intensified.

The American took a seat next to him. "You need medical attention. The embassy is close by. I can get you there."

Miguel knew he needed stitches. The laceration on his arm felt deep—very deep. Not to mention his other injuries that he couldn't see.

"Okay," he said wearily. "I'll go with you, but I need to know why you're following me?"

The captain nodded, "I went to Antonio's to ask about Sergeant Gournsey and found you doing the same thing, which means you're extremely diligent about crossing your 'Ts' or you're having doubts. I suspect the latter and I also suspect that you're a good detective. Following you felt prudent. Maybe you'd find other clues about last night that could exonerate my guy. Then I spotted those two skulking in the bushes like snakes and things got interesting."

Miguel didn't like any of what the captain said. He kicked himself for not noticing the American or the two thugs. But most of all, he didn't like not knowing the complete picture of events and felt like a man wandering through fog, hoping not to fall into a hole.

Unsteadily, he raised himself up and hobbled over to the

men on the ground again. One still had a little life left in him. The dead man had a skewer sticking out of his neck. The kind you got from a street-side kabob vendor. Miguel kneeled and searched through their pockets. Both men had large wads of cash. New bills. Not the well-worn paper that usually circulated through the informal economy. Miguel took the money as recompense.

"You might need this," said the American, who held out Miguel's lost pistol.

"Did you have that the entire time?"

"More or less."

"Why didn't you use it?" he demanded.

The American frowned. "Not worth the noise."

Miguel hadn't considered such a detail and would have gladly used the weapon without a second thought, but he knew that two American killers would make the political situation exponentially worse.

"Are we walking back to the embassy?" he asked, already weary from the thought.

"No," replied the captain and pointed to a pair of head-lights wobbling in the distance.

Sherman had not intended to get involved in such local matters. He'd spent the day prepping for the worst-case scenarios. Having completed his tasks, Sherman sent Lopez to retrieve the CIA's expert from the airport and then headed out himself.

The logical stop was Gournsey's favorite watering hole. The sergeant had found it on night one of their time in-country and was a regular. If he'd gone anywhere, it was to Antonio's.

He bought a couple of kabobs from his usual lady around the corner from the embassy and ate leisurely on the walk. Arriving at the bar, he spotted the lanky cop deep in conversation with the bartender. Sherman stayed in the shadows and listened. He liked the way Ondo operated. Carrots and then stick. A tried-and-true method. Personally, he was more a stick kind of guy, even if it meant stabbing someone in the eye with an especially pointy carrot.

Once he spotted the two interlocutors deep in the shadows across the street, Sherman decided there was more at play.

What came next, on the darkened street, did not surprise him. Violent intent trailed behind the duo like cans clanking behind a 'just married' car. They were too focused on the cop to notice him and too cocky to watch their six. Once things started, Sherman improvised. The first guy took a chunk of asphalt to the skull. The second, a kabob skewer to his jugular. Neither act bothered Sherman in any moral sense. If the men would have left after a few sharp words, he would have done so, but men like that were not deterred by broken Spanish or loud English.

As the headlights grew closer, Sherman saw blood ooze down Miguel Ondo's arm from a wicked cut. His head didn't look much better, and his pants had dark lines of blood too.

Tough guy, thought Sherman.

Most people didn't stand up after a beating like that.

A moment later, Lopez arrived driving a white Land Cruiser, that universal sign of Westerners in Africa. Sherman opened the front passenger door for Miguel, who looked weary beyond words. Lopez gave Ondo's injuries a once over and motioned for Sherman to get in the back quickly.

Only when Sherman opened the back door did he realize Lopez had come straight from the airport. The CIA expert sat in the back seat with a half-amused smile. Sherman didn't smile back.

"Hi, Frank," said the woman.

Sherman chuckled at the unexpected. "Hi, Charlotte. Long time, no see. Still expanding the empire?"

Charlotte McMillan.

One-time girlfriend years earlier. Twice over ex-lover.

Lifetime CIA agent.

Not the expert Sherman had expected.

The last time he'd seen her was in Ghana when she was still undercover as some mid-level UN bureaucrat, climbing the ranks to further US policy.

She looked the same. A few more creases around the eyes but still nice to look at. Only now, she'd traded in the pantsuit for some yoga pants and a pair of Converse.

Chapter Seven

The laceration in Miguel's arm steadily closed with each stitch of Lopez's sure hands. One more wound tended in a list too long to recount. Sherman sat across the room and watched the precision with which Lopez worked. Had he not been one of the finest shooters in any army, the man would have made a fine surgeon.

A metal chair gave a brief screech as Charlotte slid it closer to him and sat. He hadn't seen her in years. Not since another chance encounter in West Africa. Back then, he didn't know she was a spy, but neither did anyone else.

Her dark hair was shorter than he remembered, but the devil-may-care grin remained, along with the shrapnel scar along her jawline.

"We need to stop meeting like this," said Sherman.

"At least you picked me up from the airport and not a kidnapper's car," she teased.

Her luck had improved in that regard. Back in Ghana, Sherman's team had saved her from some unsavory characters who intended to sell her off for cash.

"Are you still with the UN?" he asked.

She was the last time he saw her. A CIA mole climbing the bureaucratic ladder in one of the opaquest of international institutions.

"Not anymore," she answered, almost wistfully. "I'm with the State Department now."

No one like Charlotte McMillan just worked for the State Department. Spies don't go back to the grind. People of her ilk didn't change. They couldn't give up the game. Espionage flowed in their veins.

"Working directly for the agency then," said Sherman.

She gave one of her famously dismissive smiles that said *what a silly idea* on the surface but had a sharp undercurrent of unease, which told Sherman she hadn't changed at all. Still a spy and working for the CIA. Still wearing the sheep's clothes, just a different sheep.

"Tell me about Raylan," she said, ignoring his remark.

"He got caught in some stickiness. The police arrested him for murder this morning."

Charlotte looked at her watch and frowned. "We're already behind."

"Care to elaborate?" asked Edward, who'd wandered into the room. He'd come straight from making calls to various government ministers and had not noticed Miguel or the bloody mess covering the table that Lopez used as his workstation.

Sherman pointed at the makeshift operating table and said, "She means that we're playing catch-up with the situation."

Upon catching sight of the bloody gauze and fresh stitches, Edward gave a little yelp and retreated a step.

"Wh-what happened?" he stammered. "Wait… is that Lieutenant Ondo?"

Charlotte gave Sherman a look that conveyed her general disdain for the quality of employees in the building.

"He's sharper than he looks," said Sherman.

"You must be the Chief Political Officer," said Charlotte, being charming and condescending all at once.

"Edward Rake," said Edward and extended his hand.

"Nice to meet you, Edward. I'm Charlotte McMillan, Regional Director for West Africa."

Edward must have recognized the name or title, maybe both, because his eyes practically jumped out of his skull and ran down the hall.

"I'm sorry, ma'am, I didn't know you were coming. No one told me."

"It's alright, Edward. I hope it's okay if I call you that."

He smiled back like a puppy.

Sherman groaned.

They might have recalled her from deep cover ops, but Sherman could tell she still commanded respect.

"Where are we with the local angles?" she asked. "Do we have any good points of leverage?"

"I've called the Ministers of the Interior and Defense. They all pointed me to the other. No one will talk with me about options."

"And we're sure Sergeant Gournsey is innocent?" she asked.

Sherman gave her a hard look but said nothing. Charlotte knew Rayland and that knowledge answered her question a thousand times over.

Edward interjected to answer, but Charlotte raised her hand.

"Apologies, that was a rhetorical question. I believe the sergeant."

"But that's the thing..." added Edward. "Sergeant

Gournsey doesn't remember the twelve hours leading up to his arrest."

Charlotte whirled toward Sherman. "And you didn't think to mention that, Frank!"

Miguel, who'd been unconscious, stirred. Charlotte hissed at Sherman and pulled him into another room across the hallway and closed the door.

"Why didn't you tell me?" she whispered.

"I assumed it was in the report they gave you."

"It most certainly was not. This changes things."

"I'm aware," said Sherman.

"Have you secured his access cards and laptop?"

"Yes, they never left embassy grounds. I retrieved his gun from the hotel as well. It smelled clean, so I don't think it was fired after he cleaned it."

"What about the cop in there?"

"Seems legit. He was out chasing down a lead that might help clear Gournsey when those thugs jumped him."

"Could be a coincidence," she said.

"You don't believe in coincidences," Sherman reminded her.

"You're right. I don't."

"Where does that leave us?" asked Sherman.

"Swimming with sharks," answered Charlotte.

"Should we get a drink?"

"Yes, we should."

Sherman exited and popped his head into the conference room. "Lopez, don't let Miguel leave before tomorrow morning. I don't want him getting whacked on his way home."

"Copy that."

The hotel bartender accommodated their request for a private table with a knowing nod, greased by an extra-large tip. Charlotte paid with US dollars straight from the American taxpayer. Sherman sat with his back against the wall, surveying the few patrons left in the bar. Unwilling or unable to give up the vantage, Charlotte took a seat next to him. It made them look even more like a couple, which, as camouflage went, was just fine with Sherman.

Charlotte ordered a whiskey, neat.

Sherman got a beer—local and cheap.

The bartender delivered their beverages and retreated with a deference towards their privacy. Charlotte let out a deep breath as if she'd held it in all day.

"Long day?" asked Sherman between sips of beer.

"And getting longer."

Sherman nodded in agreement and said, "Tell me about these sharks and whatever else you didn't want to say around Edward."

"Let's start with the basics. Do you think Gournsey was drugged?"

"Without a doubt. You've seen how much that man can drink. No way he blacks out for twelve hours and doesn't have liver failure."

"And the dead woman in his room. Do we know anything about her?" she asked.

"Unknown, but they said she was a sex worker."

"A little cliché," said Charlotte. "But it certainly makes the optics worse, which I assume is by design."

"A fall guy," said Sherman, repeating what he'd suspected from the start.

"Tried and true," she added. "The question is, who is pulling the strings?"

"I bet you have an answer," he said. Sherman would have staked a house on it… if he owned a house.

"The obvious culprits are China or Russia."

"I've seen a lot of Russian flags around the city," said Sherman.

Charlotte sipped her whisky and gave a little choked giggle. "Those flags are cool or hip or whatever the kids say these days. Russia is picking up our security scraps and mining contracts in the process. Better to have your capital overrun with corrupt mercenaries than some jihadist offshoot of ISIS. What's surprising the suits back home is the speed at which Africa is ghosting us."

"Everything surprises the suits back home."

"Simple math, if you ask me," she continued. "America has the attention span of a toddler. Every four years, our priorities get tipped over, mixed up, and then thrown out. Imagine basing your national security on the whims of the US electorate. Insanity."

Sherman raised his bottle to insanity.

"The Chinese are playing the same game but with bread instead of bullets. They offer all this money to build big state projects like dams or railroads, except the loans get tied to natural resource contracts. When the country can't pay, then they can kiss goodbye all that oil or timber or rare earth minerals."

"Edward mentioned a lithium deal," added Sherman.

"A rare win for the State Department. We secured a limited deal to mine the seafloor around Bioko Island. Apparently, it's littered with lithium-rich rocks."

"Against competing bids, I assume."

"Correct," she replied and sipped her whiskey with elegant ease. "The Chinese were quite annoyed, as were the Spanish, who think we're mucking about in their backyard, not to mention the British who are still pissed about giving away the island two hundred years ago."

"That's a lot of sharks."

"This place is teeming with spies and plots."

"Present company included," said Sherman.

"I'd tell you but then I'd have to kill you, and that would cost me a fortune."

Sherman laughed. "Hint taken. I'll stop asking."

"Thanks. It saves me the explanations and poison."

"Knowing what you know now, how do we get Gournsey out of this mess?"

"To be honest, it would be easier if he was guilty. We could have bribed the police chief or prosecutor to drop the case quietly, but I doubt that's possible with external forces involved. They'll have bought off someone important to make sure the case doesn't disappear. Or that's what I would have done in a similar, completely hypothetical situation."

"Since we're talking hypothetically, what if this person of import supporting the case mysteriously disappeared? Would that speed up the release of my man?"

Charlotte paused with her whiskey midway to her lips. "The agency won't approve of that, not without justification and, let's be honest, your team is just one very sharp spear in a large arsenal."

"I don't disagree. The brass won't do anything either, but I'm here and they're not. So, what I say goes."

"You're not seriously considering kidnapping a government official in their own country?"

"Hypothetically," said Sherman as a reminder, but he was happy to burn down the police station if need be.

"I'd counsel against such an action. You don't know how deep this goes," said Charlotte.

"And extracting him from the police station?"

"Judging by your expression, you already have that

planned out. As a last resort, sure, but you're not a man who waits that long."

True, thought Sherman.

He had no intention of waiting for the situation to deteriorate.

"I have a contingency plan," he said.

Charlotte raised her eyebrows in mock surprise.

"Not what you want to hear," she said. "But we wait and see what plays out."

"Major Sanders isn't going to like that answer either," he replied.

"No, I don't imagine that old bastard will, but the major knows the game. I'll get the analysts working on the possibilities and see if we caught any Russian or Chinese chatter. Something like this takes planning. They'd have to move assets into the region."

"Wait and see?" asked Sherman.

Charlotte nodded. "Wait and see."

Chapter Eight

When Miguel awoke in the morning, his entire body hurt at the same time. Not quite the racking pain of dengue fever he had as a teenager, but he wasn't a young man anymore. Injuries took longer to heal, bruises lasted weeks, and Miguel acutely felt his forty-three years of life.

He didn't remember moving to a cot, but he was on one. Someone had covered him with a blanket, too—a gesture he appreciated but caused him significant unease. Nothing came without a cost. He'd learned that lesson the hard way.

The American who spoke flawless Spanish sat at a nearby table cleaning a wicked-looking rifle. Miguel remembered the man's kindness and clinical precision from the night before, but he was a killer. Plain as day. A proficient, meticulous taker of human life. People like him frightened Miguel, not because of the capabilities—all people can take a life under the correct blend of stimuli—but because they could switch off that innate human trait of compassion whenever the need arose. Take the captain from the previous night. He killed two men with almost no effort and certainly no remorse. The act carried no more emotional weight than taking out the trash or buying groceries.

Miguel did not have the same constitution. He sympathized and empathized with people from all walks of life. He wanted to make his city, his island, his country a better place. Violence wasn't the way to accomplish those lofty goals. Lots of dictators on the continent tried that and all failed eventually. Even the Equatoguinean president knew bread over bullets wins the day. Miguel didn't think the man actually believed such a notion, but he was smart enough not to cross the line into outright repression.

Although, after forty years in power, and no end in sight, the young grew restless. Miguel saw it on the faces of high school graduates with no job prospects. Even college graduates fared only marginally better and most left the island in search of sustaining work. Those who stayed grew disillusioned, bitter, and radical.

Miguel knew he was lucky to have a job. His father was a cop during those first heady years of independence and his grandfather before that policed his own people for the Spanish. Following in those footsteps was all but guaranteed. If Miguel had a choice, he'd never known it.

Rising from the cot took effort and caught the attention of the young American. He offered Miguel a cup of coffee and two ibuprofens.

"*How are you feeling?*" he asked in Spanish.

"*Old,*" replied Miguel, downing the pain pills with one big swig of coffee.

"*You're in good shape for an old guy,*" replied the soldier.

"*Thanks to you. I appreciate your hard work stitching me back together.*"

"*My pleasure. Captain Sherman left you some clean clothes on the chair over there.*"

Miguel found a pair of clean pants and a shirt roughly in his size sitting on a nearby chair. "*I don't think I can accept the hospitality,*" he said.

"*Honestly, sir, I don't think you have a choice,*" said the American. "*The captain is very persuasive and rarely takes no for an answer.*"

"*I've learned,*" said Miguel.

"*You can change in there.*"

Miguel followed the soldier's outstretched hand.

"*Thanks. I apologize, but I don't recall your name.*"

"Corporal Lopez," said the American in English.

"*Well, Corporal Lopez, thank you for what you did last night.*"

Lopez smiled. "*Take it easy with that arm for the next few days. I put fourteen stitches in there and I'd hate to see them break.*"

"*Understood,*" said Miguel. It wasn't his first serious injury.

"*I can drive you home if you'd like,*" offered Lopez.

"*I'm going to work and, no offense, but it wouldn't look appropriate if I showed up in a US embassy car when there's an American sitting in my holding cell. Bad optics.*"

Lopez held up a sniper scope. "*This is the only optic I care about.*"

Miguel wasn't sure if that made the corporal's life easier or not. Easier because he didn't have to deal with corrupt politicians or co-workers who wished they were corrupt politicians. Or worse because the choices were life and death. No gray area or fudging of facts. Just ballistics.

"*I'll remember that,*" said Miguel, then he went to change his clothes, which didn't quite fit but weren't crusted over with dried blood. At least he still had his badge and gun.

Relatively clean, Miguel left sheepishly through the front

gates, waving to the guards who looked perplexed at how the local entered in the first place.

He walked a few blocks, stubbornly insistent that he could make it to the police station under his own power. He couldn't. That much was abundantly clear. The injury to his leg, while superficial, caused a good deal of pain and his knee swelled.

A taxi skittered by, and Miguel flagged down the driver, who flashed a sympathetic smile.

"*Motorbike accident?*" asked the man behind the wheel.

Miguel appraised his general state and, having thought of no better explanation, nodded in agreement.

The driver accepted Miguel's explanation and his money. Congestion worsened as they neared the city center by the police station. Throngs of people cheered and sang and danced. Most were young and unemployed.

"*What's this?*" asked Miguel.

"*Protest,*" answered the driver.

"*Of what?*"

The man looked around and shrugged. "*Of life, I suppose.*"

Many of the protesters carried Russian flags. Miguel didn't have an opinion on that other than he didn't want foreign mercenaries swarming his city, be they Russian or Chinese or American.

"*I see,*" said Miguel, which was partly true. He saw poverty and the empty promises of jobs and the rising unemployment rate and the uptick in crime and the general sense of hopelessness. He did not see how waving Russian flags would change any of that.

Out of the taxi, Miguel felt the crowd's surging restless energy. Chants of *freedom*, unheard for forty years, rippled through the masses. *El Presidente* would not approve of his people advocating for a regime change. Not when he was close to handing over the reins to his son. President for life part two. Fed from a golden spoon. Heir to a fortune stolen from the people.

Miguel understood the chants but also knew they came at a significant risk. The Army had crushed any expression of outrage in the past, and he considered this outlook equally grim.

Traversing the crowd took time. Traffic clogged the roundabout as protestors poured past cars and brought everything to a standstill. Blaring horns amplified the chanting.

Why here? Miguel wondered again. *Why not in front of the legislature?*

By the time he made it to the front steps of the police headquarters, the mood had changed. Freedom was no longer the word of choice. Several people in the crowd unfurled a large, professionally made banner that read '*Down with America*' in Spanish.

Not as dramatic as the Iranian catchphrase, '*Death to America*', but the sentiment took hold, and thousands chanted the slogan.

More and more police officers streamed outside, and Miguel directed them to form a cordon around the police station entrance.

The chief stepped outside to survey the problem. His eyes widened like saucers.

"*We need to move the American,*" said Miguel. "*If they storm the building, he won't survive.*"

"*Sometimes the will of the people outweighs the rule of law,*" replied the chief.

Miguel had never heard the man babble such nonsense and he didn't like it.

"*I'll get more men*," said Miguel and retreated inside the nearly empty building.

He spotted a few officers reporting for their shifts and directed them outside. In his cell, the American paced the length of the cell in two long strides.

"You need to leave," said Miguel in English, making sure nothing was lost in translation.

The man stopped moving and turned to face him. His head was almost a full foot taller than Miguel's. "I wondered if you'd come back."

"I'm not leaving you to the whims of a mob," retorted Miguel.

"Then I suggest we leave now," replied the American.

Miguel held up a pair of handcuffs and tossed them through the bars. The soldier caught them with a sympathetic look.

"If they make you feel better, I'll put 'em on," he said.

"Will they matter?" asked Miguel.

"No."

Miguel considered insisting upon the cuffs but knew better. The American could kill him a dozen different ways with the restraints.

"Can I have your word that you'll not try to escape or kill me?"

"Do you trust me?" asked the sergeant.

"No, but I trust your captain and he trusts you."

The American pointed to the fresh stitches on Miguel's arm. "Is that Corporal Lopez's work?"

Miguel nodded.

The admission mollified the sergeant.

"Okay," he said. "No escape or murdering you."

"Okay," replied Miguel. "Let's go."

Miguel found the cell key, unlocked the door, and

stepped back. The American lumbered out and stretched his arms up, taking advantage of the increased space.

Outside, chants for the downfall of America grew louder as the crowd moved closer.

"They're coming," said Gournsey.

"Out the back," said Miguel, motioning towards the rear exit. "We can take the side street away from the roundabout."

Miguel cracked open the door and poked his head out. He didn't see any protestors or colleagues. A nearly empty parking lot stood between them and the street towards safety.

"Are they chanting 'Death to America'?" asked Gournsey.

Miguel cocked his head and listened as the chanting echoed around the building. Minutes earlier, the protestors had followed the banner, but the tenor had changed. Down became death. Rancid furor grew in the multitude of voices.

This is what feasting sharks sound like, thought Miguel.

"Yes, they are," he replied.

"Were they earlier?"

"No. No, they weren't."

The sergeant shook his head slowly and said, "Lead the way."

Miguel held open the back door to let the American out as pounding cascaded through the building like falling rocks. Hard, hungry fists slammed against the front door. The sound of pent-up anger stored over a generation of undelivered promises erupted all around them.

"Go," urged Miguel and pointed across the parking lot towards an unassuming gate on the other side.

They ran, heads hunched low, legs churning hard in the

thick morning air. Miguel's leg burned from his injury and the stitches threatened to pop.

Gournsey reached the other side first and stopped.

"Keep going," urged Miguel.

"It's locked," replied the American.

"What?" said Miguel in surprise. The gate was never locked, yet a shiny new padlock prevented their escape.

Miguel looked up but broken bits of glass topped the walls and climbing over was not a great option.

"Don't you have a key?" asked Gournsey.

"It's not usually locked."

The American shook the gate. It rattled and creaked.

"Stand back," he said.

The soldier turned and kicked like a mule just below the metal hinges. With a cruel screech, the rusted metal hinge sheared off from the wall, twisting outward, leaving a human-sized gap at the bottom.

"That works too," said Miguel, now further convinced the American could snap him like a dry twig.

Behind them came shouts—loud and urgent. Out of the police station streamed a raucous crowd. They looked like they'd lost something and were in the process of searching.

"Go," urged Miguel again and herded the American away from the crowd in the parking lot.

Sirens blared in the distance—shrill yet muddled in the humidity. They grew closer and closer as the duo moved on.

"We can't stay on the streets," said Miguel, which was more of a comment to himself, but he blurted it out anyway.

The American pointed toward a narrow alley between two apartment buildings. "We can stay out of sight for a bit, but you need to trust me and call this number."

Gournsey held out a business card with a local number printed on one side. The back was blank.

"Who is it for?"

"The embassy emergency line. Call that and hand me the phone."

"Does our agreement still stand?" asked Miguel, figuring it did not.

"Can I amend it to add 'Until you're satisfied of my innocence?' I feel convincing anyone else is a tall order."

On the sergeant's innocence, Miguel had few doubts. He just couldn't prove it to anyone else but himself.

"Yes, that works for me," he said and dialed the number.

They stood in the shadows of the narrow alley as Gournsey spoke. Sirens shrieked and Gendarme trucks whizzed by, loaded with heavily armed men.

No riot gear, thought Miguel. *Shouldn't they prepare for the crowds?*

Chanting echoed down the street like distant thunder, inspiring both awe and fear.

The call ended and Gournsey handed the phone back to Miguel.

"We stay here. The embassy is sending a car to get us."

Riding in an American embassy vehicle didn't strike Miguel as the brightest idea, but he couldn't walk the sergeant down the street. More pedestrians streamed by their hiding spot every minute. They were no doubt curious about the not-so-distant happenings. Soon enough, those pedestrians would turn into protestors and come looking for the giant American they might have seen lurking in the shadows. Better to risk a car ride than be dragged out by a frenzied mob.

Chapter Nine

Sherman's morning began identically as the day before, with coffee and conversation. Diego, the waiter, arrived at his customary table in the corner with a pot of coffee and cream. He didn't look surprised to see Charlotte sitting next to Sherman. He merely retrieved an extra cup.

"Good morning," said the waiter.

"*Bonjour*," replied Sherman.

"*Bonjour*," added Charlotte.

Diego smiled in the early morning light and gave a little bow.

"*Bonjour, madame. Puis-je t'apporter autre chose?*"

Charlotte smiled back at the waiter and answered his question by ordering a pastry and fruit in Spanish. Diego looked at him for an order.

"The same," he replied.

"You haven't changed," she said.

"I'm stuck in my ways," he replied. "But you learned Spanish."

Charlotte sipped her coffee and smiled knowingly. "I learned it a long time ago, you just never asked."

Another layer in the mystery of Charlotte McMillan, thought Sherman.

The woman had the complexity of an ancient oak, each ring revealing a secret covered by the next. After all those years, he still didn't know who she was at the core.

Across the patio, Diego appeared carrying two croissants and a worried expression. He set the plates down on the table and leaned in close to Sherman's ear.

"One of the staff says there is a protest gathering downtown. They are chanting 'Death to America'."

"Where in downtown?" asked Sherman.

"The police headquarters."

"Thank you, Diego," he replied and motioned for Charlotte to get up.

"What is it?" she asked.

"We need to leave," he answered and placed a hundred-dollar bill under his cup as a tip.

"Frank," hissed Charlotte. "What the hell did the waiter say?"

"There's a crowd shouting 'Death to America' outside the police station where Gournsey is being held."

"Shit," she said.

They ran the two blocks toward the embassy. Charlotte had her phone out and was talking to an analyst in DC. She barked orders between breaths of humid morning air.

As they rounded the corner near the front gate, Sherman spotted Lopez returning from a morning run on the beach. Sweat drenched through his shirt and bits of sand glittered on his arms and face.

"Captain," he said, looking alarmed to see Sherman running with Charlotte at his heels. "Why the rush?"

"There's a protest by the police station and they're chanting 'Death to America', and Gournsey is still locked inside."

"This ain't Tehran, that makes no sense," said the corporal.

"Exactly, and neither does Gournsey's arrest, so I'm headed down there to see what's going on. I need you to lock down the fort here and prep for an extraction. Let Scott know what's going on."

"Copy that. There's an old Peugeot parked in the back lot if you want to go incognito."

Sherman turned to Charlotte, who was still on the phone, and said, "Stay inside. I'm going to check on the protest."

She flipped him the bird and shook her head. "Not a chance," she mouthed.

"Fine. Meet me in the back lot in five minutes."

Sherman went straight to the conference room with all their gear. He grabbed the bag he'd prepped the day before along with his HK416 rifle and an extra tactical vest for Charlotte. A local embassy staffer leaped out of his way as he hustled out the back door and toward the sedan. The car wasn't new, but it had tinted windows and enough dings to blend in with the traffic.

Charlotte was already behind the wheel with the engine running. He slid inside and handed her the vest and a Glock 21. She didn't bat an eye at either item. Slipping on the vest, she press-checked the pistol and holstered it with practiced ease.

"Did you learn that a long time ago too?" he asked.

"A girl is allowed her secrets," she answered and slipped the car into gear.

"Fair enough. What did Langley have to say about the protest?"

"A sophisticated social media campaign organized the protest," she answered as they exited the embassy compound. "Nothing about 'Death to America', but it's tapping into decades of pent-up rage. A clever bit of social engineering."

Sherman knew little about social media and didn't want to. But he understood people. "Are you saying someone staged this?"

"The spark always comes from somewhere."

"Do you know who's behind the campaign?" he asked.

Charlotte took a corner at speed and Sherman held onto the door handle.

"Nothing yet," she answered. "The profiles and accounts are local, but it resembles Russian meddling in the Central African Republic."

"Nothing like a giant angry crowd to get the government to change their minds," said Sherman.

"It would jeopardize the lithium deal," she added. "Anti-American protests plus an American in jail for murder."

"Double whammy," he added.

"Convenient for whoever swoops in and snags the mineral rights," Charlotte added.

"Slow down and take this next right," Sherman instructed. "We should have a decent line of sight toward the police station."

Charlotte turned onto a narrow residential street and eased onto the shoulder. They were three hundred yards away from the chanting crowd. Sherman pulled out a compact spotting scope and surveyed the situation. He'd seen plenty of angry crowds in Iraq and Afghanistan. At least this one didn't look armed to the teeth.

"What do you see?" asked Charlotte.

"Hundreds of angry young men."

"Not great."

"Not ideal. They certainly seem energized and organized. I see banners. Professionally printed ones. The first one says, *Abajo con Estados Unidos*. Second one reads, *Sacar a Estados Uniods*."

"Down with America and Get Out America. Quotidian if you ask me, but the professional bit is worrisome."

"Suggests planning," said Sherman.

"Exactly, but the crowd is chanting, *Muerte a Estados Unidos*. Things are escalating."

Sherman didn't need a translation. He'd heard Death to America in several languages, though Spanish was new.

"I don't like where this is heading," he added.

Charlotte fidgeted in the driver's seat. "Nor do I. They're moving closer."

The buzz of a vibrating phone pulled Sherman's attention away from the restless crowd that inched closer to the police station. The call came from the embassy. He answered.

"Captain, this is Agent Scott. We just received a call on the emergency line. Priority Alpha."

"Who?" asked Sherman while motioning for Charlotte to start the car.

"Sergeant Gournsey, sir. He's holding near the police station with the local cop. He said things were turning pear-shaped, whatever that means."

"It means things are going to hell and I'm watching it happen. Did he give a location?"

Scott relayed the cross streets. Sherman knew the spot. They weren't far.

"The sergeant requested that you hurry. Something about a dam breaking and the flood washing us out to sea."

"Understood," said Sherman and hung up.

Charlotte shifted into gear and waited expectantly for directions.

"Make a U-turn. We'll circle around from the other side."

She nodded and the old sedan lurched into motion.

They weaved north then east with Charlotte driving and Sherman navigating. Brightly colored buildings whizzed by in a blur as they sped down narrow streets in the oldest parts of town—the part planned by the Spanish during an ad-hoc expansion of the city. Signs for churches, barber shops and bars slid past in a flurry of cheerfully hand-painted signs.

Nothing like those banners, thought Sherman.

"Take the next right," he said.

The tires groaned in protest as Charlotte turned hard, then quickly slowed. A small crowd loitered on the street in front of dilapidated two-story apartment buildings. The crowd was pointing and yelling.

Charlotte inched closer.

In the searing morning light, Sherman saw a gap, an alley, between the buildings. It hid in the shade. Two men from the crowd swarmed toward the alley like hungry dogs chasing a bone. Moments later, they came back out like bags of trash tossed to the curb, bouncing and rolling across the pavement.

Another man ran into the gap, shoulder lowered like a battering ram. Again, he exited mid-air and landed next to the others.

"Drive into the crowd," Sherman instructed.

Charlotte balked. "What if they don't move?"

"Humans are good at self-preservation. They'll move the same way the guys on the ground aren't."

She frowned but moved forward.

"You can honk if that makes you feel better."

Charlotte lay on the horn as they picked up speed. As expected, the crowd dispersed, scattering in all directions except down the alley. In the shadows, almost as wide as the gap, stood Gournsey. Behind him was Miguel. He'd broken a few stitches on his arm and blood dripped in long red lines.

Sherman jumped out and opened the back door. "Your taxi, sirs."

Gournsey smiled and pulled Miguel toward the sedan.

"Frank," yelled Charlotte.

The crowd congealed again, thickening around the vehicle. They were loud and angry, rightfully so. One young man in his late teens picked up a chunk of broken concrete. He cocked back his arm and made to throw it at Sherman's head.

Sherman shouldered his rifle, hoping to dissuade the young man. He didn't want to end a life over economic disappointment and poor choices.

"No," he shouted, thankful that the word did not need translation.

The teenager dropped the projectile. Sensing danger, the crowd backed away, unwilling to turn their backs to the man with the rifle.

Sherman slid inside the car. "Now would be a good time to back up," he said.

Charlotte slipped into reverse. The gears ground. The crowd took a step forward. Anger bounced and rippled, rising with each shout and raised fist.

The sedan jerked backward.

Rocks smashed into the windshield with a tremendous crunch. Thin cracks spread out from the craters.

"Shit," muttered Charlotte.

With her head over her shoulder, she hadn't seen the stones mid-flight.

The car careened into the junction. Charlotte turned hard and the Peugeot slid ninety degrees right, facing toward the ocean and the embassy.

"I can't see a damn thing," she said, bobbing her head about to find an unbroken view.

Sherman reclined his seat back over Miguel, brought his boots up, and kicked hard against the shattered windshield. The window didn't pop out in one clean go but peeled outward like a stubborn sticker resisting removal. Soon enough, Charlotte had a clear view and stomped on the accelerator.

For the next few blocks, they drove in silence, except for the wind whipping through the mostly missing windshield. Smoke rose from tires burning down the streets and alleys. Sounds of protest echoed around them. Chanting. Shouting. Jeering.

"*Liberte*," rang thousands of voices.

"*Revolución*," came the reply.

Sherman picked up his phone and called the emergency line at the embassy. Scott answered. Sherman spoke in measured tones.

"I want you at the front gate in three minutes. Tell the guards to open it up. They will not want to, but make sure they do."

"Are you okay?" asked Scott, sounding nervous.

"Fine, just be there. We'll be the car with a giant hole in the windshield."

He hung up and glanced backward. Crammed behind

Charlotte, Gournsey looked like an overstuffed sausage filled to bursting. A large man stuffed into a small space. His head bent to one side because the roof was too short. His knees shot upward at odd angles.

"I hate sedans," he said with a smile.

"I'll remember that for your next rescue," said Sherman.

Next to Gournsey, Lieutenant Ondo had a torn-off shirt sleeve pressed against his arm. Blood flowed freely from the torn stitches, dripping onto his pants and the car seat.

Sherman pulled out a roll of gauze and handed it back.

"Thank you," replied Miguel.

Gournsey took over the operation and wrapped Miguel's arm. Red blotches spread through the white fabric.

"How'd that happen?" asked Sherman.

"He tried to reason with the crowd," said Gournsey. "They weren't enthused about the conversation."

"I don't blame them," added Miguel. "Young men have no place in this country anymore. No work. No families. No money. No purpose. They're angry and the government does nothing."

"Someone is tapping into that anger," said Sherman. "Intel suggests an external party organized the protests on social media."

"The Russians did something similar in the Central African Republic last year," said Gournsey.

Miguel watched out the window, a forlorn expression on his face. "This island is no different than a sugar cane field. Soon enough, the fire will come and burn it all down. Then someone else will come and harvest all the riches."

A deep pessimism hung on his words, but Sherman sensed a tenacity and willingness to fight in the man. Giving up was not in his DNA.

The car skidded around another thin ribbon of broken asphalt and into sight of the embassy. True to orders, Scott stood out front as the gates slid open.

Charlotte didn't let up and the sedan bounced over the speed bumps in a shower of sparks. They didn't stop until the back parking lot, out of sight from prying eyes.

All four occupants peeled themselves out of the car, slick with sweat and, in Miguel's case, blood.

Lopez appeared a moment later in combat gear, carrying a trauma kit. He surveyed the scene for a moment before trotting over to Miguel.

"*I told you to take it easy with that arm*," he chided the lieutenant in Spanish.

Miguel took a seat on the curb and held out the bloodied appendage to receive care.

"*I'll try harder next time.*"

Lopez smiled and got to work.

As the corporal stitched, Charlotte paced, her phone to her ear. The conversation was tense. Sherman only heard one side, but he was glad not to be on the receiving end of her venom. Even Agent Scott, who'd run up like a kid late to a birthday party, stepped away from her rage.

"What happened?" Scott asked Sherman.

"Pent up anger and manipulation," said Sherman.

"Sir, what does that mean?"

"It means you need to secure the ambassador. The protest is growing in size and volatility."

"She's at her residence," replied Scott, suddenly fidgeting with nervousness.

"What's your evacuation plan?" asked Sherman.

"Hold here until the Marines arrive."

"That's a shitty plan," said Sherman. "Nearest QRF is

at least eight hours away and they won't launch without a clear and present danger."

Scott pointed to the shattered windshield. "Doesn't that count?"

"That's because the sergeant broke a few bones, and I pointed my rifle at an angry crowd. You don't call in the cavalry over a few well-aimed rocks."

"I'll go and get the ambassador," replied Scott.

"Good idea," said Sherman.

As Scott ran off, Gournsey moved in and clasped Sherman on the shoulder with a baseball glove-sized hand.

"That was fun," he said with a grin.

Sherman smiled. "Glad to have you back in one piece."

"Thank Lieutenant Ondo, he let me out as the crowd came in. He even tried to reason with the people who found us hiding in that little alley."

"I take it that didn't work," said Sherman.

"No, not really. A group of teenagers saw us in the shadows. They were on their way to the protest with these hand-painted signs saying *Down with America* on one side and *Freedom* on the other. When they spotted me, they stopped."

"You're hard to miss."

"Genetics," said Gournsey, ever so sheepishly. "Anyway, Miguel here tried reasoning, then threatening them with his badge. Neither worked. Stubborn kids. They pushed. I shoved. Then you showed up."

"At least he got you out of the police station."

Gournsey nodded. "We have an agreement about that."

"You and the lieutenant?" asked Sherman.

"I promised not to escape or murder him until he's satisfied that I'm innocent."

Sherman choked down a laugh. "That's mighty kind of you. What happens if he thinks you're guilty?"

The sergeant didn't miss a beat in his response. "You'll have to murder him."

"Let's hope it doesn't come to that. I quite like the guy."

"Me too," said Gournsey.

Charlotte emerged from her call, fuming. "It's the fucking Russians. Or they're working for someone else. Either way, it's the fucking Russians."

Sherman and Gournsey exchanged a look of amusement at Charlotte's ire. Although, the content of her rant was no laughing matter. Russian influence on the African continent had only grown in the previous decades since the American distractions in the Middle East. Leave a bone unattended and another dog will sniff it out.

"Have your analysts figured out an end goal behind the protests?" asked Sherman.

"The running theory from State is an attempt to scuttle our lithium mining deal."

"You don't sound convinced," said Sherman.

"The Russians never operate so linearly. Think of their plan like a big roundabout. The first exit ruins the lithium deal. The second exit pulls President Mbasogo out of his pro-Western orbit. Maybe the third exit is his premature departure. Our file on his son is slim, but we think he harbors sympathetic views of China's Belt and Road approach to development. And we can't rule out a coup as a final exit either."

"What happens if the thing goes all the way around to the start?" asked Sherman.

"The Russians lose," answered Charlotte. "A possibility they always accept when starting an operation like this."

Politics, Sherman knew, was a complicated endeavor— angles upon angles, layers upon layers. He didn't care for it or its practitioners, but he understood contingencies: plans upon plans. Russians didn't fight without contingency plans, the same way he never had just one exfil location. That the social media campaign and the protests were the only plan made no sense. Why risk it all on one horse when they could run a herd?

"You mentioned this island is crawling with spies," said Sherman. "What if the Russians have other assets in play?"

Charlotte nodded in agreement with his logic. "And they say you're just a pretty face, Frank. You have them all fooled."

Gournsey laughed at Sherman's expense.

"We haven't caught any chatter about other assets in the area, but your idea fits with the Russian playbook."

"Wagner?" asked Gournsey, referring to the mercenary group serving as a pseudo-army.

"They're too busy in the Central African Republic," answered Charlotte.

"That's not far away," said Sherman.

"Nothing shows they're in the mix," she said, then added, "At least not yet."

"But it's a possibility," added Sherman.

"Given recent events," said Charlotte, "I'd say it's an eventuality."

"If things turn sour, I don't like our odds here," added Gournsey, sweeping his arm toward the too-weak fence and the local guards.

"Neither do I," agreed Sherman. "This place only has the illusion of safety."

"And people say I'm the paranoid one," added Charlotte.

"Think of this as a roundabout," joked Sherman. "We're the first turn for angry mobs or mercenary armies."

"Point taken," she replied. "But we haven't seen President Mbasogo's reaction yet. He could throw out some concessions and this might all blow over."

"Or?" asked Sherman.

"Or we have a long wait for the Marines," said Charlotte.

"Exactly."

The embassy back door swung open and Edward tumbled out into the late-morning air looking frazzled. "You're gonna want to see this. President Mbasogo is addressing the protestors on national television."

Chapter Ten

Sherman, Gournsey, Edward, and Charlotte rushed into the embassy, stopping to switch on a television at the first office they passed. President Mbasogo's dour face flickered to life. He wore a dark suit, steel-rimmed glasses, and a deep scowl. Seated behind a large wooden desk and windows overlooking construction cranes, he looked every bit the polished dictator playing a president.

"Citizens," he began in Spanish. *"We are a small but mighty nation. Great powers grovel at our feet for the wealth we hold. Stores vast enough to power our ascendency. Wealth enough for all, if we act under the greater good."*

"This guy is out of touch," said Gournsey.

"Look," said Edward. "He's not even on the island. Those cranes are on the mainland."

Sherman looked at the open windows behind the president. Edward was right. The guy was thousands of miles away.

"We must not fool ourselves into thinking we can rise to greatness without help and sacrifice," continued Mbasogo. *"We take from*

these westerners the knowledge we need to succeed, but it is our sweat that builds this country, not theirs."

"Imbecile," muttered Miguel, who'd entered behind Lopez.

"*Some of you want the Americans gone. You've taken to our lovely streets in Malabo, trampling them with your anger. I understand you. I hear your wish to build a stronger country.*"

"No, he doesn't," said Charlotte.

"*But you, dear citizens on the streets, are mistaken. It is not the Americans who make us weak. It is disunity, divisiveness, and disorder. I say this as someone who fought for our freedom and knows the cost of genuine sacrifice. Go home. Leave the streets. Stop protesting. Burn these banners of misplaced hate. They have no place on our island. Only through hard work will we prevail. Discord is for the weak. We are not—*"

The video suddenly cut out. Static reigned. Sherman's instinct was to thump the television like his dad did when he was a kid. Edward picked up the remote and switched channels. The next one worked fine. He went back to the static.

Charlotte paced, agitated by the timing.

"Odd," said Miguel. "Usually, he goes on for hours."

As if on cue, the static switched to black, then a new image.

The man on the screen was not the president. He did not sit behind an ornate desk overlooking the mainland. He was not old, nor did he wear an expensive suit. The man was youngish, dressed in a freshly pressed blue uniform, and stood overlooking the protestors. His wide, round face bubbled with energy.

"*My apologies for the interruption, but I can no longer sit idly by and listen,*" said the man in Spanish.

"Oh, shit," said Charlotte.

"Crap," added Edward.

"*I am General Asumu, leader of the Gendarme, and protector of this magnificent island. Brothers and sisters, this is our home, our land, and Mbasogo sullies it with his dirty deals. We break ourselves for his gain. The wealth of our great island flows out like the tide. It drifts into the pockets of corrupt politicians and neocolonial governments. The oil we draw from the ocean floor does not power our homes. It buys fancy cars for Mbasogo's sons. It feeds the fat, opulent men in the fake capital they are building. And now this president-for-life wants to sell our most precious metals to the Americans for pennies. Our riches. Our minerals. Extracted and shipped away so the west can get a new smartphone every year.*"

"He's not wrong," whispered Miguel.

"*Well, I say enough,*" continued Asumu. "*It is time we stand up to these plunderers.*"

The crowd behind him roared with approval, loud enough that Sherman heard it in the distance.

"*As of noon today, I, General Asumu, have assumed control of Bioko Island and its government. We shall rid ourselves of the neocolonialists and their collaborators once and for all. To the Army and Navy, to those fine men and women, I say, join our cause. We wish you no harm. But to those who stand in the way of freedom, we will show no mercy!*"

Again, the crowd behind the general roared with enthusiastic cheers. Again, Sherman heard the cries echo through the neighborhood.

"*To the true patriots of Malabo, I command you to risk and fight with us. To our families and friends, I urge you to stay inside. The sound of freedom will ring loud and true.*"

The screen cut to black again and silence filled the small office for a moment.

Then chaos ensued.

Chapter Eleven

Sherman moved first. He set the timer on his cheap Casio watch for eight hours, hoping it wouldn't take the Marines longer—an inherent pitfall of being in the middle of nowhere, twenty-five hundred miles from Camp Lemonnier in Djibouti. A little further to Italy. Double that to the East Coast. All of which meant at least eight hours across the breadth of Africa. Assuming the Marines landed safely, they would still have to fight from the airport into Malabo.

Best case, ten hours, he thought.

Sherman updated his timer and picked up the landline to call Agent Scott.

The call went nowhere.

Sherman grabbed his satellite phone and called again.

"Captain," whispered Scott. "Am I glad to hear from you."

Whispers are not a good sign, thought Sherman, except for sweet-nothings, and he wasn't much for those.

"Status?" asked Sherman in a low voice.

"I've got the ambassador, but we didn't make it out of

the compound. Two Gendarme trucks are parked in front of the gate and I hear some unnerving radio chatter about capturing Americans."

Sherman was already in motion, moving towards the gear. Gournsey and Lopez followed.

"Understood. Are there other exits?" he asked.

"The back gate is sealed shut and everything else is surrounded by walls."

Sherman recalled the map from his prodigious geographic memory: a lone house, long driveway, surrounded by palms and overlooking the beach. Great spot, except for the current circumstances.

"Move towards the back wall but stay out of sight. We'll be there in ten minutes."

"Please hurry," said Scott.

"I'll call when we arrive."

"Okay," said Scott and ended the conversation.

Sherman pocketed the phone and found his men fully kitted and ready to go.

"Lopez, take the long guns and get on the roof. Try not to make the front-page news, but if anyone tries to get past the fence, you bury them."

Lopez merely nodded and headed for an interior ladder that led to the roof.

"Gournsey, grab Edward and meet me at the front door in a minute."

The sergeant disappeared into the crowd while Sherman grabbed an extra bag of goodies. As he left, he saw Charlotte pleading into the phone for support. She didn't look pleased at the response.

Gournsey and Edward stood by the front door—a four-inch-thick mass of bullet-resistant glass and steel. Sherman pulled Edward into the command booth, which controlled the front door and front gates.

"This is your job until we get back," said Sherman, pointing at the control panel. "You'll open the door and gate for us. After that, you don't open shit until I call you. Are we clear?"

Edward glanced down at the phone in Sherman's outstretched hand, then across at the control panel. He gulped.

"It's easy," said Gournsey. "Green opens things. Red closes them. Don't hit the green buttons until the captain calls."

Edward took the phone and nodded. "What if they start shooting?"

Gournsey smiled and said, "The door and windows can stop a fifty-caliber round, plus the extra bit encasing this booth. Besides, Lopez is on the roof. Anyone aiming this way catches one to the head."

Edward did not look pleased to receive such graphic assurances, but he gave a timid thumbs-up.

Sherman and Gournsey walked to the front door. It opened with a mechanical click. They exited and waited to hear the same noise in reverse. Edward did his job and they ran to the remaining armored SUV, of which the embassy had two. Scott had taken the other.

The front guardhouse was empty. Wisely, the local guards disappeared after the announcement. Sherman didn't blame them—not their fight. After the gate slid open, Gournsey gunned the engine and they careened onto an empty residential street.

Within two turns, they were on the principal thoroughfare heading towards the airport. The ambassador's house once belonged to Chevron or some other oil conglomerate, which rented the place to the US Government out of goodwill and a significant amount of money. Nothing was free in the tangled web of government procurement.

The highway was empty. Word, it seemed, traveled fast. Just at the horizon, barely visible in the thick island air, sirens flashed blue and red. The Gendarme had already blocked the road to the airport.

No way out. No way in.

"Take the next right," said Sherman.

The SUV bounded onto a muddy dirt road, sloshing as the heavy vehicle plowed through an endless string of puddles.

"Left past those trees," instructed Sherman, creating a new route from memory and instinct.

Gournsey swung onto a walking path, veering between trees and the occasional shack that materialized out of the thick vegetation. They bumped forward for several minutes until the path widened.

"Here," said Sherman.

Gournsey swung the SUV around to face where they'd come from and parked, ready for an escape.

As they exited and shouldered their rifles, Gournsey asked, "Rules of engagement?"

Sherman didn't like fluid situations draped in layers of gray. He didn't want to hurt an innocent bystander but took a logical leap. Any paramilitary officers surrounding the ambassador's house were enemy combatants.

"If they raise up, we put them down," Sherman answered.

"You know I love holler rules," said Gournsey.

From the SUV to the compound wall was less than a half-mile. Sherman called Scott on the way.

"We're three minutes out," he said to a barely audible DSS agent.

"Hurry. Movement at the back gate and breaching at the front."

"Understood. Hold tight," replied Sherman.

He picked up the pace. Gournsey followed.

The waist-high grass and bushes fell away as they crossed the property line. Manicured palms swayed in the breeze. The compound wall topped with razor wire lay ahead of them.

Sherman veered right. He stopped at the corner of the compound and peeked towards the back gate. Four soldiers in blue Gendarme uniforms were busy trying to pry open the back gate with an industrial-sized crowbar. The break-in was a failure and all four ignored the outside world as they kept trying.

They didn't see Sherman and Gournsey close the gap. The soldiers focused on the crowbar, the gate, and their repeated failure.

In a fleeting moment of chivalry, Sherman considered giving the soldiers a fair chance to surrender.

He did not.

Instead, he and Gournsey descended upon the soldiers like hungry lions. In a brief spasm of violence, four bodies slumped to the red earth. Three soldiers took suppressed pistol rounds to the face. Not lightweight 9mm bullets, but the heavier .45 caliber rounds from Sherman's Heckler & Koch. Gournsey extracted his knife from the fourth soldier's neck.

The air smelled of blood, piss, gun smoke, and the ever-present rot of tropical places. Gournsey pulled the bodies aside like large sacks of flour while Sherman examined the gate. Their attempts to open it were not in vain. They'd nearly pried apart the rusty hinges from the concrete wall.

"You're up," whispered Sherman, passing Gournsey the crowbar.

The sergeant stepped up, jammed the crowbar, and pulled hard. Metal screeched. Bolts popped. The hinges sheared off. He repeated the process with the bottom one. Sweat dripped down his neck from the effort and adrenaline.

Gournsey pulled open the broken gate and Sherman slipped inside. He was in the expensive back patio—fancy chairs and a teak table, a pool beyond that. A storage shed with a corrugated tin roof leaned against a wall to Sherman's right, the type gardeners used.

Loud crunches of metal-on-metal echoed from the front gate—the sound of imminent conflict.

They're breaching, thought Sherman.

He moved toward the shed and hissed, "Time to go."

One eye poked out of the shed door followed by an extremely relieved-looking face. Scott edged out. Ambassador Duggan followed—an early forties woman with a prominent brow, pale topaz eyes, and a professorial aura. She appeared frightened but did not panic.

"I owe you big for this, Captain," whispered Scott.

"You can pay up once you're stateside. Head through the back gate, Sergeant Gournsey is waiting."

Scott nodded while the ambassador gave a relieved smile.

Wait until they see what's outside, thought Sherman.

Once they were through, he moved to Scott's SUV, which was parked alongside the house. By the sounds coming from the front gate, it was still holding. Carefully, he pulled the pin on a grenade and wedged it under the front tire, leaving a nasty surprise for whoever moved it.

Then Sherman ran like hell back to the gate.

Agent Scott and Ambassador Duggan stood behind Gournsey, trying not to look at the bloody mess of recently breathing human beings on the ground.

"Time to go," said Sherman. "You two stay behind me and in front of the sergeant. No stopping. No yelling. Nothing but what we say. Understood?"

Scott nodded with understanding and put the ambassador behind him, sandwiched between the soldiers.

Sherman edged to the corner of the compound. Shouts came from within—angry shouting. They called for the ambassador to come out using slurs that Sherman could only roughly translate.

"They're in the compound," said Gournsey.

Sherman looked down the outside length of the wall towards the driveway, suddenly begrudging the wide gap of manicured lawn between them and the uncut forest. From the chaotic sounds, most of the soldiers were busy looking for the ambassador.

Raising his hand, Sherman motioned forward.

Twenty paces across the well-cut lawn and under the hand trimmed palms, Sherman saw a man step around the wall. Silhouetted against the vibrant green, his blue uniform looked almost black.

The figure stopped.

Fifty yards separated them.

The soldier looked at Sherman.

Sherman took a knee. The others kept moving, urged on by Gournsey.

The soldier raised his rifle—a newer AK variant. It

shined with gun oil, fresh out of the crate from some Eastern Bloc country.

Sherman didn't hesitate—no second thoughts or political considerations. He opened fire.

Five quick suppressed shots caught the soldier center mass, no louder than a paintball gun and barely audible amid the chaos in the compound. The guy tumbled backward, his finger squeezed tightly around that shiny new trigger.

The air roared with an entire magazine worth of gunfire. Loud cracks reverberated off and over the wall. The shouts from within grew louder and more concerned. Boots pounded. Gear clinked.

Sherman ran hard.

As he reached the tangled edge of uncut trees and thickets of bushes, he found Gournsey covering his retreat from behind an old hunk of concrete covered with vines. The sergeant opened fire as Sherman slid into the undergrowth next to Scott and the ambassador. Both looked terrified but lucid.

"Moving," Sherman shouted over his shoulder.

Soon, the crack of a Soviet caliber overwhelmed the dainty sound of Gournsey's suppressed rifle. Bullets hissed and snapped, zipping through the leaves like angry hornets.

Sherman stopped twenty yards further, behind the thick trunk of an ancient tree. Scott and Duggan clung to the bark with fervent hope.

"Stay crouched. Be ready to move," he told them.

A moment later, Gournsey crashed by, practically pulling the two Americans along like toddlers yanked away from the road by a protective parent.

"Moving," he shouted to Sherman.

Sherman emptied his magazine into the forest, still

hissing and snapping with incoming fire. Then he too retreated.

Twice more, they leap-frogged back to the SUV. Each time, the enemy's fire slackened. The Gendarme did not want to follow them into the unknown.

When they reached the car, sweat poured down their faces. The adrenaline and exertion stretched eyes wide and mouths taut. They piled into the SUV without a word.

Gournsey drove while Sherman watched behind them.

"Ma'am, lay on the floor and keep down. I'll tell you when it's safe to move," Sherman said, instructing the ambassador what to do.

Duggan gave him a look of resigned disdain.

The SUV bumped wildly over ruts and potholes while Gournsey struggled to maintain control through the mud.

He turned right out of the forest walking trail and onto the dirt road. Sherman swiveled right towards the driveway and the airport and the distant sirens they'd seen on the way in.

The main road approached ahead of them.

"Clear right," he said.

Gournsey flung the wheel left and the SUV vaulted out of the mud and onto the blacktop. The tires screeched. The engine groaned.

Sherman shifted again to look behind them.

A quarter-mile back, a blue truck bounced onto the road with two men in front. A third stood in the truck bed, trying to steady his rifle in their direction.

"Contact rear," Sherman said, his voice dry and even like someone reciting baseball stats after the game.

Gournsey mashed the accelerator in an all-out race to the next turn. The dry bark of gunfire howled behind them.

Bullets smacked into the rear window with a heavy crunch, leaving impact craters in the thick glass.

"Let me out past the next turn," said Sherman.

"We can beat them to the embassy," said Gournsey.

"I don't want them to know we got that far."

The sergeant shrugged. "They'll assume."

"Just past the next turn," repeated Sherman.

"Copy that."

The V8 rumbled and the turn toward the embassy quickly loomed. Gournsey cut hard and braked fast.

Bullet-resistant windows don't roll down. Too heavy. Sherman had no chance for a Hollywood-style car chase with him leaning out the window firing like crazy. Not a possibility. Thus, the unplanned ambush. Better than nothing.

Sherman jumped out at a run and made for the nearest bit of cover, which was a Toyota sedan several shades of blue. Placing himself behind the engine block, Sherman put an extra magazine on the hood and switched his HK416 rifle to full-auto.

As the SUV receded, Sherman heard the truck approaching. The brakes squealed. The tires chirped. A newish Nissan truck barreled through the corner's apex with three guys. Two in front bracing against the dashboard. One at the back hanging on for dear life.

All realized their mistake too late.

Sherman fired. The air thrummed. His ears hurt. Brass tinkled against the car hood before tumbling to the ground. The universe slowed and condensed into that moment. Everything boiled down to him, the gun, and the truck.

He emptied all thirty rounds in the magazine in a few heartbeats. The truck rolled past covered in blood and broken glass. Sherman grabbed the magazine from the hood and reloaded.

The truck rolled to a stop against a corrugated metal fence. Sherman walked up and fired three more times. Unnecessary shots, but he was thorough.

Gournsey backed up the SUV.

Sherman got in.

"You can sit up now," he told the ambassador.

Duggan glanced through the back window, webbed with cracks, at the truck covered with blood and bits of bodies. She gazed at the sheer violence for a long moment of silence. Then she turned back to Sherman and said, "Thank you, Captain."

Chapter Twelve

Charlotte McMillan paced the conference room floor in great lion-like strides. She kept her head high, chin out, and phone glued to her ear. Since the coup began, she'd made no less than sixteen calls.

Her first call to her real boss, the Assistant Director of the CIA, did not go as planned. The man did not enjoy looking bad, and an unpredicted anti-American coup made the intelligence agency look anything but intelligent.

"Why the hell didn't you see this coming?" he demanded.

Charlotte did not like the use of a singular noun in his question, but she was the regional specialist, so she plowed on.

"The situation developed quicker than our analysts could foresee," she replied.

"Don't bullshit a bullshitter, Charlotte."

"Fine, we missed it," she admitted.

"We need that lithium, Charlotte. They just revised the

estimates. Enough to power two generations. It's worth trillions."

Charlotte didn't respond to that mistake of sizing, which had she known, would have changed American strategy in the region.

"Our goal is to keep President Mbasogo in power," continued the assistant director. "He signed the deal. We need to keep him in control of the island."

"Sir, I can hear fighting on the streets. From what I can tell, the Gendarme general is already attacking the army base nearby. My primary goal is surviving the next twenty-four hours."

"Your job is to keep that deal alive," he replied and hung up.

Charlotte wanted to scream. The man was an absolute ass-kissing, short-sighted son-of-a-bitch, but he wasn't wrong. The view from the top was clear. America needed those minerals for any chance at a 'green' energy independence from China, who controlled most of the world's supply of lithium. Lithium was the linchpin in the renewable energy and technology sectors. Without it, America would inevitably fall behind and succumb to the whims of China.

Yet, Charlotte couldn't do a damn thing if she was dead. A fact the assistant director did not appreciate in its totality.

In a flash of pure Machiavellian genius, Charlotte crafted a plan. When the Marines arrived and if President Mbasogo invited them to stay as peacekeepers, then perhaps he could maintain control of the island he'd abandoned in favor of the mainland. America might take a knock in the media for propping up a dictator, but State could spin it as preventing a bloody coup. A sign of multilateral cooperation, even as progress, depending on the news outlet and their definition of the word.

At least, Charlotte hoped it would work.

First, she needed to make sure the Marines were coming. That meant the traditional channels. No circumventing the process. That would raise suspicions. It needed to come from within the embassy. Americans under attack always justified force.

She went to get Edward and found him in the fortified booth overlooking the front door.

"What are you doing?" she asked, perplexed by his strained conversation and general lack of activity.

"Waiting for Captain Sherman. He told me to stay here and open the gate when they return."

"Have you called the emergency line?"

Edward glanced at her. "No, not yet."

"Call the damn line," she ordered.

"But the gate," he protested.

Charlotte glanced at her watch. "The captain left ten minutes ago. I'd say you have ten more before he comes back. Make the call now."

Edward nodded and pulled out the red emergency binder. He fumbled through the pages laying out the plans for various scenarios. When he found the correct number, he picked up the landline, but Charlotte stopped him.

"Use the satellite phone," she said. "They cut all the phone lines."

"Right," mumbled Edward before he dialed.

Charlotte went to the window overlooking the front gate and the city beyond. Black smoke rose from downtown. Thick columns—a dozen, maybe more. The wind mingled them together so she couldn't tell how many fires burned.

Behind her, Edward was progressing through the chain

of command, raising the red flag at each stage. Several massive explosions boomed toward the port. Edward looked up in alarm.

"Keep going," urged Charlotte.

She walked towards the center of the building and the ladder leading to the flat roof. Taking a breath, she climbed to the top. Corporal Lopez was in one corner gazing down the road through his scope.

"Any updates?" asked Charlotte.

Lopez didn't turn to answer. "They just blew up part of the port. My guess is they sank the Navy's one and only frigate. That's what I would have done."

"And the army base?"

Lopez swiveled to look towards the thickest column of smoke. Gunfire rattled from that direction. An occasional tracer streaked through the smoky sky.

"I don't have a clear view, but I'd say they took a pounding."

The sheer scale and organization of the coup gave Charlotte pause. Something felt off, just like the protests. Russian interference somewhere meant Russian interference everywhere.

"Any movement near us?" she asked.

"A few SUVs went down the road," said Lopez.

"Gendarme?" she asked.

"No."

"Care to hazard a guess who?"

"Above my paygrade," replied the corporal.

"Humor me."

"If I were to speculate, which I'm not, I'd say they were armored SUVs. Springs were stiff from the weight. Windows stayed up because they couldn't roll them down.

I'd say four occupants per vehicle based on the silhouettes. Certainly not Americans, but similar."

"Mercenaries?"

"Your word, not mine."

"But you agree," she said.

"I don't disagree," said Lopez.

Charlotte headed back down the ladder with a frown burrowed deep into her forehead. She didn't think there'd be a direct confrontation between Sherman and the Russians, but the fallout of that possibility was not something she wanted to consider. Russia regarded the mercenaries as a proxy army and might retaliate with force if they were killed.

In the command booth, Edward had only progressed a few bureaucratic layers.

"Yes, sir. That's what I've been saying. Yes, it's urgent. No, I haven't been drinking. No, this is not a prank. Please, things are out of control… Okay. Thank you."

Edward muted the call and looked at Charlotte in frustration.

"This is taking forever," he said.

"They don't send in the Marines for just anything," she replied and went back to the front window.

Down the road, a family crossed, clutching a few possessions. The youngest child rode on the mother's back. Even from a distance, Charlotte understood their fear. It made her wince. Things would get uglier before they got better, and her job wasn't to make anything better, not for people like that.

From around the corner thundered a white SUV with embassy plates. It was missing a mirror with bullets pockmarking the back windows. Charlotte crossed her fingers that Sherman was inside. Those three soldiers were the only thing standing between her and a very unpleasant end.

She motioned for Edward to open the gate.

He didn't see her.

Charlotte yelled. He ignored her.

The SUV barreled toward the gate.

Charlotte ran into the booth, shoved Edward aside, and slammed down the green button.

The gate slid open.

Seconds later, the SUV bounced over the speed bumps and screeched to a halt. Charlotte held her breath, only releasing it when all four doors opened.

She buzzed Sherman inside, followed by Gournsey, Agent Scott and a very frazzled-looking Ambassador Duggan.

Sherman stopped by the booth as the others went to rest. He looked wired. Charlotte knew the look—pure adrenaline in action. Knowing the captain, a wild ride wouldn't elicit that much of a response. Dark specks of blood dappled his vest like an abstract canvas.

"How did it go?" she asked.

"The Gendarme already had the place surrounded when we arrived," he said.

"That's awfully quick."

"They've blocked the road to the airport as well."

She glanced at the still wet blood splatter. "I'm guessing they didn't just let you in."

"I didn't ask," Sherman replied.

"Good work," said Charlotte. "When you have a minute, we need to talk."

Sherman nodded. "I'll meet you on the roof in five," he said before turning to Edward. "Do you have an ETA on the Marines?"

It was the same question dangling from Charlotte's lips.

"Twelve hours," said Edward.

Sherman tapped a couple of buttons on his watch but said nothing. He turned and left, rifle in hand.

"Why so long?" asked Charlotte.

"Thunderstorms over the Congo. They must divert south and then refuel."

"Not good," said Charlotte.

"I was afraid you'd say that," replied Edward.

"Worrying about it will not make it better. I need you to pull together the personnel lists. Make sure we account for all Americans in-country."

"What about the locals who work here?" he asked.

"We couldn't get all the interpreters out of Afghanistan after twenty years of war. I'm afraid all they'll get is kind words and a sympathetic press release."

"That's crap," he replied. "You heard the general's speech. Americans and collaborators."

Charlotte nodded. "I heard."

"And you're not going to do anything?"

"I'm going to do everything I can," replied Charlotte, her voice rose despite her best efforts to remain calm. "And that still won't be enough. And people will still die."

"Okay," said Edward softly. "Okay, I'll start on the lists."

"Thank you. Bring them into the conference room when you're done."

Charlotte gave Edward an encouraging slap on the back that she hoped didn't betray her own doubts, then headed back to the roof.

Twelve hours is too damn long, she thought.

She found Sherman sitting on an upturned beer crate, pouring a bottle of water over his head. Behind him, Lopez hadn't moved from his overwatch position, still hidden behind the raised lip of the roof.

She took a seat next to Sherman.

"The Marines won't land until midnight," she said.

Sherman glanced at his watch. He looked tired and wired at the same time.

"I'm aware," he replied.

Smoke still filled the sky like endless gray geysers. They billowed and rippled in the wind.

"What happened out there?" she asked.

"Seven or eight less people to shoot back."

"All Gendarme?" she probed, hoping the captain hadn't started something larger.

Sherman glanced at her without moving his head. "No Russians, if that's what you're asking."

"It's a page from their playbook," said Charlotte. "Besides, the corporal saw some suspicious SUVs earlier."

Sherman twisted towards Lopez. "Is that true?"

"I saw 'em. Who they are is just a guess."

"Are we talking twenty or eighty percent certain?"

"Seventy," said Lopez.

"Why didn't you say so?" said Charlotte. "Seventy is strong."

"Seventy is big enough to drive a tank through what you don't know," said Sherman.

"A lot of green," added Lopez.

Charlotte assumed that was a billiards reference and not golf-related. She couldn't imagine the corporal in a collared shirt. Besides, she was more of a shuffleboard kind of woman. All that sand made for some mystery.

"Langley will take seventy percent. Add that to the ninety percent certainty the Russians are behind the protests, and we come to a thoroughly acceptable eighty percent."

"If you say so," said Lopez.

Charlotte looked to Sherman for an opinion. Streaks of dirt ran down the shirt under his vest. Red dirt or maybe blood.

"The only hostiles I've seen wore blue Gendarme uniforms, but I'm not discounting the bigger threat. First Gournsey, now this. It feels like we're spinning in a much bigger wave."

"I just need you to be careful out there," she added and gestured towards the city. "Our situation here might lead to an actual shooting war if we blow up the wrong guys."

"Don't kill the Russians," said Sherman. "How confusing that would have been to my father!"

Charlotte frowned. The point was valid despite his cynicism. "Just keep an eye on the longer game. That's all I'm asking."

Sherman looked at her with his strange orange-green eyes that reminded her of a cat. A big, dangerous, hungry cat.

"And what is your long game?" he asked in a flat, dry tone.

Charlotte said nothing. Not at first. He knew her too well.

"I'm here to do my job, just like you," she said after a pause.

Sherman nodded and opened another bottle of water, this time to drink.

"Have we accounted for all Americans?" he asked.

"Edward is working on that now. We should have the list finalized soon."

"Do you know how many people work here?" he asked.

"Usually, five or six for a place this low on the totem pole."

"Anyone else in country that we need to protect?" asked Sherman.

Charlotte knew he meant other CIA assets. Given the situation, it was a fair question.

"No one they told me about," she answered.

"That doesn't sound definitive," said Sherman.

"It never is."

"Does Langley have any surveillance assets in the area? We could use extra eyes."

"We'll get an hour of satellite coverage around two this afternoon, but this isn't a high priority tasking at the moment."

"Drones?" he wondered.

"Nothing within range," she said, which was mostly true. The CIA base in Mali could reroute a Reaper, but it would take hours before it arrived on station, assuming a minor coup in a country most people assumed was in South America garnered enough attention.

"On our own again," he said. "Should be an interesting day."

"You've seen worse," said Charlotte. She meant the comment reassuringly, but it came out nearer to a question.

"They're not shooting at us… yet. That's a plus."

Charlotte did not think that would last but said nothing. The chaos of Benghazi flashed in her mind. She knew Sherman and his team were in for a long night.

Chapter Thirteen

Miguel had a problem, a problem with no immediate solution and many unsavory outcomes. He couldn't leave the embassy grounds, not now, not during the day. Prying eyes no doubt lingered on the periphery. But he couldn't stay either. Eventually, they would come. Who exactly they were, Miguel couldn't say. The Gendarme, perhaps. Others too. The officers he knew in the Gendarme weren't any better than the police or army for that matter—better paid, yes, but not better trained. About equally corrupt too, if he was honest with himself. But the crowds were real and angry and large. He didn't want to be on the wrong side of history or a machete.

Besides, it was his fight... or that's what he told himself while sitting in the conference room as controlled chaos simmered in the halls. He was not a fan of President Mbasogo. Neither were many of his friends. They tolerated the man because that was all they knew and, in a twisted sense of irony, Mbasogo did not tolerate dissent. That duality had existed for all of Miguel's life.

Don't rock the boat if you can't swim, his father said. Miguel preferred a different boat altogether, but General Asumu was not that ship.

With nothing else to do but watch the frenzied destruction of files, Miguel searched for a fresh breeze. The harshness of air conditioning got under his skin like a rash.

Unnatural, he thought and found a ladder to climb up to the roof.

What he found was a city consuming itself. Smoke snarled up into the thick cumulous clouds overhead. In almost every direction, something burned. There was fighting too. Gunfire echoed through the streets and the occasional shell whistled in the distance. Explosions rumbled like deep fissures erupting under the earth.

Miguel realized he'd taken stability for granted. Faced with the sheer force of change, he couldn't accept the cost. What was the point of exchanging rocks for rubble?

Captain Sherman spotted Miguel frowning at the destruction and ambled over.

"I appreciate your support, Lieutenant, but this isn't the safest place to hang out. I wouldn't blame you for taking off."

Miguel cast his head upwards, squinting at the heavy tropical sun. Burning plastic wafted on the breeze, tainting the afternoon air.

"I suppose it's not the best time to leave," continued Sherman. "I can try to get you out tonight."

"But no promises?" said Miguel.

"Afraid I am all out of certainties."

"The old order is burning as we speak," said Miguel.

Sherman looked unfazed.

"You've seen this before, haven't you, Captain?"

"I'm afraid so," replied Sherman.

"How does it end?"

"Usually on a spectrum of bad to terrible, although there are always exceptions," Sherman answered.

"Like Kosovo or Rwanda," said Miguel, his mind wandering to the darkest corners of the human heart.

"I guess that all depends on what side of the fence you're on. Judging by your expression, you don't seem a fan of General Asumu."

"I'm a loyal son of Malabo, Captain Sherman. I don't want my city reduced to ashes and blood."

"Then I suppose you need to pick a side," said Sherman.

"There is no good side," said Miguel.

Sherman nodded thoughtfully and replied, "Make your own then."

Miguel chuckled softly at the idea of change, but he appreciated the idea—an example of that unbridled American optimism that he always mistook for hubris. Perhaps it had a purpose or maybe he just needed to try.

"Can I help?" he asked.

"How are your eyes?" asked Sherman.

"Keen," replied Miguel.

"The corporal over there could use a spotter, if you're willing."

Miguel considered the request, which he knew would end in bloodshed. That much was clear about the Americans.

"What are his orders?"

"Shoot anyone shooting at us," answered Sherman.

Miguel nodded. If he wanted to make his own side, helping defend the embassy was a start and he couldn't change anything from the grave.

Sherman glanced at his watch—eleven hours until the

Marines landed. The sun set at 6:30 pm and full night an hour after that, which left him five and a half hours of light and a nearly equal amount of night.

During his mental math, Sherman's satellite phone rang —a Pentagon prefix number.

"Major," he answered, a logical guess. Few people had his number; fewer still would call.

"Captain, I've got some anxious people on the line. What can you tell me?"

"We secured Ambassador Duggan and most of the American staff members at the embassy."

"Any resistance?"

Sherman visualized the Pentagon room on the other end of the line—the stars and suits, staffers from State and the CIA, coffee and pastries on the table, tense looks all around.

"The Gendarme had her residence surrounded and ready to breach when we arrived. We neutralized four hostiles during entry—one on the way out and three more during exfil to the embassy."

The major didn't miss a beat in responding but Sherman heard grumblings or mumblings from the others.

"Any casualties?"

"Not ours," answered Sherman.

The sound cut out as Sanders muted the line. Questions were brewing in the room. Political considerations. Plans and alternatives. Sherman hated the back and forth, even when he wasn't privy to the conversation.

"Captain," Sanders continued. "What can you tell us about the situation on the ground?"

"Gendarme units blocked the road to the airport. Heavy fighting downtown, presumably near the army base, but I can't confirm. Smoke is rising from multiple directions and the streets are empty."

"Any attacks on the embassy?"

"No, sir. Nothing yet. We've seen some scouts, but they were in unmarked SUVs."

"Gendarme vehicles?"

"Unknown, sir."

They placed him on mute again. Sherman waited.

"What's your best guess on the occupants of the SUVs, Captain?"

"Best guess, sir, is Russian mercenaries."

The pause on the other end lingered long enough for Sherman to imagine a wide range of responses, most of which would handicap his operational scope.

"Captain," Sanders continued. "We believe the Russians are no longer operating under Kremlin orders, but we cannot confirm."

"Does this change my rules of engagement?" asked Sherman.

"You are authorized to defend American lives if threatened. No offensive operations," replied Sanders.

"Understood," said Sherman.

"Marines' ETA to the airport is twenty-four hundred hours. They will move to your position from there."

"Copy that. They're in for a fight."

"I don't think they'd have it any other way," replied Sanders. "Stay safe out there, Captain."

"Thanks, sir."

Sherman hung up and digested the conversation, which, in his opinion, only contained bad news. Untethered Russians were far worse than those on the Kremlin's leash.

"Any good news?" asked Lopez.

"They're airdropping in cases of beer," Sherman joked.

"We're on our own then," said Lopez.

"Correct. The major also mentioned our neighborhood Russians are playing their own hand, so keep an eye out. I'm sure they'll be well compensated for blowing us up."

"Crazy Ivans," said Lopez.

"Looks that way," said Sherman.

"Am I free to fire?"

"If they get out and give you a dirty look, yeah, put them down."

"Copy that," said Lopez.

"I'll be downstairs if you need me," added Sherman and retreated down the ladder.

Chaos and fear greeted him. Edward paced back and forth feverishly writing names on a whiteboard while Ambassador Duggan and Agent Scott circled locations on a giant map spread across the conference room table. Charlotte stayed in an office across the hall, phone to her ear.

"Captain," called Edward. "Where have you been? We have an issue."

The others glanced up as Sherman stepped into the room.

"You've got my attention," he said.

"We're missing two embassy staff members. Jim Parker and Evelyn Ramos."

"Have you contacted them?" asked Sherman, starting at the beginning.

"I called on the satellite phone. No answer."

Not one for worst-case scenarios or fear-mongering, Sherman looked at the map laid out on the table. Red lines circled two buildings near the embassy, which Agent Scott had labeled in blue.

"Do they normally answer on a Sunday?" he asked. "Did they have any trips planned?" Sherman could have gone on with many reasons someone would not answer their phone.

"Not… always," said Edward. "Jim likes the… uh, nightlife and Evelyn—"

"Likes to wander," Scott interjected. "A free spirit type."

"How far does she wander?" asked Sherman, hoping she took a vacation to Italy or Newark—anywhere out of the country.

"She's seen more of the island than most locals," Scott answered.

"A real connoisseur of local culture," added Ambassador Duggan. "She has contacts from all walks of life."

Sherman always kept his sat-phone with him, but he knew not everyone was so diligent.

"What number did you call?" he asked.

"Their emergency phones. They still have signal despite the network blackouts."

"Do you carry your emergency phone at all times?" he asked Edward.

"Well, no," admitted Edward.

"Perhaps we ought to knock on their doors first, before chasing wild speculation," said Sherman.

No one in the room raised their eyes to meet his, which meant no one wanted to leave the compound.

"That's settled," he said. "Edward, grab a vest from that table over there and meet me at the front door in five minutes. We're visiting your co-workers."

"Out there?" asked Edward in a small voice.

"Yes, Edward. Out there."

If Edward had more complaints, he did not voice them, though his body language suggested many objections.

Sherman went to find Gournsey, which was easy. The man took up half a room.

"I'm taking Edward to find some stragglers. Make sure they don't burn the place down in a panic while I'm gone."

"I'm good at babysitting," said Gournsey.

"Which is why I'm asking you and not Lopez."

"High praise indeed, Captain."

Sherman smiled. "Keep them calm. Radio if something changes."

"Copy that. Good hunting."

Sherman left and walked out the front door with Edward close behind. His lanky frame made the vest look comically short—not great for survival but humorous to behold, like a teenager wearing a toddler's shirt.

Past the bullet-resistant glass, Edward did little to inspire Sherman's confidence. As they crossed the open grassy expanse surrounding the embassy, the man hopped about as if the ground was lava.

"Edward, calm down. You'll draw attention jumping around like that."

"Sorry," said Edward a bit sheepishly. "I move a lot when I'm nervous."

"I see that," said Sherman. "Try not to. Movement catches the eye. It's hard-wired into our brains."

Edward stopped jumping. "Why do you need me?" he asked.

"Your colleagues trust you," said Sherman.

"You're persuasive enough for the both of us."

Sherman stopped behind a car at the edge of the street. "I've got the gun, so people usually listen, which is what I need you to do right now."

The comment sank into Edward's brain. He focused on Sherman's face.

"Good. Come on, Jim's house is one block up."

Edward said nothing, which is exactly what Sherman wanted. No words. Full attention.

They crossed the normally busy street without seeing a soul. An enormous explosion rattled windows and set off distant car alarms.

"What was that?" hissed Edward.

"Ammo depot or storage building," said Sherman, guessing logical places to store dangerous items. Lots of things exploded under the right circumstances. Even flour exploded when dispersed into the air and ignited.

"Echo One," radioed Lopez. "I'll lose line of sight when you round that corner. Over."

"Echo Three, understood. Out."

Sherman glanced down the next block and saw only an empty dirt street edged by gated homes. Concrete walls adorned with barbed wire crowded the shoulder of the road like miniature prisons, one after another. Jim's house was the fourth one down on the left.

"How do you get through the front gate?" Sherman asked.

"Usually, the guard lets me inside."

"Let's assume there's no guard," said Sherman, hoping they didn't run into one.

"There's a code," said Edward.

"Do you know it?"

"No, but Scott keeps track of them in the security binder."

"Echo Two," radioed Sherman. "I need a front gate code for Jim Parker. Check the security binder. Over."

Gournsey answered, "Echo One, confirmed. Wait one. Over."

More of the house came into view as they moved down the dirt road. All the buildings on the short block were identical save for the exterior color, which alternated between adobe and blue. Nice places as far as government rentals went.

The street ended a few yards past the last house. Beyond that was untamed forest and beyond that lay the ocean, churning against the beach just within earshot.

"What does Jim do at the embassy?" asked Sherman as he stepped carefully forward.

"Technically, he's an economist, but he has a background in mining."

Lithium, thought Sherman.

"And he likes to party?"

"He's still pretty young," answered Edward, who didn't look all that old.

When they reached the thick metal gate leading into the walled courtyard, they didn't need a code.

The gate was open.

Sherman motioned Edward back and peeked through the opening. The guard was gone. A metal chair lay toppled and playing cards covered the lawn. They'd left in a hurry.

Not his fight, thought Sherman.

He radioed Gournsey. "Echo Two, the outer door is open. Moving in. Over."

Beyond the walls the sound of water gurgled from a fountain. Sherman found himself in a lavish courtyard built of brick and surrounded by Kentucky bluegrass. Facsimiles of American life abounded. A gas barbeque and smoker stood to one side, cornhole boards on the other.

Past the fountain was the front door, a white chunk of wood that resembled any myriad of suburban homes, replete with keypad and lock.

Sherman stopped.

The front door was open too.

He didn't like unguarded gates and open doors.

"Echo Two. No need for the codes. The front door is open. Making entry. Out."

Edward's mouth gaped like a tunnel entrance.

"Stay behind me. Do as I say. Nothing more. Nothing less. Am I clear?" whispered Sherman.

Edward nodded, probably more out of habit than any mental state of readiness.

Sherman didn't hesitate. He slipped inside, rifle shouldered, ready for all the terrible possibilities. Beyond the door was a hallway that ran through the entire first floor to the back door. On the right side were stairs and doors to rooms unseen. The left side opened into a living room and kitchen or dining area. Sherman didn't know what they called it anymore. He didn't own a home.

He didn't see anyone. Not in the flesh.

Papers covered the floor like great rectangular snowflakes. Couch pillows lay scattered on the rug. Water pooled by an overturned cup.

Sherman wondered if they were taking hostages or just executing them.

He cleared front to back, through the living room, and into the kitchen.

Nothing.

No bodies. No blood. Just evidence of a struggle.

Someone locked the back door from the inside, so Sherman circled back towards the stairs leading to the second story. He cleared a spare bedroom and a bathroom on the way.

The steps were concrete like the house itself. Wood rotted too quickly. Sherman took them slowly, listening with each upward movement.

A faint rustling filtered down the stairwell—the sound

of papers falling or being spread out. Sherman pointed to his ear and then up. He hoped Edward understood.

The stairs ended on a landing and what Sherman guessed was another straight shot hallway down the length of the second floor.

When he reached the top, he stopped again. Despite the narrow exterior, the house felt large. Two doors were on his right—one to his left and one straight ahead. Both right and left doors were wide open, the master bedroom straight ahead was only open a crack.

More sounds of a search came from his left. File cabinets opening. Drawers shutting. Methodical work, performed in silence. No profanity or anger or broken glass. A focused search.

Sherman padded across the carpeted floor like a cat. Edward, less so, but he didn't clomp about. They reached the left door.

Sherman paused to listen.

Then he stepped through.

Three shapes caught his attention.

Two men stood over a third, who kneeled on the ground, searching through papers.

The two standing wore olive-green fatigues and balaclavas, despite the heat outside. No visible insignia on either shoulder. They carried rifles, somewhat blocky and made of polymer, but unmistakably Russian. Newer AK variants in the 100 series. Sherman knew that much in a glance.

Not Gendarme, thought Sherman.

Despite their concern over the papers on the floor, the men sensed Sherman's arrival. They whirled toward him with practiced ease.

As they turned, Sherman fired from right to left.

Two bullets each. Not fifteen feet away.

Pop-pop. Dead. Repeat.

It all happened so quickly that Edward didn't move. He stood there, stunned at the unmitigated violence. Sherman had to push him aside when he turned back toward the hallway.

A moment later, the master bedroom door shredded in a blizzard of splinters. Gunfire roared as bits of sheetrock and chunks of concrete cascaded through the air, peppering Sherman and Edward.

Sherman dove to the floor next to the two dead men and crawled backward over a carpet slick with blood and sprinkled with dust. He tried to get an angle through the doorway and down the hall toward the shooter.

He rolled right and found the geometry: a narrow angle out of his door and down to the master bedroom.

The shooting stopped long enough for a reload then resumed with terrifying force. The sheer power of it all still amazed Sherman. He'd never lost that respect. Doing so would be fatal, like a sailor losing respect for the sea.

Bullets hissed, cracked, and snapped.

Edward whimpered.

Sherman watched and waited.

A faint shadow flickered down the hall. Dark edges of a figure flashed through the bullet holes. Not much, but enough.

Sherman fired. Two consecutive bursts thumped and whooshed in the small office room.

A cry of pain rang out from down the hall—visceral and raw—then moaning, then silence.

Sherman didn't move. He covered the angle and waited. Through the gap, he could just make out a face lying on the floor, hidden by a black balaclava and covered in red.

Edward hissed and pointed to the third man, the one in

shorts and a shirt that Sherman guessed was Jim in that split-second when he decided who to shoot.

Jim was on his ass, leaning sideways against a wall. His face was pale, his breathing ragged. He clutched at his side. Blood oozed through his fingers.

Not good, thought Sherman.

He rolled to one side and took out a field dressing designed to control significant hemorrhaging. From what Sherman could see, Jim needed more than that.

He handed the bandage to Edward but kept his rifle aimed at the door.

Sherman spoke slowly, pausing at each instruction. "Unwrap that, lift his shirt up, place the white side against the wound, press hard, and wrap the sticky sides all the way around his back."

Edward complied.

His hands shook. Jim moaned in pain. His face went paler and clammy. Shock began to set in.

Sherman stood up. He didn't have time for any more waiting or cat and mouse games. Jim was bleeding out. He had minutes—not hours—to get help.

He pulled the pin on a grenade and tossed it down the hall and into the master bedroom. Then he heaved himself over Jim and covered his ears.

The explosion rocked the house. The conclusive blast sent papers flying and bits of concrete wall pinballed about. Smoke alarms blared.

"Pick him up," yelled Sherman. His ears rang like Sunday morning bells.

Edward didn't know how. Sherman mimed the fireman carry twice before it clicked, and Edward struggled to his feet. Jim was a much larger human and the chief political officer sagged from his weight.

Sherman stuffed the papers from the floor under his vest before swapping rifle magazines.

Reversing their entrance, Sherman went down the stairs and toward the front door, but not outside.

Not yet.

The courtyard was still empty and the front gate ajar. Still, something was off.

He radioed Lopez. "Echo Three, I need your eyes. I have one critical and multiple tangos down. Over."

"Echo One, the cross-street is empty, but I have no visual down your road. How copy? Over."

"Understood. Did anyone pull up while we were inside? Over."

"Negative, Echo One. All quiet. Over."

Sherman took one last look at Jim to make sure they weren't carrying a corpse. The American moaned in pain.

Good enough, thought Sherman.

He motioned for Edward to follow, and they crossed the courtyard and onto the dirt road. Edward, with his thin frame, wobbled. Jim clearly liked the finer things in life and his naturally robust frame had filled out accordingly.

"Hang in there," said Sherman as they slogged towards the paved road and the embassy beyond.

"Are you talking to me or him?" huffed Edward.

"You," answered Sherman. "Jim here can't do shit to save himself right now."

"He's heavy," said Edward. "And bleeding on me."

"They do that."

The trio had almost reached the end of the dirt road when Sherman's earpiece crackled to life with Lopez's voice.

"Echo One, contact left. Black SUV. Approaching fast. Over."

Sherman saw the vehicle speeding down the paved road to his left. He remembered Lopez's guess of seventy percent and the uncertainty it contained. He also recalled the masked men in Jim's house and their clear European ancestry.

Russians, he thought.

"Echo Three, bury them. Out."

Sherman pointed at a sedan parked on the other side of the street, next to the grassy buffer in front of the embassy.

"Edward, run to that car and stop. When I tell you, haul ass across the field to the embassy. Clear?"

Edward said nothing, but he nodded. Fear danced in his wide eyes. He turned and ran.

Sherman positioned himself behind a concrete wall at the intersection of the dirt and paved roads. The growl of a V8 grew louder as the SUV approached. Peeking around the corner, Sherman saw a boxy black shape hurtling down the residential street.

He raised his rifle and waited.

Chapter Fourteen

Corporal Lopez knew the ranges, distances, and variables. He'd considered the windage and the humidity. He calculated everything out and memorized it all.

The world around him fell away.

No more Miguel Ondo or embassy or distant gunfire. Everything that mattered existed inside his scope.

One black Mercedes SUV. Tinted windows. Occupants unknown. Armor unknown.

Inhale. Exhale. Gentle squeeze.

Crack!

The .338 Lapua bullet zipped across 200 yards and shredded the front tire of the SUV. The driver swerved left and then overcorrected right. With a tremendous crunch, the Mercedes crashed into the trunk of a gnarled mango tree.

From forty to zero in the blink of an eye.

Lopez chambered another round and waited.

Further down the street, Captain Sherman began advancing toward the crash.

"*The skinny one is running back here*," said Miguel in Spanish.

Lopez didn't look. He kept his attention on the SUV, never assuming the occupants were anything but a threat. They weren't dead until he sent them there.

Seconds passed. Sherman leapfrogged forward from trees to parked cars. Miguel checked on Edward. Lopez didn't move.

The rear door of the Mercedes budged, then opened. A man in green fatigues stepped out. He wore a black balaclava and a tactical vest and gripped a newer AK rifle.

Lopez fired without thought or consideration for the person at the other end—just a mental calculation of ballistics and the gentle squeeze of the trigger.

The bullet found flesh just under the man's armpit, inches above the vest. With only a couple of ribs to slow it down, the bullet tore through organs like tissue paper.

The Russian fell back into the car, already dead.

Inside the SUV, Lopez spotted another target. Same uniform. Same black balaclava. The guy reached across to close the open car door.

Lopez fired again.

This time, the bullet found a skull, but Lopez didn't see the visceral mess. He chambered another round and focused on the front seat. The goo dripping down the back window didn't even register in his mind.

He tapped the transmit button on his radio. "Echo One, two targets down. Proceed with caution. Over."

Next to him, Miguel let out a low whistle and said, "*God help us.*"

"Echo Three, I see movement in the driver's seat. Over," came Sherman's voice.

Lopez aimed at the driver's side window and fired. A

baseball-sized crater appeared, but the window held. He chambered another round and fired again—same spot but different results.

Bullet two tore through the glass, shattering what remained and revealed a gruesome scene inside.

The driver had no lower jaw while the passenger had not worn his seatbelt and took the sudden stop with the top of his head.

"Echo One, two more down in the front. Over."

Sherman reached the SUV and slowly circled around the mess. Lopez watched as he retrieved something from the driver's pocket.

As soon as Sherman got back to the embassy, Lopez immediately started looking for another threat.

By the time Sherman caught up with Edward, he'd handed Jim off to Gournsey, who carried the large man like he was a toddler. Edward lay panting just outside the front door. Sweat poured down his face and his shirt. Sherman's watch read 1300 hours—eleven hours until the Marines landed.

"You did good," he told Edward and held out his hand.

Edward accepted and wobbled to his feet again.

"What... just happened?"

Sherman ushered him through the front door and into a chair on the other side. Shock or disbelief filtered across Edward's face—not an unusual reaction given the circumstances.

Charlotte appeared with water bottles and juice boxes.

"Drink this," said Sherman, handing Edward a juice. "You need the sugar."

Charlotte pulled Sherman aside as he drank his own. He too needed the sugar.

"What the hell happened out there?" hissed Charlotte.

Sherman held out the phone and wallet he'd taken from the SUV driver.

"These guys were in Jim's house, holding him at gunpoint while they searched for something. I intervened, but he caught a round."

"Shit," said Charlotte. "And the SUV that Lopez shot?"

"Same guys. I took these off the driver."

Charlotte flipped open the wallet. "Russian ID, so that's confirmed. Local cash. Nothing much else to go on."

"I also grabbed these," said Sherman as he pulled the ream of slightly damp paper from under his vest. "Jim was going through them while the Russians watched over his shoulder."

Charlotte took the papers and frowned at the specks of blood. "I'll take a look… and, Frank, I'm glad you're back."

Sherman shared the sentiment. He moved deeper into the embassy and found Lopez hunched over Jim in a makeshift operating room. Several chucks pads covered the table, and the ambassador held a desk lamp above Jim's torso.

Lopez worked feverishly to stabilize the American, but he was no doctor and time was running out. They called it the golden hour—that time window between life and death when everything came down to getting to a trauma center.

"How bad is he?" asked Sherman.

"No exit wound, so what hit him is still inside," said Lopez. "He needs a surgeon."

"Understood. Do what you can."

Never one for excess words, Lopez nodded and went to work, but Sherman understood the unspoken. Without intervention, Jim would die before dark.

Sherman moved on and found Edward resting on a couch in the embassy break room.

"Is Jim going to make it?" he asked as Sherman entered.

"That depends. Do you know any trauma surgeons?"

Edward's eyes cast about in thought then distress. "No," he replied. "Maybe the hospital."

"Can't go there," said Sherman. "It's likely overwhelmed from the fighting and surrounded by Gendarme."

"Even the private hospital?" asked Edward.

Sherman frowned. He didn't recall seeing a private hospital on any map or reading about one in the briefing.

"Where is it?" he asked.

"East of town. Where all the rich people live."

"Follow me," said Sherman, then he marched off to the conference room with the whiteboard and map. He crossed off Jim's name, then smoothed out the map.

"Where is the hospital?"

Edward pointed to a clump of buildings east of the city along the coastal road. The houses were large and widely spaced. A golf course meandered between them. The drive from the embassy was long on a good day with normal traffic and no hostile forces controlling the streets.

"Not doable," said Sherman. "Too much ground to cover. We don't know the extent of the fighting or Gendarme locations."

Edward's shoulders slumped forward in defeat. "Poor Jim," he added.

"Always have a backup plan," said Sherman. "What's our next best option? A doctor or a nurse. Know any of them?"

"The Navy rotates in a doctor every few months, but we fell off the schedule. It's cheaper to fly us out than bring someone in."

"No doctor. Check. Any nurses—practicing or otherwise?"

Edward sat down and leaned back on two legs of the chair. Suddenly, he rocketed forward and snapped his fingers. "Evelyn… she used to be a nurse in the Air Force."

Evelyn Ramos. The last name on the whiteboard. Location unknown.

"I guess that's two birds with one stone," said Sherman. "Did you find her location?"

Edward resumed his slump. "No."

Undeterred, Sherman picked up his phone and dialed Major Sanders, who answered before the first ring ended.

"Captain, status update?"

"Multiple mercenaries KIA. One American civilian in critical condition. One more still missing."

"Name of the missing American?"

"Evelyn Ramos. Last location unknown."

"Wait one," replied Sanders and the line fell silent.

Sherman waited. He had nothing but time and no time at all. Ten plus hours for the Marines to arrive and less than one to find Jim help.

"I have an active ping, sending you the coordinates," said Sanders, returning to the call.

Sherman's phone dinged and he wrote the string of numbers.

"Copy that," he said.

"What can you tell us about the mercenaries?"

"Russian IDs. Nice kits. Otherwise, dead."

"Understood."

"I scooped up a phone and some pocket litter. Ms. McMillan has the intel."

"And the critical case?"

"Jim Parker. Economist. Gunshot wound to the lower abdomen. Critical and fading."

"Options?" asked Sanders.

"Limited. I'm told Evelyn Ramos was an Air Force nurse. Can you pull her record?"

"Yes. Getting it up now."

A din of clacking keyboards and shuffling papers ensued.

"Confirmed. She was a trauma nurse at Balad Field in Iraq."

"Good. Better than a doctor," said Sherman. Nurses of her pedigree saw more carnage in a week than most doctors saw in a lifetime.

"Do you have an extraction plan?"

Sherman looked down at the map and the small X he'd drawn. According to her emergency locator, Evelyn was five miles due south of Malabo. The map showed a cluster of buildings on the side of the mountain.

"Grab and go," Sherman answered.

"Good hunting, Captain."

Sanders hung up, leaving Sherman staring at a map thousands of miles from help and a diminishing chance of survival.

"Do you know what's down there?" he asked Edward, pointing to the map.

"I think it's an eco-resort. Go and stay off the grid. Unplug and all that."

"That would explain why you couldn't find her," said Sherman.

Edward traced the route with his finger, south from the embassy and out of the city. "She's far away," he said, almost absentmindedly.

By degrees, he was correct. Five miles was not far in America—an eight-minute drive on a highway. But five miles on rutted roads, dodging Gendarme units, was another beast.

Two birds, one stone, thought Sherman.

"I need to restock," he said and turned towards the stash of ammo.

"You're going?" asked Edward,

"You're staying," said Sherman, hoping to give the man some relief.

"I can go."

"While I appreciate your willingness," said Sherman. "Now is not the time for bravery."

"They say guilt is the underbelly of bravery," replied Edward.

"I've heard. You can unburden yourself over a beer stateside. For now, stay here and help Sergeant Gournsey."

"Who's going with you?" asked Edward, looking somewhat relieved.

"The only person around who knows the island," Sherman answered.

Edward glanced around as if expecting to see someone. "You can't mean Lieutenant Ondo? You don't know his loyalties. He wasn't exactly booing General Asumu. How do you know he's not playing both sides?"

"I don't, but he's my best chance of getting across the city in one piece."

With that, Sherman grabbed extra gear and headed towards the ladder up to the roof, leaving Edward to fuss over needless questions.

Upon his arrival, Miguel and Lopez were deep in conversation in Spanish.

"*You seem of this place*," said Miguel.

"*It is not so different from where I grew up*," said Lopez. "*Same language, same heat, and same people just trying to get by.*" He paused and glanced at the verdant green trees. "*But with humidity and malaria.*"

"*What is the world without thick air or the red earth?*" asked Miguel.

"*Dry and hard,*" replied Lopez.

Miguel nodded at this wisdom as Sherman joined them.

"We have Evelyn's location," said Sherman.

"Is she far?" asked Lopez.

"Five miles due south of here."

With a slow arc of his head, Lopez gazed south at the thick plumes of smoke curling from downtown.

"Good news for you, there are no major military targets in that direction."

"And the bad news?" asked Sherman.

"Everything else, plus the Russians."

"The Russians," echoed Sherman.

"Are you going alone?" asked Lopez.

"I'm hoping to convince Miguel to guide me," said Sherman.

Startled by his name, Miguel carefully set the binoculars down and turned to face Sherman.

"Me?"

Sherman nodded. "I need your help dodging the Gendarme. I'm guessing you know where they'll set the roadblocks."

Miguel nodded.

"I figured as much, but will you help me?"

"I'm already helping, why should I risk more by going down there?"

"I can't answer personal questions," said Sherman.

Miguel paused for a moment to digest the statement or perhaps just to translate.

"Why now?" he asked.

"Jim, the injured one, will die today without medical

attention. Evelyn used to be a trauma nurse. Right now, she's our best bet for saving Jim."

"Lots of people will die today, why should I help you save an American over my neighbors?"

"Asked and answered," replied Sherman. "If you needed external motivation to do your job, you would have quit long ago. Which leaves some sense of duty or purpose. Therefore, it is a personal question, and I can't answer those."

Miguel smiled. His teeth flashed and cheeks crinkled. "Alright, Captain Sherman. I'll go with you, but it won't be easy."

"Show me how we get there."

Miguel agreed and they descended into the still unfolding chaos of the embassy. Gournsey met them at the conference room table. Sherman pointed to the X he'd drawn and handed Miguel a marker.

Leaning forward, Miguel traced a route, narrating as he went. He circled likely roadblocks and choke points. Many of them were in the city, fewer existed as the roads opened into the countryside. Tracing his finger south, Miguel came to a final crossroads and tapped loudly.

"This is our biggest problem," he said and stopped tapping.

Under his finger, at a village of fifty, two main roads intersected. The north-south route they would take bisected an east-west road crossing the island—a strategic point of interest no doubt on any coup planner's list.

"Options?" asked Sherman.

"You can detour west," said Miguel. "But the roads are bad, and it will add hours."

"Which we don't have. Can we drive through the village and skirt the checkpoint?"

Miguel shook his head. "Too open. They'll see us."

"How close can we get before they notice?"

Miguel's finger trapped the northern edge of the village. "After here, they'll see us for sure."

"How many should we expect?" asked Sherman.

"Two trucks, maybe more. It's hard to say."

"Six guys minimum," said Gournsey. "Not great odds. If you want me to come—"

Sherman cut him off. "Not a chance. I need you here if things get shady."

Gournsey nodded. "Heard."

"Good. Can you make sure Lieutenant Ondo has whatever gear he needs? I need to talk with the spook before we leave."

"His ex-girlfriend," Gournsey told Miguel, sniggering.

Sherman checked several rooms but only found Edward and the ambassador shredding files. She wasn't in any office or with Jim, who looked paler.

Frustrated, Sherman headed out the back door and almost ran Charlotte over as he exited.

"I was looking for you," said Sherman.

"I wasn't hiding."

"Standing outside right now is a bad idea."

She shrugged. "Life is filled with bad ideas, Frank. That's what keeps it interesting."

"I'm taking Miguel and going after Evelyn."

Charlotte sniffed in the thick afternoon air redolent with smoke. Gunfire echoed in the distance like a long stretch of ripping canvas.

"Why take Gournsey?" she asked.

"I'm not," replied Sherman, confused at her question.

She turned to face him. "No, not right now. I'm talking about earlier. Why did they set him up for the murder?"

"He's an obvious target. A very large obvious target. What are you getting at?"

"The papers you found at Jim's house. They list lithium deposit locations. Few people have that information."

"Are you saying Jim was the target?" asked Sherman.

"If you told someone to go after the big American without knowing Gournsey, their target would be Jim."

"Spell it out for me," said Sherman, anxious to get moving.

"I think the Gendarme or the Russians or both were looking for leverage on Jim."

"To get at those documents?" asked Sherman, pivoting to the gray areas of his world.

"Two birds, one stone," answered Charlotte. "They'd search his home with a warrant, get the documents detailing the mineral deposits, and scuttle the American lithium deal."

"A real win-win," said Sherman. "But doesn't the coup work against them? Assuming we're only talking about the Russians."

"Yeah, I haven't figured that part out yet."

Sherman glanced at his watch. Time was seeping away. "You can tell me the end when I get back."

Charlotte gave him a wistful smile and he thought she might wish him a contrite 'good luck', but she surprised him.

"Take the gloves off, Frank. No mercy."

He had shown none thus far, but he understood the sentiment. Come back, no matter the cost.

Chapter Fifteen

Getting from A to B was not the problem. Miguel knew as much. He knew the city. He knew the police and their operations. Evading the patrols and dodging the roadblocks... those things were simple. Guiding the American was not the issue. The real problem—the one that gave him pause—was what the American would do upon arriving at point B.

He considered this as they loaded gear into an unmarked Mazda SUV with Equatoguinean plates. The best-case scenario was uneventful. They passed through unmolested and returned unscathed.

Worst case—they both died.

Most of the in-between scenarios involved scores of dead countrymen and a good amount of damage. While Miguel was no fan of the Gendarme and harbored his own suspicions, he loved his country and the people. His people. The people he'd sworn to protect as an officer of the law.

The American had taken a similar oath, but his loyalties did not lie with a West African nation famous for smuggling and human trafficking. The captain cared for his people the same way Miguel did.

That was the problem.

Miguel started the SUV. The steering wheel thrummed under his fingers. He didn't want people to get hurt and wanted no more death.

"You ready?" asked the captain.

No, thought Miguel.

"Yes," he replied.

"*Vamos*," said the American.

Miguel exited the embassy front gate and headed south, avoiding the major roads. He snaked back and forth on the narrow streets and claustrophobic alleyways choked with trash. They passed colorful homes, now locked up tight from the fighting. The normally teeming streets were empty. The silence hurt Miguel's soul, which took great pride in his island and his people.

The going was slow.

Captain Sherman looked at his watch often, but he said nothing to Miguel about hurrying up. He said little at all. The silence suited Miguel. Talking and concentrating didn't mix—one or the other, but never both.

They pushed farther south.

To the west, a battle raged. Small arms fire echoed down the streets like tin cans blowing in the wind. Behind that came the chest-pounding booms of artillery. Mortars thumped. Machine guns rattled in long mournful stretches of chaos.

The world—Miguel's world—was ending.

He saw it in the billowing smoke and empty roads and terrified faces poking out from behind curtains. Their fear seeped into the pit of his stomach, churning like a night of too much palm wine. It hung in the air, thick and pungent.

Past the city limits, the battle receded into the background, only occasionally punctuating the rhythms of rural life. Distant thumps mingled with the cackle of macaws. The road opened into grassland on either side as the horizon tilted up towards *Pico Basilé*—the volcano dominating the center of the island.

The stillness and simplicity reminded Miguel of childhood visits to his grandfather who grew maize on the side of the mountain with those grand vistas. It was the first time Miguel saw so much of the sea at once. How it sparkled.

"We're close," said the captain.

Miguel surfaced from the detour into his past. The American was right. They were close. The edge of the village loomed in the distance. A smattering of simple homes clustered around the intersection of two ribbons of asphalt. His parents stopped there for Fantas on the way to visit his grandfather. Miguel had not been back for many years, but things had not changed.

The road south curved just after entering the village— nothing dramatic, but enough to block those at the crossroads from seeing them approach.

Captain Sherman pointed towards a cluster of small concrete homes just before the corner, at the village's outer limits.

"Pull over there," he said.

Miguel complied and stopped the SUV on a thin patch of dirt behind the homes.

"Thanks for your help, Lieutenant. You got us this far, but I think it's best you wait here. I don't want to put you in a difficult position."

"Are you sure?" asked Miguel.

He had mentally prepared himself for more but didn't want to hurt his countrymen. Some of his friends worked for the Gendarme. What if they guarded the road? Miguel wouldn't forgive himself if he pulled the trigger. Yet, through some moral gymnastics, he'd accepted that the American might and he could live with that.

The American nodded.

"I'll be here," said Miguel.

"Give me twenty minutes," said Sherman. "If I'm not back by then, head back to the embassy. Tell Sergeant Gournsey what happened. Keep the car and get the hell away from there. Understand?"

Miguel understood, although he didn't like the idea of abandoning the remaining Americans to their fate. Besides, he still had a deal with the sergeant.

Sherman slipped a long tube over his shoulder and repeated, "Twenty minutes," before disappearing into a patch of trees.

Navigating from his memory of satellite photos, Sherman kept wide right of the buildings, staying in the thickest foliage, passing through verdant patches of wide palm fronds and knifelike grass. He didn't want to run into an unsuspecting villager or Gendarme officer on patrol.

Five minutes later and slick with sweat, Sherman emerged within sight of the intersection. Two blue Nissan trucks occupied the middle, blocking traffic. A couple of flimsy wooden barricades did little to fortify the roadblock. The lights atop the trucks whirled blue and red, but the sirens remained off.

Three soldiers leaned against the trucks, smoking and laughing. Two more stood in the truck beds manning the mounted machine guns. A pair of battered Soviet designed PKMs.

Five on one. Not as bad as Gournsey predicted, but still not good odds.

Sherman unslung the tube from his shoulder. It was an M72 shoulder-launched anti-vehicle missile, a weapon his father used as a young man in Vietnam. No need to replace a proven tool.

An exposed gap of waist-high grass separated him from the soldiers. Seventy yards of uninterrupted openness. He wasn't getting any closer without being seen.

Sherman extended the tube, armed the launcher, and aimed at the three unsuspecting men leaning against the Nissan truck. He took a breath, checked his back blast, and fired.

The weapon whooshed then thumped as the rocket ignited towards the target. The soldiers never saw the instrument of their demise. Nothing could have changed the outcome. In a couple of heartbeats, the projectile hit the truck and detonated.

Four men disappeared in a cloud of smoke and debris. No great fireball, but equally deadly. The remaining Gendarme soldier standing in the other truck froze in a long moment of terror and shock.

Sherman dropped the spent launcher and shouldered his rifle.

He fired three times. Three successive shots.

The soldier slumped then fell backwards into the truck bed. Red smears trailed down the back window.

Sherman stepped into the heavy equatorial sun and moved towards the destruction. The dense grass slowed him down, like wading through a great green river. Steamy heat clung to his body.

He almost didn't see the man in blue step out from the shadows of a nearby building or raise his rifle.

Instinct took over in the moment that followed as the sharp crack of gunfire punctuated the afternoon. Sherman dove to his right, disappearing into the grass. Bullets hissed and hit the muddy ground with a sucking thwap. He had no solid cover, no hope, but his momentary disappearing act.

The firing stopped.

In the recesses of his mind, something said more was coming. The magazine was not yet empty. He kept crawling. Sludge coated his arms and legs. Putrid, vegetal rot clung to his nostrils.

More bullets tore through the grass.

The roar stopped.

Now, he thought.

Rising from the muck, Sherman caught sight of the Gendarme soldier reloading his AK-74. An unshaven teenager, standing in the open and fumbling for the next magazine.

Sherman raised his rifle.

"*¡No!*" yelled a woman, running out of the house behind the young man. "*¡Esta mijo! Por favor, no dispares.*"

Sherman stopped. He understood her cries of fear and agony. The woman kept pleading and gesturing towards her son, who looked like a deer caught in the headlights. The soldier glanced from his mother back to Sherman. His rifle remained unloaded.

The woman didn't stop scolding her boy and pleading with Sherman. Most of her words didn't translate but her son understood her fear. Using his free left hand, Sherman motioned for the soldier to put down his rifle.

"*Lentamente,*" said Sherman, hoping he'd picked the right verb.

Hesitantly at first, but with more conviction with each plea from his mother, the man lowered his weapon to the dirt. Sherman moved closer. He snatched up the gun and slung it over his shoulder.

The young man winced at the sight. Losing your rifle was, no doubt, a punishable offense.

Sherman pointed to the magazine in his hand. "*Dame las balas,*" he said in broken Spanish.

The mother grabbed the magazine out of her son's hand and passed it to Sherman.

"*No más,*" said Sherman, then added, "Get a new career, kid."

The young man slowly nodded, his mother's tears flowing freely. She pulled him into her arms and blew kisses to Sherman as she led her son inside the house.

Conflicted over his decision, Sherman headed back to the SUV. He didn't like loose ends and the kid was nothing less.

Miguel stood waiting by the vehicle with the engine running.

"You didn't have to do that," said Miguel.

"I told you to wait here," Sherman replied.

"I did for a while. Then I heard explosions and gunfire and came looking. You didn't have to spare him, but it was the right thing to do."

Sherman handed him the battered Soviet rifle. "We'll see about that. Now, please get in the vehicle."

Miguel followed the instructions, and they pulled back onto the road heading south. Upon seeing the carnage at the intersection, the Equatoguinean's face twisted with displeasure. His pace slowed as he passed the corpses, his gaze taking in the wreckage around him.

"You would have shot that kid if his mother hadn't come out," said Miguel.

It didn't sound like a question, more a statement of fact, but Sherman answered.

"Yes."

Miguel grunted something inaudible, then added, "You stink."

Sherman raised his muddy arm and gave it a sniff. Miguel was right. He stank.

Chapter Sixteen

Further south, past the roadblock, Sherman experienced the true grandeur of Bioko Island and its central mountain. Rising slowly from the center of the island like some green behemoth, the volcano teemed with monkeys and birds. The trees seemed taller and older than time, a primordial forest unmarred by the logger's ax.

The road narrowed as they drove upward, Miguel slowed his frenetic pace. Soon enough, they rose above the oppressive heat and into cooler air.

"The Spaniards used to come up here to hide from the humidity and mosquitos," Miguel explained.

Sherman glanced backward over the island's expanse. "Not a bad view either," he said.

"I came up here as a boy during the dry season," said Miguel. "My grandfather grew cacao."

"Mine was a colonel in the Marine Corps. The only thing he grew was a temper."

"And your father?" asked Miguel.

"The same. Different war, but not different men."

Miguel smiled. "And you?"

"Different war," answered Sherman.

"And the temper?"

Sherman shrugged. "It comes and goes. What about your father? Since we're on the subject."

"Police, like me. Grandfather too, before he retired up here."

"Runs in the family," said Sherman.

"The expectation does," replied Miguel.

"Fathers and sons," said Sherman with a shrug.

"And their long shadows," added Miguel, and Sherman knew exactly what he meant.

The conversation fell away, and the two men enjoyed a comfortable silence for the next few miles up the mountain before wooden signs appeared, announcing the Eco Resort. Sherman focused on what came next.

Miguel eased the SUV off the paved road and onto a thin ribbon of red dirt that meandered between trees so tall and thick they blocked the sky.

A modest building made of timber and thatch materialized from the forest. Out front were a few cars and small signs branded with the resort's logo.

Miguel pulled into a parking space next to a silver BMW with government plates. It seemed to hold his attention.

"I know that car," said Miguel.

"Who is it?"

"A Gendarme captain named Ngomo."

Sherman swung open the door and leaped out.

"Wait," said Miguel. "You'll scare the staff looking like that. Let me ask which room Evelyn is in."

Covered in stinking mud and tactical gear, Sherman

struck an imposing figure, downright frightening for most people.

"Fine," he said and stashed his rifle in the car. "But use your badge."

Miguel nodded and jogged up toward the guest check-in. Sherman took out his knife and used the time to slash all the BMW's tires. Better safe than dead.

He was checking his service pistol when Miguel returned.

"She's in the Cloud Suite. They said it is up the mountain a bit, but—"

"Let's go," said Sherman, cutting him off.

"Wait, she's not alone. The room is for two."

Sherman swiveled back to Miguel. "With Captain Ngomo?"

Miguel nodded. "He paid for the suite."

Sherman shook off the news. "Doesn't matter. We need her help."

"What if she's working with them?" asked Miguel.

A typical cop question, thought Sherman. *Always looking for the angle.*

"Then we take her back at gunpoint," said Sherman and set off up the hill, following the signs for the Cloud Suite.

They passed a spring-fed pool and an outdoor bar that blended into the towering trees. It was Sherman's kind of resort. All nature and booze.

A few dozen stairs later, they approached another timber and thatch structure smaller than the main hall. Laughter emanated from within.

Sherman motioned for Miguel to knock on the door while he stood off to the side and out of sight.

Miguel knocked politely, more like room service than a cop.

"¿*Que?*" asked a man's voice.

Miguel knocked again and stepped aside as footsteps shuffled inside. A lock clicked and a broad man with no shirt and a scowl opened the door. Annoyance at the intrusion shown on his face.

Sherman hit him hard in the solar plexus—not as hard as he could but enough to double the man over in pain. He coughed and retched and hit the floor hard.

Evelyn didn't say a word. She smashed a wine glass and lunged at Sherman.

Sherman caught her by the wrist and flipped her onto the ground in one swift movement, trying not to break any bones.

"That's enough, Ms. Ramos," he shouted.

Evelyn's eyes widened at her name. "I know you," she exclaimed.

"Captain Sherman, United States Army. I'm here to extract you."

"What are you talking about?" she demanded.

Ngomo struggled to his feet.

Sherman drew his pistol and leveled it at the man. "Not another step."

"Please," said Evelyn. "Don't hurt him."

Sherman pulled Evelyn to her feet.

"We need to go. He's staying here."

"I'm not moving until you tell me why," she yelled.

"General Asumu started a coup. The city is burning. We need to leave. Am I clear?"

Evelyn processed the information quickly like the trauma nurse she used to be. She turned to Ngomo and pointed a finger.

144

"Did you know?" she demanded in Spanish.

Ngomo groaned and spat some bile out on the ground. *"No. I've been here with you."*

Evelyn's eyes flashed with anger. *"You planned this to get me out of town while you burned it down."*

"It wasn't my idea," protested Ngomo. *"I told him to wait."*

Sherman understood enough to key in on the admission. "I want specifics. Plans, timings, goals, troop strengths." He turned to Evelyn. "Translate that."

She did in quick succession. A stream of Spanish that Sherman marginally understood punctuated by expletives that he did.

Ngomo shot back some macho bravado and ignored the questions.

Sherman reached out and broke his finger in one seamless movement.

Ngomo howled.

Evelyn didn't blink. Her anger remained blistering with intensity.

"Details," said Evelyn.

With his finger and dignity both broken, Ngomo sat on the floor, sulking like a defeated child.

Miguel stayed out of sight, but Sherman didn't need him to translate. Evelyn stepped up to the task.

"Tell him or he'll do far worse," she continued.

"I don't know anything more," Ngomo replied.

Evelyn launched into another string of harsh language. Ngomo broke bit by bit until he gave her what Sherman wanted.

"Did you get all that?" she asked.

"Assume I didn't," he replied.

She nodded. "What we have here, Captain Sherman, is a bunch of greedy bastards who weren't happy enough with their lot in life. They took it all rather than just the crumbs. General Asumu, it seems, got wind of the lithium deal and decided he could eat his cake and pie too. I guess that's what kicked off this coup."

"Two questions," said Sherman. "Did he set up my man for murder? And what are the Russians doing here?"

Evelyn asked. Ngomo nodded sheepishly at the first questions, then shook his head vehemently.

"Yes to the first part," she said. "Arresting the American was part of the plan. But he said the Russians aren't on the island. They only helped organize things online."

"Their corpses say otherwise," said Sherman.

Evelyn understood quickly. "*You fool*," she said to Ngomo.

"We need to go," Sherman said. "Because we need your skillset."

"Who's hurt?"

"Jim."

"How bad?" she asked.

"GSW to the abdomen," explained Sherman.

"You should have led with that," she replied and hastily packed her bag.

"*Don't follow us*," said Sherman in his broken Spanish. He didn't want Ngomo to join the fight.

Miguel met Sherman and Evelyn at the SUV.

"Is he with you?" she asked.

"Lieutenant Ondo, meet Evelyn Ramos."

"Miguel is fine," he said and started the Mazda.

Evelyn smiled. "Nice to meet you, Miguel. How'd you get involved in all this?"

Miguel glanced in the mirror as they drove off. "I arrested the American."

"For murder?" she asked.

"The Gendarme set up my sergeant for murdering a local woman."

"What!" exclaimed Evelyn.

"But we think they were after Jim and got my guy by mistake."

"I need to reevaluate my standards," said Evelyn with a sigh. "My recent track record with men is shit." She leaned forward from the back seat. "How long ago was Jim shot?"

"Over an hour," said Sherman.

"How?"

"Russians," said Sherman.

"If you're here, then where are the Marines?"

"Delayed over Central Africa," replied Sherman as he looked down at his watch. It read 1400 hours. "Wheels down in ten hours."

Evelyn sank back into the seat. "That's a long time."

Sherman nodded. "Yes, it is."

The drive down the mountain proceeded in silence. Even the carnage at the crossroads didn't faze Evelyn. Sherman knew she'd seen worse in the war. Her nerve reassured him. With ten hours of uncertainty on the horizon, they needed all the nerve possible.

Two miles out from the embassy, Sherman radioed Lopez.

"Echo Three, Echo One. Is the perimeter clear? Over."

"Echo One, some local creepers keeping tabs on us, but nothing significant. What's your ETA? Over."

"Two miles out, but slow going. The Gendarme closed the major intersections. Have the sergeant prep Jim's room. Over."

"Already done. Over."

"And the patient? Over."

"Significant internal bleeding and weak vitals. Echo Two is with him now. Over."

The corporal didn't mince words or sugarcoat. Sherman appreciated his directness. It cut through all the bullshit.

"Understood. We're inbound from the southwest. Over."

"Copy that. Out."

Sherman looked at Evelyn. She had her game face on—that mask of calm and focus that pushed away the surrounding chaos, if only for a few more hours. Taking off the mask caused a mental and emotional crash, but that was the price they all paid.

He turned to Miguel. "You should stop up there. We can go on foot. Take the car. Go somewhere safe."

Miguel blinked in disbelief. "I can't do that."

"You certainly can and should," said Sherman. "Consider this a first payment for helping Sergeant Gournsey."

"I can get you closer," said Miguel.

"Good," said Sherman and then turning backward, asked, "Evelyn, you ready?"

"No, but it's happening anyway."

"Thanks, Miguel. Stay safe," said Sherman.

Miguel pulled into a muddy alley just south of the embassy. "Good luck, Captain Sherman. Even though I don't think you'll need it."

Sherman and Evelyn jumped out and Miguel sped off.

"You gave away our ride," she said.

"I paid off a debt," Sherman replied.

They waited in the shadows of stocky palms as he radioed Lopez again.

"Echo Three, Echo One. Change of plans. We are one block south of your location coming in on foot. Over."

"Echo One, good copy. How many? Over."

"Party of two. Over."

"Ready to receive. Out."

Sherman gave Evelyn's shoulder a squeeze. "Stay behind me. Don't stop unless I tell you."

The run around to the front gate took two long minutes. Sherman sensed eyes boring into his back, following his every movement, but nothing happened. No incoming rounds. Just the sound of feet slapping on pavement and his heart pounding in his ears.

Chapter Seventeen

A thick, smoky haze hung over the embassy, yet the sun still singed exposed skin like a hair dryer. Sherman sat on the roof under a makeshift shade structure Gournsey fashioned out of tablecloths and folding chairs. The playful haphazardness reminded Sherman of childhood forts built from blankets and couch cushions. He drank the coldest can of soda he could find in the fridge and tried to rest while Gournsey took overwatch.

Lopez was down below, assisting Evelyn Ramos. She'd charged in and taken control of Jim's care, but Sherman didn't expect miracles. Given the trauma and blood loss, Jim didn't have long, not with their current supplies and tools.

Hungry, Sherman moved on to a protein bar and bottle of water. He poured half of the bottle over his head and chugged what remained. Tendrils of exhaustion crept into his mind. Less than ten long hours remained until the Marines landed. Sherman grabbed another snack, knowing he needed the calories.

The satellite phone on top of Gournsey's makeshift command post rang. Sherman looked at the Pentagon number and answered.

"Captain Sherman," said the reassuring voice of Major Sanders. "I've got a room full of anxious people looking for an update."

Sherman tried to recall their last conversation hours earlier. So much had occurred since then.

"I secured the remaining American, Evelyn Ramos."

A round of clapping echoed in the background.

"However, Jim's condition is critical."

There was no clapping for the second part.

"Understood," said Major Sanders. "Do what you can."

"There's more," said Sherman.

"We're all ears."

"Do you remember the documents I mentioned?" asked Sherman, but he plowed on without waiting for an answer. "The Russians were searching for documents in Jim's possession. We think he was the intended target for the frame job of that woman's murder."

"What documents?"

"Detailed layouts of the lithium deposit locations."

"Wait one," replied Sanders and the line fell silent.

Sherman watched seagulls ride the breeze, interrupted by mortar explosions near the army base—the same base at which they trained local soldiers only days before, soldiers who were likely dead.

"Captain, did the mercenaries successfully retrieve any documents?" asked Sanders.

"Unknown, sir. They didn't carry any out, but they might have digital copies. Ms. McMillan has the material I removed."

"Understood."

"Anything else, Major?"

"Our satellite is now overhead. I'll patch it through to your end. Next check-in at 1600 hours."

"Copy that. Out."

Sherman placed the phone down and opened the laptop sitting atop a beer crate. He loaded the satellite feed. The images revealed the devastation they'd only heard. Small pixels conveyed the sheer magnitude of the destruction.

The small navy base no longer existed. A ship's prow sticking above the water served as the only memory of the Navy's sole frigate. This was no Pearl Harbor scale attack, but scuttling the ship prevented any future naval assaults by the president's supporters. The sinking also opened the area to drug smuggling and piracy, a problem for the future king of Bioko Island.

Across town, the army base burned a blurry orange on the laptop screen. Sherman squinted at the images. What he saw made little sense.

Sherman slid over to Gournsey for confirmation.

"Hey, check out the satellite images. Do you see what's parked out front of the army base?"

The sergeant glanced at the screen once, then twice. His expression lifted in surprise.

"I do believe that is a Chinese tank. A first-generation Type 69."

"Or Type 79," added Sherman.

"That's not good for us," said Gournsey.

"No. That did not appear on the threat assessment list."

"Nope. Maybe a recent addition in preparation for the coup?"

"Quite the oversight," said Sherman.

"Seems like this whole debacle was an oversight," Gournsey replied.

"Debacle," repeated Sherman. "That's a nice ten-dollar word."

"I read," said Gournsey in protest.

"What's left in the armory?" asked Sherman.

"Since you used our only LAW. One AT-4."

One anti-tank missile.

"Don't miss," said Sherman, half-jokingly.

"Is it time for a tactical withdrawal?" asked Gournsey, using a polite term for getting the hell away from the embassy.

"If that thing moves, so do we," answered Sherman, and switched topics. "Have you seen Charlotte? I want an opinion on General Asumu and if he's crazy enough to send a tank to blow up a US embassy."

Gournsey gazed up at the still curling smoke. "She was in an office last time I saw her."

"Take a break and go find her. I'll stay on overwatch," ordered Sherman.

"Copy that. Charlotte and snacks," repeated Gournsey, adding in his own priority.

"And the blueprints of this place," added Sherman. "I don't want any surprises."

"Heard," said the sergeant. "Charlotte, snacks, and blueprints."

"Good luck," added Sherman as Gournsey disappeared down the ladder.

Sherman shouldered the long gun and gazed through the scope. A magnified world of unseen details met his eye. Patterned blue curtains, the faded red door, and a bike down the street with flat tires all came into vivid focus. So too did the Russian's SUV with blood-splattered windows and corpses inside.

Time slipped away inside the scope's constrained view.

Ten minutes passed, then twenty. Sherman scanned methodically, checking windows and shadows—anywhere he'd hide in a similar situation.

The steady crackle of distant gunfire eased to a methodical pop-pop before stopping altogether. Sherman raised his head to listen for more, but none came. He put down the rifle and opened the laptop. Only a few minutes remained before the satellite passed too far overhead for a clear image.

Tiny smudges gathered in front of the army base as the soldiers regrouped after the battle. The tank turned and lumbered forward. No one remained to occupy the Gendarme. No one except the Americans.

"Shouldn't you be aiming at something?" said Charlotte as she eased herself onto the roof.

Sherman glanced over the small wall and shrugged. "Look at this."

Charlotte scooted close and he turned the screen so she could see.

"Is that a tank?" she asked, her voice rising with alarm.

"It is."

"That wasn't in the threat assessment," she said.

"Nope."

"Shit," she muttered.

"Indeed."

"What now?" she asked.

"That's what I want to ask you," Sherman replied. "What are the odds General Asumu attacks the embassy? Does he risk a war over that?"

Charlotte leaned back against the wall and looked up at the sky in concentration.

"Like I said earlier, our file on the guy is slim. We know

he rose through the ranks. Not a political appointment, which suggests a level of competence."

"The destroyed army base supports that conclusion," added Sherman. "He took the gloves all the way off."

"This coup is an all-or-nothing play. He can't go back to his old life if they lose, so he's cornered himself in some sense."

"Risk and reward," said Sherman. "He knew the risk. He garnered support. Planned it out. So, it's got to be about the reward."

"Trillions of dollars' worth of lithium is certainly an excellent motivator. But why risk that? If he'd played his cards right, the State Department would have recognized his government."

"Bigger reward," said Sherman.

"If he's after cash, then he'll likely leave us alone. If the reward is political, he might come after us."

"Which leads back to my original question," said Sherman, returning to the rifle. "What are the odds that tank rolls in our direction?"

Charlotte's fingers ran through her brown hair, and she sighed. "Fifty-fifty, unless we learn more."

"Go and talk with Evelyn. She was seeing one of the General's aides."

"What!" exclaimed Charlotte. "You failed to mention that earlier."

"It's been a long day."

Charlotte whirled around and headed back to the ladder. "Don't forget to rest," she said before disappearing down the hole.

I'll rest tomorrow, thought Sherman.

He watched the empty neighborhood for a few more

minutes before Gournsey returned with snacks, an arm full of blueprints, and a small civilian radio.

"Ah, potato chips and a ball game. You're just like my grandfather," joked Sherman as Gournsey took a seat.

"I'm an old soul," said the sergeant.

Sherman smiled at the idea before asking, "How is Jim doing?"

"Alive, thanks to Evelyn. She pulled out the bullet and stitched things up, but I wouldn't put money on the man pulling through."

"Charlotte thinks the Gendarme meant to set him up, not you," said Sherman. "And I agree."

"We look nothing alike," Gournsey protested.

"Big, loud Americans. You both fit the bill."

"Why Jim?"

"He had access to documents detailing the lithium deposits," answered Sherman and the dots suddenly connected in his mind. "Papers we now have."

Gournsey eyed him. "Are you suggesting the Russians might come here looking for them? That's bold."

"Evelyn's Gendarme friend didn't know they were in country, which means General Asumu didn't hire them to take out Jim. They did that on their own."

"Documents equal leverage," added Gournsey.

"Exactly, but they'd need to act fast and secure everything before the Gendarme showed up on our doorstep."

Gournsey cocked his ear toward the strangely new silence bereft of gunshots. "If you're right, the Russians have little time left. The Gendarme already won the battle."

"Come on, we need to get Lopez up here," said Sherman, then headed towards the ladder.

"You didn't ask me what I found," said Gournsey, still cradling the blueprints under one arm.

Sherman paused. "Okay. What did you find?"

Gournsey stepped onto the ladder. "Tunnels," he replied before descending.

Sherman jumped in after him.

"Tunnels! What tunnels?"

Chapter Eighteen

Gournsey spread two sets of blueprints across the conference table. One was old, the second older. Both showed the layout of the aging embassy.

"Alright," said the sergeant. "The left one is from 1982 when they remodeled the place. The plan on the right is from 1967 when they built the place."

Sherman compared the two, quickly glancing back and forth like a game of spot the differences. It took him a few moments to see what Gournsey found. A set of dotted lines headed across the street.

"Edward!" shouted Sherman.

The Chief Political Officer poked his head into the room.

"You called, Captain."

"Do you use any of the buildings across the street?"

Edward rubbed his neck. "Yeah, I guess we use an old house over there for storage. Nothing important though, just old chairs and stuff."

"Which house?"

Edward glanced toward the road even though he couldn't see it. "Behind the white wall."

"The entire block is behind a white wall," countered Sherman.

"It has a blue metal gate," added Edward.

"Sergeant, I leave this with you," said Sherman.

Gournsey frowned. "Small spaces and me don't get along."

"Everything is small to you," retorted Sherman.

"Genetics," replied Gournsey with a shrug.

"Fine. Edward, go with the sergeant in case he gets claustrophobic."

"Why would he get claustrophobic?" asked Edward.

"Tunnels," said Sherman.

"What tunnels? We don't have any tunnels."

Sherman turned to Gournsey with a grin. "All you," he said and walked away to find Lopez.

He found the corporal sitting with Evelyn outside the makeshift operation groom. They shared a chocolate bar between them along with stories of Afghanistan.

"How's the patient?" asked Sherman.

"Dying," replied Evelyn. "He needs a blood transfusion, surgery to repair his large intestine, and antibiotics."

"Options?" asked Sherman.

"Hospital or medivac."

"Not on the table," said Sherman.

"Have you asked General Asumu?"

"We're not in touch," Sherman answered.

"Maybe you should try," said Evelyn.

Sherman thought of the dead soldiers at the ambassador's house and the crossroads and the destruction at the army base.

"What's that saying—in for a penny, in for a pound?" asked Sherman.

"I guess," said Evelyn.

"The general went all in. I don't think he'll negotiate."

"Plus, the captain here killed a bunch of his guys," added Lopez.

"The general doesn't care about his men," said Evelyn. "The general only cares for fine wine, expensive cars, and the rich life he fervently believes is owed to him."

"Chump," said Lopez.

"That's how it works here," she continued. "You take whatever you can get away with."

"Including the island?" asked Sherman.

"I didn't think he had the balls, but it seems to be working," answered Evelyn.

"What do we offer for payment in return for helping Jim?" Sherman asked.

"Not my department," replied Evelyn.

"Charlotte!" yelled Lopez and Sherman simultaneously.

Their calls went unanswered. Sherman checked every room and the back lot. Lopez found nothing on the roof.

"Scott," yelled Sherman.

The DSS Agent appeared from the control booth. "What's up, Captain?"

"Have you seen Charlotte?"

"Ms. McMillan? Not recently. Why?"

"We can't find her," Sherman replied.

"Let me check the cameras," said Scott.

He disappeared for a moment and then returned with a puzzled look on his face. "It's weird, the cameras along the rear wall just stopped working."

"Corporal!" yelled Sherman. "Contact rear! Get to the roof."

Scott's eyes went wide.

Sherman grabbed him by the shirt and leaned close to be sure the man understood. "Get everyone to the conference room. Lock the doors. Understood?"

"Yes, but what about Jim?"

"He's dead either way," said Sherman before heading toward the rear door. Sherman radioed Gournsey on the way. "Echo Two, get your ass back now. We are under attack. Out."

Sherman was halfway to the back door when an explosion shook the walls and sent picture frames shattering on the floor.

"Rear wall breach," yelled Lopez. His tinny voice echoed down the ladder.

A lone rifle cracked, followed by the roar of suppressive fire. Lopez's curses tumbled down the shaft. Sherman glanced up at the hole for information.

"Eight breached the rear wall," yelled Lopez. "Got one, but they've got a good angle on me."

Bits of building tumbled down the opening and Sherman knew things had turned terrible, quickly.

"Start tossing grenades, then get your ass inside before they return the favor," he yelled back up.

"Copy that," replied Lopez.

"Echo Two, what's your ETA? Over."

"Echo One, three minutes. Out."

Sherman rushed toward the short hallway leading to the back door. Unlike the front, the door was solid metal and built to last. Unfortunately, no matter how robust the door was, the guys on the outside were coming in. A few inches of steel would not stop them, nor would the bullet-resistant windows or reinforced walls.

A string of grenade blasts exploded outside and the

hatch to the roof slammed shut. Sherman pulled a heavy wood table into the hallway as Lopez arrived. Concrete dust covered his face and arms and blood trickled down his cheek.

"You functional?" asked Sherman.

Lopez patted his face and nodded. "For now," he said.

"Good, start leaning these tables on their ends."

They slid two heavy tables down the short hallways and flipped them on their ends, creating a five-foot-tall wooden screen.

"I got one more with a grenade," said Lopez between breaths.

"Six to go," said Sherman and pushed the table a few inches in toward the center, creating a small field of fire towards the rear door. "Cover this angle. I'll watch the other one."

"Copy that," said Lopez.

The back wall of the embassy didn't have big traditional windows. Most were small rectangles set high on the wall—less chance of getting hurt by flying glass that way when a car bomb went off. The walls, according to the updated blueprints, were reinforced with steel plates back in the eighties, save for one spot—the old servant's entrance.

The door was long gone, bricked over during the remodel, but they hadn't reinforced the wall. Sherman knew because he'd noticed the issue on day one of their deployment. Such details stuck in his brain like annoying TV commercial jingles or repetitive radio advertising phone numbers.

He raced down the hallway towards the far back corner of the building and the old entrance. Eight feet of storage space and boxes crowded against the wall, separating the door from the hallway where he stood. Lopez remained twenty feet to his right. Both hid around corners, waiting for the inevitable.

Sherman grabbed a fragmentation grenade from his vest, pulled the pin, and held on tight.

The breaching charges blew with a tremendous bang and great whoosh of air. Bits of wall whizzed past Sherman. His ears pulsed at the pressure change and thunderous sound.

When the last chunk of debris hit the ground, Sherman tossed his frag grenade around the corner. He followed up with a stun grenade immediately afterwards.

The two grenades exploded almost simultaneously—one lethal, one not—each with their own purpose: to create an opportunity.

Sherman seized that opportunity, that moment of confusion. He turned the corner and waded into the chaos.

His first target stood dazed in the gaping hole that used to be a wall. Sherman sent him to the ground in a burst of rifle fire. The man hit the floor with a wet thump.

Beyond the broken wall, Sherman spotted a second target crawling toward his rifle several feet away. Sherman didn't let that happen. He stitched the Russian's side with another four rounds.

The sound of gunfire reverberated from his right, showing that the attackers had successfully breached the door defended by Lopez. In a hurry to help his man, Sherman almost missed the third target.

Tucked in around the outside wall was another merce-nary. Bleeding and deaf from the grenades, but unwilling to give up the fight, he lunged into the gap wildly firing his pistol.

The ballistic plate in Sherman's vest took the first bullet

dead center. The second round grazed his ear, while his abdomen caught the third.

As the man kept firing, Sherman grabbed his wrist and pushed the pistol upward. He sent his elbow swinging through the guy's face—nothing fancy, just brute force with enough power to break bone and cartilage.

There was a loud popping sound and blood splashed across Sherman's arm.

The firing stopped and the attacker slumped to the ground. Sherman stepped over him, firing a single time as he went. Bits usually only seen by neurosurgeons and coroners splattered across the dirt.

Intense gunfire still came from his right as Lopez tried to hold off the attack.

Sherman leaned out of the hole that used to be a wall and glimpsed two more mercenaries shooting into the embassy. A third lay lifeless on the pavement with a hole in his neck and blood on the ground.

The two remaining men didn't see Sherman step out of the building. Lopez consumed all their focus.

Sherman lined up the shot and emptied his magazine into the two men—not his usually disciplined self, but he was pissed and bleeding.

"Cease fire," he yelled. "All clear."

"All clear," replied Lopez, who stepped over the mangled steel door and into the sunlight.

In the rear parking lot was another body, shredded by the grenade Lopez tossed from the roof. Beyond that, by the back compound wall, lay the final mercenary. He only had half a face left and Sherman didn't bother checking for signs of life.

"You're hit," said Lopez, pointing at Sherman.

Sherman grabbed his ear, which burned like hell. His hand came back smeared with blood.

"Just a scratch," he replied.

"Not there," said Lopez. "Your side."

Sherman glanced down at his abdomen. Sure enough, his shirt was sticky and wet. He hadn't felt it happen, but now that he knew, a wave of pain raced through his body. It felt like hot coals shoved inside his stomach.

"Captain," shouted Gournsey from inside.

"All clear," said Sherman, a little less loudly.

The sergeant stepped outside with a look of concern and awe. "Geez," he said quietly before catching sight of Sherman. "You're hit."

"I noticed," said Sherman with a groan. "Secure what's left of this place while I go and get better acquainted with Evelyn."

"Heard, but we need to discuss Charlotte when you're done," said Gournsey as he began dragging dead Russians around like driftwood.

"What about Charlotte?" asked Sherman.

"She rabbited out of here."

Sherman rubbed his head. "Okay, after this…"

"Come on, Captain," said Lopez. "Let's get inside before you lose any more blood."

Using the corporal for support, Sherman and Lopez made their way through the smoke and inside. Bits of concrete and shell casings littered the floor. The two tables Sherman used to create a barricade looked like an abused piece of Swiss cheese.

"Thanks for those," said Lopez as they squeezed through a gap. "They took the brunt of the breaching charge."

"Sometimes I get it right," said Sherman.

Lopez smiled, then yelled, "Nurse Ramos, I need your help."

Chapter Nineteen

The conference room door opened with a click. Evelyn poked her head out and spotted Sherman. Her entire demeanor changed in an instant. Gone was the worried embassy employee, replaced by the no-nonsense trauma nurse.

"In here, now," she ordered.

Evelyn cleared a nearby table, scattering papers in a great white tornado.

Sherman complied and laid down on the table.

What happened next was a blur of activity and considerable pain. Sherman couldn't afford the luxury of opiates or the mental fog they induced. Nine hours remained until the Marines landed—nine long, decisive hours, and he needed his wits intact. In the absence of drugs, Sherman used an old trick.

He concentrated on the popcorn ceiling and the many minuscule mountains until he disappeared into the past. He had survived being shot, stabbed, and nearly blown up before. The trauma was indelibly etched into his flesh, just

167

as this one would be too. But those weren't the memories that surfaced. What came up was older and, perhaps, even darker.

The day of his grandfather's funeral.

He remembered rain and the musty scent of freshly turned soil. His mother made him wear a dark suit, though Sherman couldn't remember where the suit came from or where it went after that day. His father wore his Marine dress uniform, looking impossibly tall and chiseled from stone. Save for a red necklace, his mother wore all black. She hated the formality of funerals and reminded her husband often.

Sherman was seventeen and trying to escape his father's orbit. There was pomp and circumstance. The rifle salute made him jump a bit, though he hoped his father didn't notice. A Marine couldn't have a jumpy son.

He remembered the thick thump of wet dirt on wood as they covered the coffin. His father didn't say a word—no tears or fond goodbyes. The Sherman men did not express such unpleasantness. Fears and anguish were private matters best handled over a glass of whiskey.

After the funeral, they ate Chinese food. His grandfather loved a good plate of greasy noodles, a holdover from his time in Korea. Sherman couldn't remember everything he ate, but he recalled his father ordering two beers and sliding one over, his oblique way of acknowledging the situation's gravity.

Somewhere between orange chicken and fortune cookies, Sherman stepped outside for some unadulterated air. The restaurant was not in the nicest part of town and Sherman, wearing a dark suit, caught the attention of some local hooligans. They came over to inquire about his wallet and wondered if he would part with it peacefully.

Sherman said no.

The kids disagreed with his answer.

The first boy stepped in to push him and Sherman broke his nose with a straight right jab to the face. What followed was not pretty or sportsmanlike. There was biting and gouging, kicking and scratching.

Outnumbered, Sherman got thoroughly beaten.

Towards the end, when the boys grew tired of punching him, Sherman's father yelled, "Enough!" His voice carried the sharp edge of violence, and the kids ran. Only then did Sherman realize his father had been standing there for quite a while and did not intervene.

"Did you start that?" he demanded.

"No," Sherman replied. "They wanted my wallet."

"Did you give it to them?"

"No."

"Did they take it?"

"No," said Sherman as he held up the wallet for his father to see.

"Good. Now, go inside and clean yourself up before your mother throws a fit. And be quick, I ordered us another round."

When Sherman sat back down in his tattered suit with bruised cheeks and cut lips, his mother did not fuss over him. She asked only one question. "Did they bleed?"

Sherman nodded.

"Pass the broccoli," she replied and that was that.

Lesson learned, they surely thought. Sherman wasn't so sure.

Even as Evelyn finished stitching him up, he wasn't sure what his parents thought they'd instilled in him. The only lessons he learned that day were to make sure someone had his back and broken noses don't stop fights. Broken femurs did.

"You can come back, Captain," said Evelyn, taking off blood-covered gloves.

"What's the damage?" asked Sherman.

"Five stitches in your ear and twelve on each side of your abdomen."

"Through and through," said Sherman.

"Your luck holds, Captain. Nothing major nicked, but you should have a professional check that out."

"I just did."

"I want to build schools, not patch up bullet holes."

"You're doing both and I thank you for that," said Sherman as he eased himself into a sitting position.

Everything hurt, but less so. He popped a handful of ibuprofen in his mouth and washed the pills down with a bottle of water.

"I'd say take it easy," said Evelyn, glancing down the hallway at the missing wall, "but I don't think that's an option."

"No, but neither is staying here," said Sherman.

"Couldn't agree more," she replied.

"Good. Can you prep Jim for a move?"

"Moving might kill him," she replied.

Sherman took out the cracked ballistic plate from his vest and found a replacement on the table.

"Right," said Evelyn. "He's dead if he stays here."

Sherman nodded. "Is thirty minutes enough?"

"I'll manage."

Sherman moved towards the door.

"Thanks for all that," she said and pointed down the hall towards the destruction and chaos.

Sherman smiled. "Thirty minutes, Ms. Ramos."

His side still hurt but now was not the time for a nice nap or wallowing. Sherman set about looking for Gournsey and found him outside next to a neat line of dead mercenaries. Out of respect, the sergeant had not piled them in a heap like firewood and lit them on fire, which Sherman would have done out of spite.

"Where's Charlotte?" asked Sherman.

Gournsey looked up from his morbid task and smiled with relief.

"Glad to see you too, Captain."

Sherman nodded but said nothing. They could hug it out later, if there was a later.

"I don't know where she went," said Gournsey.

"What happened?" asked Sherman.

"She took the tunnel before us and dipped."

Sherman's mind, still foggy from pain, took a moment to put the pieces together.

"She knew about the tunnel," he concluded.

"I guess so," said Gournsey. "The doors were unlocked when Edward and I went through. Fresh footprints in the dust. She's the only one wearing Converse and they leave a pretty distinctive mark."

Questions piled up in Sherman's mind like stacks of unopened mail. Through the clutter, two salient points stood out. First, she left before the attack. The second one he hoped wasn't true.

"Follow me," said Sherman, leading Gournsey back inside to the office Charlotte used.

"What's up?" asked the sergeant.

"We're looking for the documents I took from Jim's house. Charlotte had them."

The pair searched through the office but only found the Russian phones he'd taken from the dead men.

"It's not here," said Sherman with a growing sense of unease. He tolerated secrets as part of the job, but this felt different, almost personal.

"Care to enlighten me?" asked Gournsey.

"A trillion-dollar map," said Sherman.

"For the lithium deposits?"

"Yeah," answered Sherman.

"And Charlotte took said map?"

"Yup."

"Right before we were attacked?"

"Correct."

Gournsey scratched his stubble. "I'll admit the timing is suspect, but you don't think she's in on it, do you?"

Sherman sat down on the office chair. "She's a spook. I don't pretend to know what she is up to, but if she knew they were coming and said nothing…"

"Understood," said Gournsey and tapped his service pistol as if reading Sherman's mind for the punishment of treason.

"I better call the major," said Sherman.

"I'll leave you to it," said Gournsey.

Sherman found his phone and dialed. Major Sanders dutifully answered.

"Captain, what's the situation there?"

Sherman took a breath and answered, "We've been attacked by Russian mercenaries. They breached the outer wall and back doors. We neutralized the threat."

"Casualties?" asked Sanders. His voice remained flat, but Sherman sensed his apprehension.

"I took one under the vest, but I'm functional for the time being. However, Charlotte McMillan is missing."

"Taken?" asked Sanders.

"Negative. She bolted right before the attack. Can I get a line of sight on her mission?"

"Wait one," answered Sanders.

Getting anything concrete out of the spooks required an offering fit for the gods or a presidential order. He had neither.

Sanders returned to add, "I'm told her mission is the safety of American personnel and assets in the region."

The answer held less water than a sieve. It was the stock reply cooked up by some intelligence spokesperson and used liberally when the CIA didn't want to admit to mucking about.

"Sounds familiar," said Sherman, but he didn't linger on the lack of communication. "Can you confirm she is still on the reservation? The timing stinks."

He doubted the CIA would admit to a rogue agent, if Charlotte fell into that camp, but at least they'd have to answer on the record.

"Hold," said Sanders and the line quieted for a moment. "Nothing suggests otherwise."

"Understood," said Sherman. "We are repositioning. I'll confirm our new location shortly."

"Good luck, Captain," said Sanders, and Sherman knew he meant it.

"Thank you, sir. Out."

He pocketed the phone and chanced a glance at his side. The gauze covering his wound was still white. No active bleeding was a good sign.

Sherman poked his head into the hallway and yelled for Scott and Gournsey. Both men emerged moments later.

"We are moving across the street. Prep only the essentials. Are we clear?"

"What about Jim?" asked Scott.

"Evelyn is working on that now."

Scott nodded and ran off with a frenzied look in his eyes.

Gournsey lingered and asked, "What about Charlotte?"

"Still on our side… or so they say. No word on what she is doing."

"Her job," said Gournsey.

"That is what worries me. Her job and our survival might be mutually exclusive."

Gournsey shrugged off the idea and moved on to his tasks, which was his way of saying things happen. Sherman knew the gesture well. But an embassy full of dead Americans didn't sit well with him, even if the *greater good* prevailed. Whatever the hell that meant. It used to mean something, now he wasn't so sure.

Chapter Twenty

Three o'clock came and went and headed to four. Eight long hours until the Marines landed. Longer still until they'd be evacuated. Sherman took stock of their situation and found it wanting. Of the nine Americans in the country, one was critically wounded, one was walking wounded, six more were present, and one was missing in the late afternoon heat.

Headcount aside, their base of operations was compromised and no longer defensible. They had to move. Sherman didn't mind that part. The embassy had a figurative bullseye painted on it. What worried him was not the next stop, but the one after that and so on through the night until reinforcements arrived. He guessed Jim could survive one incredibly careful move through the tunnels to the building across the street. After that, each outing was a gamble with Jim paying the ultimate price for a loss.

Materially, they still had plenty of ammunition and supplies, but they couldn't take everything with them. It came down to the number of hops they made in the next eight hours. They could ferry supplies through the tunnel, but when they moved again, it would only be with the supplies on their backs.

Then there was the Charlotte issue.

Sherman didn't like anything about the situation. Her sudden disappearance left him simmering in anger and unknowns. Beyond his bluster, Sherman worried about her safety and the choices he'd have to make if something went wrong. At some core level, hidden behind the lies they told each other, he still cared for her.

The trail cut through what remained of a dense forest with trees so thick only pinpricks of sky shone through. Past the thick huddle of trees, the trail tacked toward the beach, opening into a wide view of frothy water churning against the thin beige lip surrounding the island.

Charlotte stood listening and watching the breakers thunder down against the sand. She loved the sound, that primal power of the surf. It reminded her of childhood vacations to the beach where all her problems and anxieties, worries, and slights disappeared into the ocean's vastness. Those waves smoothed her rough edges just as they did to rock and glass.

The water before her, crashing down on the edge of Bioko Island, did soothe her nerves but failed to sand away her angst, fear, and guilt. The latter gnawed at her stomach, twisting it into terrible knots. The heavy air became unbearable.

They're fine, she told herself over and over again.

She had been at the edge of the forest when explosions split the silence open like a giant tree crashing to the ground. She'd turned to look towards the embassy. Then came the gunfire, thick streams of sound that didn't stop.

Charlotte wanted to turn back, to run and help, but she didn't. She couldn't. That part of her died long before.

The mission matters most, she'd told herself then as she did now, watching the waves crash.

From the beach, Charlotte turned right and headed towards the towering pillars of smoke hanging over downtown. She walked tentatively, staying in the deepening shadows, listening out for lurking soldiers. The once bustling beach restaurants were shuttered. No music or laughs. No hawkers wandering the sandy space, selling counterfeit sunglasses, shoes, and watches.

Weaving between the brightly colored stalls, Charlotte felt the hot glare of eyes on her back. Silence permeated the soupy afternoon air, only to be shattered by an occasional burst of gunfire.

The equatorial sun cut low across the sky. Little daylight remained, and Charlotte still had far to go.

She hustled along the deserted streets, crunching over shattered glass and shell casings glittering on the asphalt. Curtains fluttered in house windows and the tones of low, worried conversations met her ears.

Just west of downtown, she ran into her first group of Gendarme soldiers. A series of trucks blocked the intersection and the men sat in patches of shade, smoking and laughing. They looked triumphant, not tense—the look of victors waiting for the spoils.

Charlotte did not want to be their reward.

She skirted wide and pushed further downtown.

Evidence of battle thickened as she went. Charred cars and bullet-scarred windows lined the street. A few buildings crumbled into colorful chunks of concrete like sharp-edged Fruity Pebbles.

Charlotte's luck ran out two blocks from the Gendarme headquarters as she crossed the road. Men materialized from the shadows, their blue uniforms stained with sweat and dust.

"*Stop!*" they shouted in Spanish with guns held high.

Charlotte stopped. She kept her hands high and squinted against the sun.

The men swarmed around her, hissing and leering. They reeked of booze and battle. Charlotte stared down their barrels wondering if this was the end.

"*Who are you? What are you doing?*" demanded one soldier in Spanish. He was taller and older than the others and exuded a command presence—exactly the type of person Charlotte hoped would find her.

"*I need to speak with General Asumu,*" she replied in nearly perfect Spanish.

"*Who are you?*" repeated the commander, softening his stance.

"My name is Charlotte McMillan and I work for the American State Department."

The commander tilted his head to one side and soaked up her appearance like a dry sponge. He waited a moment before asking, "And what business does America have with General Asumu?"

"I come with a business proposal and a gift," Charlotte replied.

The man smiled kindly, but his flashing eyes still reminded her of a hungry predator.

Moving the supplies out of the embassy took time and a half dozen trips. Carrying Jim took the longest of all, with Gournsey and Scott doing the bulk of the lifting. They grunted and swore in the narrow tunnel but kept the critically injured man intact. Evelyn hovered behind, waiting for his blood pressure to plummet or another catastrophic change. Nothing happened, but Jim looked worse. Sherman didn't know if his decline was from the move or just the inevitability of trauma.

They made a makeshift command center in the dining room and parked Jim on a plastic-covered couch in the living room.

"No more," said Evelyn. Her eyes focused on Jim's waxen face and shallow breathing.

"Understood," said Sherman.

He had no other option or plan. Jim would stay put until the Marines arrived or he would die while they left him behind—or he would die waiting for the Marines. All but one of those options was out of Sherman's control.

The annex, as Edward called it, was a white two-story house hidden behind an eight-foot-tall white wall with a baby blue gate. Long neglected trees drooped over the walls, obscuring the place from passing cars and prying eyes. Sherman didn't dare post a guard out front for fear of being discovered. He kept the blinds down and ordered everyone to stay away from the windows.

Anonymity was their best defense, at least for the next hour until sunset. After that, night would shield their movements like a comfortable cloak.

Gournsey sidled over to him as Evelyn tended to Jim.

"Are you still functional?" asked the sergeant.

Sherman glanced down at the bulky bandage protruding from under a blood-soaked shirt.

"I've been worse. A bit stiff, but still mobile."

Gournsey nodded and eyed the house interior. "Do you think the Gendarme knows about this place?"

Sherman had no idea. He motioned for Edward to join them. The Chief Political Officer rose with reluctance from his chair and walked over.

"Captain, what can I do for you?"

"Does the Gendarme know about this place?"

Edward squinted despite the dim light. "I can't say. The government knows. The address is written down on some piece of paper in the Interior Minister's office."

"Have you used the place recently?" asked Sherman, although the dust answered his question.

"Nothing but storage," said Edward.

"No random inspections or last-minute tours?"

"This is Equatorial Guinea. If you pay the fees, no one cares."

"And when did you pay the fees?"

"A few years ago, right after I started."

"I hope they have short memories here," said Gournsey.

"We should assume they don't," said Sherman. "I'll take Lopez and poke around. I want you to make sure no one follows us through that tunnel."

"Copy that," said Gournsey and set off towards the basement with an armful of explosives.

Sherman turned to find Lopez standing nearby, not having heard the corporal approach.

"You heard that?" asked Sherman.

"Enough," said Lopez.

"I want to scout our options."

Lopez said nothing. He was ready to go.

They gathered at the back door under Scott's reluctant gaze.

"Where are you going, Captain?" asked the agent.

"Scouting our options," said Sherman. "We'll be back in fifteen."

"Jim can't move again," said Scott.

"I know," said Sherman.

"It'll kill him. Evelyn said so."

"I know," said Sherman as he opened the back door.

In the waning glory of colonial Spain, the backyard must have been splendid. Sixty years later, little remained of that faux greatness. The fountain ran dry, its ornately carved figure lay broken on the ground and covered in green moss. Once carefully manicured plants ran wild. Sinuous vines crawled up the walls and tree branches sagged low enough to touch the ground.

The yard wasn't big—a quarter acre at most. Cloistered by nature, it felt smaller.

Rusty strings of barbed wire topped the back concrete wall. Sherman came a head short of the top. He held out his hand and Lopez passed a pair of wire cutters like a nurse handing over a scalpel.

The rusted wire broke apart with little effort and Sherman cut again. The gap he created fit an average person but not more than one at a time.

He pulled himself up and looked over the wall. Like the street beyond Jim's house, the forest encroached up to the property line.

Sherman dropped back down, and Lopez took a turn looking over the wall.

"Good for us getting out and good for them sneaking up," said Lopez.

Sherman agreed with the corporal's assessment. The thickly matted trees and grass behind the wall made for excellent concealment for anyone willing to use them.

Cooking smoke curled through the trees like fog. Voices mingled with the evening birds and insects.

Neighbors, thought Sherman.

He motioned towards one wall while Lopez walked towards the other.

Lopez bent his ear towards the top and shook his head.

Sherman did the same and overheard quiet words of worry. He pointed to his ear and over the wall next to him. Lopez understood and met him by the back door.

"Grab a few chairs and prep a quick exit over the back wall but be quiet about it."

Lopez nodded and they slipped back inside.

"That was quick," said Scott upon seeing them reenter. "What's out there?"

"Jungle and neighbors to the west."

The agent frowned.

"We'll stay inside for the time being," said Sherman. "Make sure the lights stay off. Use the red lights if you must. They are harder to spot from a distance."

"What's the corporal doing?" asked Scott.

Lopez carried two chairs and a coffee table outside.

"Prepping our exfil over the back wall."

"But we can't move Jim," protested Scott.

Sherman put his hand on the man's shoulder and leaned in. "I know, but I can move the rest of you. Sometimes the only choices left are the least bad ones. Do you understand?"

"Triage," said Scott.

Sherman patted his shoulder. "Exactly. Now, your job is to keep everyone as calm as possible. We want to stay invisible here and wait it out."

"Okay. Keep calm. I can do that."

"Good," said Sherman as Gournsey reappeared. "All set, Sergeant?"

"Whoever goes through there is in for a nasty surprise."

Sherman nodded and filled him in on the escape route and neighbors.

"I also found a cable running from the embassy."

"Fiber optic?" asked Sherman.

"Older," said Gournsey and scanned the room. He pointed to a tiny TV screen in the kitchen.

Sherman flipped the device on and two faint black and white images flickered to life—the old surveillance cameras over the front and back doors. He'd thought they didn't work anymore. At least they could monitor the old place.

"Anyone bring a deck of cards?" asked Gournsey with a jovial smile and wandered off to check on everyone.

Chapter Twenty-One

Hours passed but the guilt didn't go away. The feeling chewed on Miguel Ondo's conscience like a dog gnawing on a bone. The guilt ate through all the excuses until only the solid truth remained.

Two stones of shame weighed on his chest. The first was accepting the Mazda SUV he now drove. He shouldn't have kept the vehicle. That much was never in doubt. Nothing came for free in his world. There were always strings. He'd wanted to say no when Captain Sherman made the offer, but he didn't. He'd caved and ran away.

The second stone was older and much heavier. Miguel felt a deep and almost indescribable guilt for not fighting back—not just against General Asumu, but against the long strings of injustice perpetrated against the people of Bioko Island. Layers that transcended generations, starting with his grandfather, who assumed the badge under the Spanish against his own people. The original sin of collaboration.

His father added another layer under President Mbasogo. Policing for the dictator was no pleasant task, one

Miguel knew well. He had followed in his father's wide foot-steps. Corruption permeated everything. People expected to pay little bribes to survive, and his father expected them in return for upholding his oath. Such was life. Miguel had not changed that calculus and it ate him up.

The captain's words rang in his ears. "Be the third option."

Maybe, I can do something, he thought. *Anything.*

The Americans weren't great, but they were transparent. He knew what they wanted and what they offered. The Russians and Chinese stayed in the shadows. He never knew their goals or motives. They wanted everything, he assumed, and did anything to get it, including killing a young woman and framing their adversary.

Miguel wanted to do something. He needed to help.

Without fully considering the implications, Miguel found himself near the American embassy. Impulsively, he drove up to the front gate and honked. It had opened before. He assumed it would open again.

Nothing happened.

He honked again.

Still no movement.

Miguel felt suddenly foolish and exposed. They didn't care about him or the island. Americans only care about themselves. He should have remembered that.

He tried shifting into reverse, but it was too late.

The SUV shattered into sparks and debris.

Bullets hissed, snapped, and thudded. Metal screamed and tore. The glass cracked and bounced. The air thrummed. Miguel's world shrank.

Instinctively, he fell to the floor and slithered to the passenger side, away from the gunfire.

I'm going to die, he thought.

His stomach turned at the realization, but it did not feel strange. Subconsciously, he'd accepted such an outcome—the ultimate cost of his profession. A small sliver of peace fell over Miguel as he crawled out of the SUV.

Everyone jumped at the sudden punctuation of gunfire that pierced their small bubble of safety. Everyone but the soldiers.

Sherman grabbed his rifle and met Gournsey at the small CCTV monitor. He'd assumed the shooting was directed at the embassy. It was the logical next step for the Gendarme.

What he saw at the front gate surprised him

"Is that Miguel?" he asked.

"He came back," said Gournsey with a chuckle.

"To get himself killed," added Sherman.

"Well?" asked Gournsey in a tone that said *we're not gonna let that happen*.

"With me," ordered Sherman.

They found Lopez at the back door, long gun in hand.

"Where do you want me?" asked the corporal.

"Head east and see if you can find an angle. We'll circle west and try to get him out of there."

"Copy that," said Lopez.

He bolted out the back and cleared the wall in one swift motion.

Sherman and Gournsey followed, leaping over the back wall and landing with a muted thud in the dense grass. The air smelled sweetly of decay and the warmth of fading light. Sherman's watch read 1805 hours—thirty minutes to sunset, six hours until the Marines landed.

Intermittent bursts of rifle fire carried over the walls and dissipated in the trees. Sherman and Gournsey ran hard through a great swathe of green humming with insects until they reached a red dirt road petering out into the forest.

They turned left and met the main street that fronted the embassy. The gunfire continued—sharp pops and cracks. The occasional bullet hissed down the street.

Sherman edged past houses guarded by concrete walls until he hit the corner of the street. He peeked towards the embassy.

Not one hundred yards away, he spied Miguel sitting helpless behind the front tire of the Mazda SUV. The vehicle belched steam and gushed fluids. All the windows were gone, and it had more in common with a cheese grater than an automobile.

Miguel wore a look of deep resignation on his face and Sherman wondered how he wasn't already dead.

"Echo One, I have eyes on the shooters. Over," came Lopez's voice over the radio.

"Echo Three, how many? Over."

"Four are currently holding position down the street. They know he can't go anywhere. Over."

"This could escalate quickly," said Gournsey.

The sergeant was right. All the actions Sherman made up to that moment were in defense of American lives. They were also away from the embassy and their new hiding spot. A full-fledged battle with the Gendarme force would only snowball, drawing more soldiers to the area. The fact that it hadn't occurred already surprised Sherman. He'd assumed an all-out assault on the embassy was imminent. Maybe this was a scouting party or maybe just some drunk soldiers looking for a fight. Either way, he wanted to get Miguel out of the immediate danger, even if it was beyond the scope of his mission.

Smoke was his best option, but Sherman couldn't throw a smoke grenade that far.

Several more poorly aimed shots slammed into the SUV. Miguel didn't even flinch.

Lopez's voice came over the radio. "Echo One, I have the shot. Over."

"Echo Three, hold your fire unless they advance on the SUV. How copy? Over."

"Copy that. Out."

Gournsey glanced around the corner and gave a low whistle. "No way you're tossing smoke that far."

"Maybe from there," said Sherman, pointing to a battered van parked forty yards up the street toward Miguel.

"Long toss," said Gournsey. "Assuming he knows what to do after it goes off."

True enough, thought Sherman.

Even if he got to the van unseen, he still had to get Miguel's attention and convey his plan.

"Echo One, these boys are getting antsy and look ready to advance. Over."

"Copy that," radioed Sherman as he turned to Gournsey. "I'm going."

The sergeant took position on the corner.

Sherman ran hard in a low crouch to the van forty yards up. He remained unseen by the soldiers, but Miguel was too lost in his own thoughts to see him.

Shouting broke out among the Gendarme men. Taunts or expletives. Maybe both. Followed by bullets, like punctuation marks.

Sherman did his best to get Miguel's attention without being seen. The front gate of the embassy annex was in view. They couldn't afford a firefight, not there and not then.

"Echo One, something is happening. They are radioing and pointing at the vehicle. Over."

"Copy. I'm going to get him. Out."

Sherman pulled the pin on the smoke grenade and tossed the canister. It hit the ground with a clank and a hiss. Smoke billowed out like a caustic fog. He waited a few more seconds for the smoke to build and then took off running.

The soldiers started shouting then they started shooting. Bullets snapped over Sherman's head. Inaccurate and blindly fired, but still deadly.

Sherman covered the last yards like a man possessed. He slid in next to Miguel, whose eyes blinked rapidly as if trying to dispel a dream.

"Time to go," yelled Sherman as he slapped Miguel across the face.

The mental cobwebs cleared and Miguel matched Sherman's gaze.

"Captain?"

"Time to go. Now!" yelled Sherman.

Miguel nodded and took Sherman's outstretched hand.

"Echo One!" radioed Lopez, his voice urgent and choppy. "Tank approaching. Get out now!"

Sherman couldn't see through the smoke, but he heard the tank engines thrum and the treads clank. He yanked Miguel's arm, pulling him into a full sprint down the street in front of the embassy. Their slapping footsteps blended with his pounding heart.

The tank's engines roared behind like a fire-breathing monster hidden in its own smoke. Sherman kept his eye on the cross street, the nearest avenue of escape.

A right turn across the road led to Gournsey, who watched them run with a look of impotence.

Left led away from his team, away from support, but also away from the Americans under his protection.

A great crunch of popping metal sounded behind them as the tank ran over and through the SUV they'd just left.

Sherman turned left.

Chapter Twenty-Two

The metal chair pressed into Charlotte's spine at an odd angle, but interrogation chairs were not designed to be pleasant. They did not elicit joy, but dread and fear. Soft, cushy furniture conveyed all the wrong impressions; hard chairs did not.

The room itself was similar in design and purpose. After the Gendarme captain took Charlotte from the street, he escorted her into the bowels of a bland office building. No signs hung on the exterior, no official seals or lettering— nothing to say why the building existed or who used it.

Charlotte knew of such places. The CIA called them black sites, a polite term for hell, a place where the rules of war did not apply, a place that did not exist on a map. And since it did not exist on a map, neither did those unfortunates inside.

Two flights down, the captain had stopped and opened a metal door. Charlotte imagined all manner of terrible scenarios awaiting her, but there was only a chair, the uncomfortable piece of metal bolted into the ground on which she now sat. Nothing else—no table or cot, no bucket of human excrement in the corner, and certainly no windows.

The captain told her to sit. She sat and waited.

The room felt cold in a dry, air-conditioned way that seeped into her bones.

Still, she waited. There was nothing else she could do.

Charlotte existed outside of normal time and every interrogation manual said to make people wait. The longer, the better. She only hoped the waiting would not last all night. If the Marines landed before she got a word in with General Asumu, then her whole plan might go to hell. The irony of that word did not escape her.

When the door finally opened, Charlotte stuck to her poker face, but hidden behind that flat expression was a wide grin. Only an hour had passed and the man stepping into the room wore a crisp blue uniform and addressed himself as Colonel Nze. She'd already climbed the bureaucratic ladder—no lowly officers reeking of liquor and indecent intentions.

The colonel pulled in another chair, noticeably more comfortable, and took a seat facing Charlotte. She placed him in his early forties, with a stocky build and a wily look.

The true measure of the man was the watch on his wrist. She'd learned over the years that this specific accessory determined a soldier's level of corruption or competence. A gold Rolex told her the man could be easily bought. Something less flashy meant they could still be bought, but not so easily. A cheap Casio, like the one Captain Sherman wore, meant they didn't care about money, only time.

Colonel Nze wore a curveball of sorts: a fancy

outdoorsy smartwatch—expensive, yes, but also practical, more utilitarian than a statement piece.

"To what do I owe the pleasure, Mrs. McMillan?" he began, in only slightly accented English.

"Miss McMillan," said Charlotte. "Mrs. McMillan was my mother."

Colonel Nze gave a wry smile. "Miss McMillan, you are charged with breaking curfew and interfering in a military operation. Care to tell me why you were sneaking around?"

"I was trying to get here," she replied.

The colonel no longer smiled. "Who do you work for?"

"The United States of America," said Charlotte. "I am a regional director for the State Department."

"Hmm," mused the colonel. "And why would a regional director for the State Department risk her life to be here?"

"My government wishes to speak with General Asumu regarding the situation on Bioko Island."

"You mean our glorious revolution against the dictator Mbasogo?" asked the colonel with a knowing smile. He leaned in, waiting for her response.

Charlotte didn't think flattery would help her cause. The colonel was a company man, but not a vain one. He appeared too poised and capable to fall for sweet words.

"I mean your secessionist demands for the island."

"Go on."

"The safety of all Americans on the island is my primary concern. General Asumu's speech caused quite a stir in the State Department."

The colonel rubbed his thick, calloused hands together as if grinding her concerns to dust. "The General understands those concerns. In fact, he sent a group of his finest soldiers to ensure the safety of Ambassador Duggan, should the rightfully enraged crowds find her first. Do you know what happened when they arrived to help?"

"No," lied Charlotte, but she saw things had turned against her.

"My men were ambushed and butchered like hogs by American soldiers," retorted the colonel, his voice rising with anger.

"I'm sorry to hear that."

"No. You are not. Not yet."

Charlotte swallowed the very real thought that she would never leave the room and plunged onward.

"Given the situation, I'd also like to discuss American assets and interests in the region and reaffirm American commitments to the island." She almost said country but stopped short.

The colonel crossed his arms over his barrel chest and leaned back. "Now, we've come to the meat of it. You want to keep your lithium deal, but General Asumu did not sign that deal. General Asumu, the new President of Bioko, does not condone imperial theft. All such contracts with the dictator Mbasogo are hereby null and void. You have no power here. No authority. No standing."

"Colonel Nze, I can assure you that the United States will not accept such blatant disregard for the norms of international relations. We signed a deal in good faith and expect such a deal to be upheld, even if the reins of power change hands."

"Your citizens, your companies, your deals are no longer welcome in Bioko."

Bioko. He'd said it twice. Charlotte assumed it was the newest attempt at an African country born from a coup and supported by the barrel of a rifle.

"We provide this island significant monetary support," she added.

"We do not need or want your neo-imperialist blood money. We have other, like-minded, backers."

"The Chinese and Russians," said Charlotte.

"You say their names like we say yours," said Nze. "It puckers the mouth like rancid goat stew."

"They are not honest brokers," she continued.

The colonel stood up laughing. "And you are? Think of all your broken promises. Americans change their minds every four years, reneging on promises like a child. We cannot blindly trust you the same way I cannot stick my head into a lion's mouth and trust he ate enough breakfast."

Fair point, thought Charlotte, but she plowed on.

"Why did you attack the embassy?"

The colonel frowned. "We've done no such thing. Yet."

This confirmed Charlotte's suspicion that the explosions and gunfire were from the Russian mercenaries. It fit with her theory, the one she needed to persuade the colonel with.

"You're in bed with the wrong side, Colonel Nze. The Russians are playing you, double-crossing you, and this glorious revolution nonsense has blinded you to the truth."

The colonel said nothing, but his eyes looked curious.

Charlotte continued. "You're after the lithium, just like we are. It'll power a generation and mint millionaires."

"The money means nothing if the people don't reap the rewards."

Charlotte shrugged. "Look, I admire your plan. Blame the American for murder. Lock him up. Search his house. Confiscate the documents detailing the lithium deposits. Great stage work. Except, you drugged the wrong guy. But mistakes happen, so on to Plan B. You started the revolution.

That gets rid of the Americans altogether. So, what if you don't have the exact location of the lithium deposits? Lots of companies will gladly partner with you. Sure, you won't get as much money, but still, does a few billion less really matter?"

The colonel sat back down.

"Here's where you went wrong. You hired the Russians to drum up your revolution online, but you didn't know they wanted it all for themselves. They sent a team of mercenaries here. Those men tried to steal the lithium documents this morning and failed. In their haste, they attacked the US embassy this afternoon and failed again." At least, Charlotte hoped they failed. "The Russians double-crossed you. If they get the documents, you won't be able to stop them when their mining ships show up escorted by a destroyer and take the lithium."

The colonel's face was a mask of discontent. Charlotte wasn't sure how much of her story was true, but it had struck a nerve.

He stood up again, gave Charlotte an inscrutable frown, and disappeared out of the interrogation room, slamming the metal door on his way out.

Charlotte took a deep breath. Her pulse raced. Either her plan worked, or Colonel Nze was getting his gun and she'd end up dead on the concrete floor. She guessed that wouldn't be the first time someone died in that room. The large drain in the center assured the Gendarme could pressure-wash away the evidence.

Not over three minutes later, Colonel Nze returned. Enough time had elapsed to make a call or maybe he'd got his gun. Charlotte watched him intently for clues.

"Do you have any proof of your fanciful tale?" he boomed.

Charlotte hid her smile well and produced the ID card

Sherman took from the dead man in the Mercedes. She held it out like a peace offering.

"We retrieved this from one mercenary earlier today."

The colonel turned the piece of plastic over and over in his hand as if considering the merits of her evidence. Then he tossed it back to her.

"This proves nothing," he said.

"Taken out of context, it doesn't hold much weight," said Charlotte. "However, if you look him up in your immigration records, I imagine there will be many other Russians entering around the same time. If you don't want to do that, have your men look for the black Mercedes SUV full of corpses in front of the US embassy."

"My men surround the embassy as we speak," Nze added with a thin smile.

Charlotte swallowed her fear, wondering if Sherman was still there, which she hoped he wasn't. Surrounding the embassy might spark a slaughter. She tried not to let that fear show.

"Then it shouldn't be hard to verify what I told you."

The colonel relented. "What do you want?"

"To speak with General Asumu about a mutually beneficial future," she answered.

"Come on. He's waiting," said Colonel Nze, opening the door and gesturing for her to follow.

They walked back up the two flights of stairs out of the nameless building. Outside, a black BMW sedan idled at the curb. The colonel opened a door and pushed Charlotte inside, before taking a seat next to her.

"*The Presidential Palace*," instructed the colonel to the driver in Spanish.

Chapter Twenty-Three

Sherman and Miguel panted hard in the thick evening air, trying to catch their breath. They'd turned left and sprinted the depth of the embassy grounds to an adjacent alley. Sweat ran down Sherman's face and back. His side burned with pain and smudges of blood soaked through the bandage. He didn't bother checking but knew he'd broken a stitch or two.

Shouts and the tank's rumble lingered in the distance but didn't grow closer. Either they'd escaped unseen, or the Gendarme were not interested in following. Either way, it brought them a moment of respite.

"Why'd you come back?" asked Sherman between ragged breaths.

Miguel braced himself against a wall with one arm. "Why did you do all that?"

Sherman didn't answer because he didn't need to. The nature of Miguel's question showed he understood Sherman's motives.

"We need to find a place to lie low until dark. Then we can meet with the others," said Sherman.

"You're bleeding," said Miguel, pointing at Sherman's side.

"I pulled a stitch."

"Why do you have stitches?" asked Miguel.

Sherman pointed west and they started moving down the muddy alley behind walled-off homes. Their boots squelched and slipped in the muck.

"You didn't answer," said Miguel as he tried to maintain his balance.

"I got shot," said Sherman matter-of-factly. Years ago, he'd been embarrassed by such unfortunate events because they felt like a mistake. Age and experience taught him a valuable lesson—shit happens, even to the well prepared.

"What happened?"

"Russian mercenaries attacked the embassy."

Miguel appeared unfazed. "That's bold. Is that why no one opened the gate?"

"We moved across the street," said Sherman.

"Did anyone else get hurt?"

"Besides the Russians and me? No."

Miguel squinted at the setting sun. "That's good."

A half-built home came into view as they walked. One of dozens dotting the area. The wall around it had a hole and Sherman pointed to the gap.

"That should work," he said.

Miguel poked his head through the opening. "Looks abandoned," he said a moment later.

"Is that good or bad?" asked Sherman.

"Sometimes these attract squatters, but this one doesn't have a roof."

Slipping through the hole, Sherman understood what Miguel meant. The house had only two walls of homemade bricks held up by rotting wood braces. A pile of slowly dissolving bricks sat in one corner of the lot. Long tendrils of grass and vines threatened to consume what little human imprints remained.

Sherman found a secluded corner and settled into a deeply shadowed patch of grass. Miguel followed and eased himself onto the ground.

"Echo Two, Echo One. How copy? Over," radioed Sherman.

"Echo One, good copy. What's your situation? Over."

"We holed up nearby and are waiting for dark. What's your sitrep? Over."

"Cooking steak and watching the game. Everyone accounted for and safe. Over."

Sherman chuckled to himself. "What's the situation across the street? Over."

"The tank is still squatting on the SUV and the soldiers have cordoned off the street at least two blocks in either direction. Looks like they're setting up for a long siege. Wouldn't be surprised if the trebuchets came out. Over."

Sherman had expected as much, at least in one of his imagined scenarios. In another, the embassy was already a smoking pile of rubble. It was a good sign the latter had not already come to pass.

"They are going to knock on doors soon. Over," radioed Sherman.

"Heard. I'll move everyone upstairs, Jim included. Over."

"Good, I'll radio after dark. If you can't respond, click three times. Over."

"Copy that. Out."

Sherman sighed and leaned his head against the wall. It was still warm to the touch.

"How long have you known Sergeant Gournsey?" asked Miguel.

"You don't think he's still guilty?" asked Sherman in reply.

Miguel laughed. "No, I don't. Curiosity is my curse. You two have a good... oh, what's the word? Rapport?"

"We've been doing this together for a long time," said Sherman. "Rapport is probably an understatement."

"A bond," added Miguel.

Sherman nodded. "Yeah, something like that."

"That's not something I ever experience with my fellow officers," Miguel continued. "Everyone played the game for their own benefit."

"For survival?" asked Sherman.

"Maybe for some. We police make little money, but you can survive. Most wanted more, so they took what they could. My superiors didn't care. They did the same. Corruption ceases to be visible when everyone is corrupt. Then it is just normal. That's what it felt like."

"The normalization of bad behavior," said Sherman. "It happens all the time. Just look at politicians."

"You know what I am talking about," said Miguel, sounding relieved.

"I'm a soldier, the barbaric apex of normalization. When you strip away all the noble ideals and rationalizations, I kill people for a living. We normalized murder long ago. Don't feel bad about playing the game. It could be far worse."

"Like what?"

"Really murdering for money. This soldier of fortune bullshit."

"The Russians," said Miguel.

"And many others," added Sherman.

"You don't want the extra money? You could retire somewhere nice."

"I don't give a crap about the money and my retirement plan is a wooden box draped with an American flag," said Sherman.

"Really?" asked Miguel.

"Maybe a cheap bamboo bar on the beach if I'm lucky," admitted Sherman.

"That sounds better," said Miguel.

"My point being," Sherman continued, "that this is an all-or-nothing path we're walking. You're in or not. No half-measures. No dangling a toe in to see if the temperature feels right."

Miguel nodded with a knowing gleam in his eyes.

"You figured it out?" asked Sherman.

"I did," said Miguel, but Sherman didn't have time to find out what.

A vehicle trundled past them and came to a stop in the alley. In the briefest of glimpses, Sherman saw a black Mercedes SUV.

He put a finger to his lips and rose to his feet. Miguel followed his movements but appeared lost to his rationale.

"Russians," whispered Sherman and edged towards the broken wall to get a better view.

The SUV idled fifty feet down the alley. With no open doors and tinted windows, Sherman couldn't tell how many passengers were inside—anywhere from one to five given the capacity of the vehicle. A substantial numerical gap for one wounded soldier and an unarmed cop.

"What are they doing?" whispered Miguel in Sherman's ear.

"Scouting."

"For what?"

"Their next attack," said Sherman.

Five minutes passed. Then ten. The sun began its daily freefall towards the horizon. Sherman checked his watch. 1830 hours. Only minutes of daylight remained. Three and a half hours until the Marines landed. A lot of time and no time at all.

As the sun sank and the great curtain of night closed, the SUV's doors opened. Two shapes stepped out into the gloaming.

For the length of two cigarettes, the men said nothing. They smoked and gazed down the alley. A natural cacophony of night sounds enveloped them. Frogs, toads, bugs, and birds went about their routines indifferent to humanity as they had for thousands of years.

As the two men smashed cigarettes under their boots, they spoke. Sherman never learned Russian, other than a few phrases. His war was not the Cold War but the War on Terror. He learned Arabic, Pashto, and Farsi. But he knew the two shadows spoke Russian. That much was clear.

Sherman and Miguel listened in their hiding spot.

Midway through an exchange, one man answered a call and switched to heavily accented English.

"What news?" asked the Russian.

He listened and paced around the SUV.

"An American! Why weren't we informed immediately? What do we pay you for?" he growled.

More pacing and gesturing followed.

"They took her to see the general! Can you prevent the meeting?"

A pause followed.

"I don't care. Stop the car. Shoot the driver. They have something we need."

Another pause.

"You're the shark. Get it done!" said the Russian and hung up.

The men returned to an animated conversation in Russian that Sherman didn't understand. The phone call, however, was clear enough. The American was Charlotte, and she was speaking to General Asumu and the Russians didn't want that to happen.

Sherman already had the suppressor screwed onto his service pistol. He slipped out of the hole in the wall.

The two Russians stood by the vehicle's hood looking at a map spread across the metal surface. They held small red flashlights and jabbed at points. Their faces showed age and experience in the red glow—wrinkles, scars, broken noses, and boxer's ears. They were capable men. Commanders.

Sherman crept within fifteen feet of the pair before pulling the trigger twice in quick succession. No hesitation or remorse. The pops melted into the night, stopping the insect symphony for a moment. The pair slumped to the ground, caught by the eerie red glow of the flashlights that fell with them.

Quickly, Sherman flung open the SUV's back door to make sure no one else was in the vehicle. It was empty.

"Miguel," he hissed. "Come and help me."

Miguel emerged from the hole in the wall and examined the scene with a detective's eye.

"You think Ms. McMillan is the American they spoke of?" he asked.

Sherman pointed to the feet of one Russian. "Yes, I do. Now, please help me carry this guy into the compound."

Miguel paused as if considering the ramifications of moving the body, then grabbed on. They carried the two corpses through the broken wall and into a patch of tall grass. Sherman took a Makarov pistol off one of the men and handed it to Miguel along with an extra magazine.

"I suppose I'll need this," said Miguel, examining the weapon.

"I sincerely hope not," said Sherman. "But the way this day is going says otherwise."

"And doing this helps your friend?" asked Miguel, looking at the dead men.

"Questioning my methods?"

"They seem…" Miguel paused, searching for the word. "*Demasiado.*"

"Too much," translated Sherman. "Perhaps, but I can't afford too little." It was a sentiment he'd survived by for years: no half-measures, all or dead.

Miguel nodded in understanding. "I see."

Sherman hoped he did. The last thing he needed was an accomplice second-guessing his actions.

"We need to move," he said. "What's the best way to the annex?"

Miguel pointed to a small trail weaving between the houses.

"No," said Sherman. "What's the best way to drive?"

"We're taking their car?"

"It's armored. We might need it."

Miguel paused. "West down this alley, then loop back to the north. We can leave it by the beach, but you'll—"

"Have to cut through the forest," Sherman said, finishing the thought.

"Exactly."

"You drive," said Sherman.

"Are you sure?"

"Yeah, that gives me time to disable the GPS."

Miguel looked puzzled for a moment. "Otherwise, they will track us," he said.

"Bingo," said Sherman, handing him the keys.

Chapter Twenty-Four

The Presidential Palace had all the excessive trappings Charlotte expected in a dictator's home. Marble floors, mahogany dining chairs, great golden chandeliers, giant televisions, overstuffed leather armchairs, and even what she assumed was a genuine Rembrandt endowed the interior with an overwrought splendor—all the luxury stolen oil wealth could buy and then some. But that wasn't enough. President Mbasogo couldn't bear the simplicity of the island, so he went and built a new palace in a new capital on the mainland.

What a fool, thought Charlotte.

Dictatorships don't work in absentia. As soon as they leave, someone else takes their place. Simple math, really, and she kicked herself for not seeing it earlier.

Her team should have foreseen this eventuality, but African dictators were like stubborn warts that defy removal and cling to the body. She'd assumed Mbasogo was a survivor. She was very wrong.

The broad-faced colonel led her through several grand,

albeit empty rooms until they reached the presidential office. The door in front of her was a good eight feet tall and thick enough to have required an entire tree. Ornate carvings covered the surface. Charlotte looked closer and discovered it depicted kneeling Africans in front of Spanish conquistadors.

A trophy or something more sinister, she wondered.

"You will address the general as President Asumu. Are we clear?"

"I'll call him his holiness if it gets me in the room," replied Charlotte.

The colonel looked as if that might be a possibility, before opening the door. Charlotte found Asumu sitting with his feet on an antique desk that cost more than a Maserati.

"Mr. President," Charlotte began, but Asumu held out his hand for silence.

Charlotte bit her tongue and closed her mouth.

"I find it highly amusing to see you Americans groveling so quickly at my feet," he said in a slithery English accent Charlotte couldn't quite place.

"I work for the State Department," she replied. "We grovel when the moment calls for it."

"And this is such a moment," said the general, sweeping his arms around the room.

"It appears so."

"Have you come to congratulate me?" he asked with a smirk. His smooth face and watch glittered in the warm yellow light.

Charlotte saw it was a fancy watch, worth almost as much as the desk—a gift perhaps or maybe bought with stolen money.

"It is a rule that the State Department does not congratulate coup leaders. Such platitudes set a poor precedent."

The general laughed. None of the somber revolutionary rhetoric from his speech on television remained. This was a man of opportunity and greed, a chameleon willing to shed ideas when the need arose.

Charlotte was relieved.

Zealots made for tough negotiations. Facts and convictions always got in the way of solutions.

"You may not congratulate me, but you need me."

"The United States has many partners," she said.

The general laughed and stood up to pour himself a drink. "Would you like one? It was the former president's favorite."

"No, thank you."

"Personally, I'm a rum man. I never understood the whiskey craze, but I admit, this is quite good. How much do you think it costs?"

Charlotte knew a few labels but not that one, nor was she particularly enthused about playing his game.

"I couldn't say," she replied.

"Humor me with a guess," he pressed.

"A thousand dollars," she offered, but guessed it was much more.

"Twelve thousand," said Asumu with a shake of his head. "Twelve thousand dollars for a liter of whiskey. Do you know how many liters of water that buys? Or cooking oil? Or petrol?"

Charlotte did not like the direction of the conversation, but she'd dealt with worse men.

"And this?" asked Asumu, shaking his wrist and the shiny emblem of luxury attached to it. "I found this in a desk like a common pen. Do you know how much it costs?"

Charlotte did, but she shook her head. The revelation that the watch did not belong to Asumu threw her theory about watches to the dogs.

"Eighty thousand dollars," said Asumu with a chuckle. "It's a nice watch, but all watches tell time. Why does the ex-president deserve such a watch?"

"I couldn't say," said Charlotte.

"He doesn't. Not now, not ever. The man is a crook. He takes from his own people and pads his Swiss bank accounts."

"Why are you wearing it?" asked Charlotte, trying to get a true measure of the man. She'd heard and seen conflicting information.

The general smiled and jiggled his wrist. "I tried it on, and it fit."

"To the victors go the spoils," said Charlotte.

"I never understood such sentiments," replied Asumu. "There are no spoils in victory. Everyone takes what they deserve."

All of this only confused Charlotte. Reading the general made her mind churn. She pushed ahead with her own agenda.

"The United States government would like to discuss what you now so deservedly possess."

The general played coy and asked, "And what might that be?"

"We want assurances you will honor the ex-president's deal for lithium mining," replied Charlotte, holding her breath for a response.

"Why would I honor anything Mbasogo signed? That contract is worth only the paper and ink."

Charlotte exhaled long and slow. "Because reneging on the deal won't help you or your people."

"I disagree."

"You disagree because the Russians offered you a better deal, and if not them, then the Chinese. Nice tank by the way."

The general no longer smiled.

"I can see why you played your hand," continued Charlotte. "With the lithium deal inked, there wasn't much time left. You had to act. You framed the American for murder to get to the lithium deposit map, but you got the wrong guy. To top it off, the Russians figured out your play."

Asumu's face was a tangled mess of anger and fear.

"The Russians tried to take your precious map. They're dead or most of them. But I'm guessing you didn't know that. Maybe they forgot to tell you. Things slip through the cracks in high pressure situations such as coups."

"Enough!" bellowed Asumu. "You have no proof. This is another American ploy to rob Africa of her resources."

Charlotte slid the ID across the expensive and ornate desk. General Asumu leaned over and glanced at the Russian ID.

"This could come from anywhere," he said dismissively.

"It came from the driver of an armored Mercedes SUV intending to take possession of information that could deprive your nation of billions if not trillions of dollars. Since you don't believe me, ask your men near the embassy. The vehicle and bodies are still there."

"Near," said the general with a victorious smile. "We surrounded the embassy thirty minutes ago. Your colleagues have no means of escape."

Charlotte tried not to flinch or frown... or breathe for that matter. She wanted to project complete indifference, but screams of fear and doubt filled her mind.

Sherman wouldn't stay, she thought. *They got out. Stay the course.*

"Ask your men," she repeated.

Reluctantly, Asumu picked up the radio and asked for the information. The exchange unfolded quickly, and Charlotte tried not to smile. Everything she'd said held water. Meanwhile, the general's cheeks grew sallow, drained of vibrancy.

"Do you believe me now?" asked Charlotte once the radio conversation ended.

The general glowered and Charlotte feared for her safety a little more.

"The Russians are not the only fish in the sea," he replied. "There are other options."

"Like me," said Charlotte. "And the deal already signed."

"Like the Chinese or Indians," continued Asumu as if she hadn't spoken.

An aide opened the office door, apologized for interrupting, and spoke in Spanish. *"It's almost time for your victory speech, Mr. President."*

Charlotte choked back bile at the words *El Presidente* but didn't move.

"The nation awaits," said Asumu. "Take her back to the cage. We don't need any more American meddling. I don't care how good your offer is or how many gunboats you send."

Gunboat diplomacy died decades before, but Charlotte considered it a wise course of action given the general's stubbornness.

"We'll give you ten percent," she shouted as the general exited the office.

The possibility of millions, if not billions, gave the

general pause. He stepped back into the room with a thin smile on his face, not fully convinced.

Charlotte played her ace—the one Evelyn told her about. "And your family will get American citizenship."

"And immunity from anything that happens here," added Asumu.

A true deal with the devil, thought Charlotte, but she stuck out her hand to shake.

The general accepted and Charlotte breathed a brief sigh of relief. She'd done it. The runaway train was back on the tracks. The minerals would flow and America would stay on top. She'd accomplished a nearly impossible feat.

Any thoughts of rest quickly faded with a great thrumming roar.

Her mind said jet.

The general's expression read fear.

Then a great thunderous explosion sent her world tumbling to black.

Chapter Twenty-Five

The sound snuck in between crashing waves as Sherman and Miguel parked the Mercedes, as if there was no space between the breakers. Sherman understood before Miguel. His ears were attuned to the sounds of war.

Jets. Inbound low and fast.

Not us, thought Sherman. *Who?*

Before he could consider the answer, downtown exploded in a great geyser of flame that splintered the night.

Miguel stood transfixed as the light died and sirens trilled.

"Was that you?" he asked.

"No," answered Sherman. "But we need to find out who. Come on, we're close to the embassy annex."

The duo continued through the ancient thicket of trees until Sherman's inner map said they were close.

He radioed Gournsey. "Echo Two, Echo One. We are almost to the backyard. Can you confirm your location? Over."

"Echo One, hold for confirmation. Over."

A moment later and three houses deeper, a faint red light flashed twice.

"Copy two beats. Over," said Sherman.

"Confirmed. Over."

"We're inbound. Out."

Sherman led the way and helped boost Miguel over the wall. When he finally pulled himself up and over, Gournsey stood nearby with a finger to his lips. Silently, they moved inside and upstairs.

The annex lay quiet and musty. They passed Lopez and Scott, who greeted them with smiles and gentle arm squeezes. The silence reminded Sherman of stories his grandfather once re-told about the First World War—stories passed down from his father, rich tales about silence and the clanking of nearby German patrols.

Gournsey motioned towards an empty bedroom and closed the door behind Sherman and Miguel.

"Glad to see you in one piece," whispered the sergeant and patted Miguel on the back.

"Glad to be here," Miguel replied.

"I assume you heard all the commotion," said Gournsey.

"Got a good view back there," said Sherman. "Looks like downtown took the brunt."

"Thoughts on who?"

"Nothing worth saying out loud," answered Sherman, who felt no obligation to speculate.

Gournsey handed over a satellite phone. "I thought you might say that."

Sherman dialed Major Sanders.

"Captain, what news?" asked Sanders.

"I'm hoping you can tell me, sir. Jets just bombed downtown Malabo. Am I in the middle of a shooting war?"

"Let me get back to you on that, Captain," replied Sanders with gravel in his voice. Sherman knew someone would catch hell for not knowing.

"Understood, sir. Otherwise, we're holding position and awaiting exfil."

"I'll be in touch shortly," said Sanders and hung up.

Gournsey watched Sherman's expression before adding, "He didn't know."

"Nope," said Sherman.

"Sounds like a shooting war then."

"What do you call everything else that happened today?" asked Miguel, exasperated.

"Civil war," said Sherman. "Not to diminish any of the suffering, but it implies a unique response."

"The dead don't see any difference," said Miguel.

"I know," said Sherman.

"He means the Marines won't land," said Evelyn, who stood in the now open doorway. "Sorry, voices carry in here."

"Maybe," said Sherman.

"It's the Nigerians," whispered Ambassador Duggan, joining Evelyn at the door.

"Ma'am, care to say more?" asked Sherman.

"They consider the Gulf of Guinea their backyard and they have a vested interest in local drilling operations."

"Are you saying they're looking to intervene?" asked Gournsey.

"Yes," said Edward, whose head was just visible behind the ambassador.

"Stop lurking," said Sherman, motioning everyone inside the bedroom. "Now, tell me what I need to know."

"The Nigerians—" began Ambassador Duggan.

"If it's them," added Edward, ever the diplomat.

"If it is the Nigerians," she continued. "Then they are acting in concert with President Mbasogo. He is good friends with the Nigerian president, and local oil production flows through their refineries."

"You're telling me the Nigerian Air Force just bombed a friendly neighbor."

The ambassador nodded. "Until Mbasogo is in control again—they're not friendly. I'm afraid diplomacy is never straightforward."

"Things clear up when the shooting starts," replied Sherman.

The phone rang, cutting off the awkward silence that followed. Everyone scattered, but Sherman waved the ambassador over.

"Major, I have Ambassador Duggan with me," he answered, and they both huddled around the phone to hear.

"Good, I have an update. Ghanaian radar caught two Nigerian JF-17s entering Equatoguinean airspace twenty minutes ago."

The ambassador gave Sherman an 'I told you so' look.

"Major, this is Ambassador Duggan. Have we heard from the Nigerians?"

"Nothing official," replied Sanders.

"I have contacts there," she said. "I could make some calls."

"The ambassador thinks the Nigerians are propping up Mbasogo in order to keep the oil flowing to their refineries," added Sherman.

"By all means, Ambassador," said Sanders.

She nodded and slipped out of the room.

"Sir, any changes with our exit strategy?" asked Sherman.

"Not yet, Captain. The Marines are still en route, but this is a fluid situation as you're aware."

"Understood, sir."

"Keep your head down, Captain."

The call ended and Sherman took a seat on the floor. Gournsey disappeared for a minute, returning with cups of extra strong instant coffee. He handed one to Sherman.

"I think we're in for an all-nighter," said the sergeant.

Sherman smiled at the gesture and said, "I think you're right."

The two friends sat in silence and sipped coffee, listening to the wind and sirens slithering through the trees. Minutes passed as Sherman enjoyed the respite, letting his mind empty of any unnecessary thoughts.

"Captain," hissed the ambassador.

Sherman opened his eyes, which he hadn't recalled closing. "What news?" he asked.

"It's not a shooting war," she said.

"What?"

"My contact in Lagos said that President Mbasogo is fighting back. He struck a deal with the Nigerian government. If they help him back to power, they get a cut of the lithium deal."

"Not much of a deal for anyone on the island," said Sherman.

"The resource curse," added Gournsey.

"Did your contact say what comes next?" asked Sherman.

"They couldn't provide specifics, but the Nigerians are motivated to keep Mbasogo in power."

"Because of the lithium or mutual friendship?" asked Gournsey.

"Does it matter?" asked the ambassador.

"No, it doesn't," said Sherman. "What matters is how far they're going to take this."

"My understanding is that they'll take it to the end."

"Ground troops?" asked Sherman, unhappy with the idea of citywide battles.

"If necessary. They can claim they're coming to the aid of a regional ally and stopping a coup. No one needs another coup in Africa."

"Like all good allies, it comes with a cost," said Gournsey.

Sherman wished Charlotte hadn't disappeared so they could bounce ideas around.

"Captain," said Evelyn, poking her head into the room again. "I think I made a mistake."

"Haven't we all," said Sherman. "You'll need to be more specific."

"Ms. McMillan and I were talking before the attack on the embassy and I said something to her that maybe I shouldn't have."

"I doubt you said anything Charlotte couldn't handle, but let's hear it."

"I told her about General Asumu's family and how he wants them to live in America. She asked for information about the general and I told her that was his Achilles heel."

"She asked, you answered. No harm in that."

"I saw her pack up some things after that."

"And then she left," said Sherman.

"And then she left," confirmed Evelyn.

"Sounds like a Charlotte move," said Gournsey.

"Which means she went downtown," said Sherman. He didn't need to add a conclusion to his statement. The recent bombing run served as the punctuation.

His phone rang, cutting the silence.

"Major," he answered.

"Captain, local assets near Lagos just sighted another group of jets launching about ten minutes ago. They'll be over the island in a few minutes."

"The ambassador's contacts say the Nigerians are working to keep President Mbasogo in power," said Sherman.

"That is the CIA's assessment as well."

"I'm glad we can agree on that," said Sherman. "Where does that leave the Marines?"

"They're holding in Ghana until we coordinate with the Nigerians, which will take hours, if not days. We can't have them flying into a kinetic environment without support."

"Understood, sir."

"One more thing, Captain. Charlotte McMillan's emergency beacon just activated."

"Where?"

"Southeast of your location. Near the Presidential Palace."

"Have our orders changed?"

"No, continue to safeguard American lives," said Sanders.

"Has the CIA requested assistance?" asked Sherman.

"No."

"Understood," said Sherman.

"I'll call with future intel. Out."

Sherman gave the phone back to Gournsey, who looked confused.

"Room change," said Sherman. "Everyone to the basement. Nigerian jets are inbound."

"And Jim?" asked Evelyn.

Sherman shook his head. "Leave him be."

"And the rest of what Sanders said," added Gournsey.

"Charlotte activated her emergency beacon a few minutes ago."

"Downtown?" asked Gournsey.

"Near the Presidential Palace."

"Which they probably bombed."

"Likely," said Sherman.

"Rescue orders?"

"Langley has not requested any assistance."

Gournsey's eyebrows twitched with exasperation, "So, am I going or are you?"

Sherman gave an exhausted grin. "I'm going," he said. He stood with a grimace, thought better of going solo, then added, "And Lopez."

Chapter Twenty-Six

Another wave of Nigerian jets roared through the dense night air as Sherman and Lopez gathered their gear. Distant explosions rolled in from the west near the airport and further east.

"Full kit?" asked Lopez.

"Light and fast," said Sherman.

The streetlights flickered, then abruptly went out as the city lost power and tumbled into darkness.

"And extra batteries for the NVGs," he added and clipped the night vision goggles onto his helmet.

They finished their checks in a pale red glow.

"Radio when the major calls in the next round of bombers," Sherman told Gournsey.

The sergeant nodded, "Good hunting, Captain."

Sherman and Lopez left over the back wall in absolute darkness. A moonless night with stars smudged out by smoke.

Only when Sherman flipped down his goggles did the

world around come into view. A tangled web of green pixels danced before his eyes.

"On me," said Sherman and they headed into the vertiginous forest.

From the annex, they headed north towards the beach before turning east towards downtown. Sherman reckoned Charlotte took a similar route.

Fires glowed in the distance as bright swirling columns in their night vision goggles. Smoke wafted on the sea breeze, thick and caustic—a mix of plastic, chemicals, and flesh.

As they moved away from the beach and crossed over into the denser downtown area, the smoke thickened into a fog. Entire sections of town lay in rubble with homes reduced to crumbled bits of concrete. Screams filled the streets, undulating across the broken asphalt.

Sherman and Lopez tried to stay on the smaller, less damaged roads, but the closer they got to the town center, avoiding the carnage became impossible.

On one block, an errant Nigerian bomb had landed smack in the middle of a tightly packed group of homes. Nothing remained but rubble and small fires burning meager household items. Two women knelt on the street, howling with grief into the sickly night air. Their wails twisted Sherman's stomach and Lopez swore under his breath.

The scene reminded Sherman of an air strike outside of Kandahar years earlier. Intel painted the compound as a Taliban command center and maybe there was truth in the story, but not when the bombs arrived. Only women and children remained. The Taliban, in their cowardice, had packed up days before.

Sherman's team arrived to confirm the strike, only to

find two wrinkled old women, grandmothers or great-grandmothers, howling into the parched summer air.

Same pain, different war, thought Sherman.

Cloaked by the night, they passed the women in silence. Words couldn't help, only grief and time would ease the overwhelming pain of their loss.

Beyond the police station, where Gournsey once stayed, the real destruction began. The Nigerians struck at the bureaucratic heart of Bioko. Once grand buildings smoldered in ruin. Gone was the old House of Parliament and courthouse. Only pieces of their regal past still stood. The odd brick wall or ionic column remained as a testament to the destruction.

Sherman and Lopez slunk through the deep shadows of night as hundreds of people dug in the rubble with only flashlights for illumination. Hundreds of tiny beams of light danced across the macabre scene, hoping to find someone still alive.

"This is more than a message," whispered Lopez. "This is punishment."

"The president built a new capital," said Sherman. "He has no reason to keep an old rebellious one."

A distant explosion rumbled across the city and the rescue workers shouted for people to work faster.

"Echo Two, Echo One. Any word on further strikes? Over."

"Echo One, checking now. Over."

Sherman and Lopez waited on one knee, eyes out, rifles shouldered.

Gournsey came back with, "Echo One, confirmation on more strikes. ETA thirty minutes. Over."

"Echo Two, understood. Confirm last ping on the GPS tracker. Over."

"Echo One, last ping is five hundred yards due east of your position. Over."

"How accurate are those things?" asked Lopez.

"Within fifty feet," answered Sherman.

"That's a lot of rubble to sift through," Lopez added, saying what Sherman already thought.

Rounding the corner, they came upon the carcass of the Gendarme headquarters. The stylish glass and steel frame façade lay shattered and crumpled. Soldiers sifted the wreckage, pulling bodies out and laying them on the street. Dozens upon dozens of them.

Generators powered a few industrial work lights and the area buzzed with activity.

"We need to move around," said Sherman.

Lopez said nothing, but Sherman knew the corporal kept a close eye on his watch.

They moved two blocks north, weaving between crowds of locals and jittery soldiers eyeing the sky. Looping around took ten tense minutes of their thirty-minute window.

Even from a distance the Presidential Palace looked more like a hill than a building. Two bombs had torn apart the western half of the structure, pulling the gleaming white stone in on itself.

Sherman and Lopez scaled an unguarded fence on the northeast corner and slipped into the manicured grounds.

"Echo Two, Echo one. Confirm ping. Over."

"Echo One. Eastern edge of the building, less than a hundred feet from you. Over."

"Copy that. Out."

"Find somewhere to cover our exit," said Sherman. "I'm going in to have a look."

"There ain't much left holding it up, Cap. Don't linger," said Lopez before trotting off into the night.

Sherman turned and approached the eastern most wing of the palace. Through sheer luck or over-engineering, a good chunk of the building remained tenuously intact.

Using a shattered window as a starting point, Sherman slipped inside the first floor. The room he found himself in didn't appear to have any purpose—perhaps a meeting room or parlor, if such things still existed. Broken glass covered a burgundy rug edged with gold. A few oil paintings hung on the walls. The rest lay smashed on the floor. Intricate vases had fallen from their perches and smashed into bits. Whatever the room's purpose, it had been luxurious.

He followed a darkened hallway further into the building, hoping to find a stairwell. He planned to search from top to bottom and then run before the next bombs struck.

Three doors later, he heard footsteps thumping on hard surfaces like tile or stone. Sherman slipped inside the nearest door and waited inside what turned out to be a giant liquor cabinet. Two rows of bottles glowed green in his goggles, but he spotted a bottle of bourbon too good to pass up and he slipped it inside the small pack, next to the dwindling bladder of water.

The footsteps passed and Sherman pressed on until he found a marble staircase leading to a second story. Part of the roof had collapsed, and chunks of concrete lined the hall.

Most of the doors along the second-floor hallway were open as if the occupants left in a panicked rush. The interiors were dark and seemingly lifeless. Sherman prowled from room to room, whispering Charlotte's name as he went.

He found nothing and pressed on.

At the corner office, under the open sky above, a light flickered under a closed door.

Sherman eased the door open a crack and then slipped through with practiced ease, scanning the room for threats. He found a shattered space with most of the ceiling on the floor. Heavy beams stuck up at odd angles like the skeleton of some ancient creature.

In the corner, lit by the pale glow of a cell phone, Charlotte sat alone. Dust covered her hair and face. Squiggly lines of dried tears streaked down her cheeks.

"Charlotte," hissed Sherman.

She blinked and gazed into the darkness as if the wind spoke her name. Sherman realized she couldn't see him. He stepped closer and spoke again.

"It's Frank. Are you okay?"

This time, her eyes lit up with recognition.

"Frank," she groaned. "What took you so long?"

As Sherman stepped into the pale glow, he saw Charlotte's true predicament. A giant wood beam pinned her left leg to the ground. Her toes were blue, and her femur was broken.

"That doesn't look good," said Sherman, stooping down closer and squeezing her hand.

"It ain't a Christmas present," she said and winced at the pain. "Who's dropping the bombs?"

"The Nigerians," Sherman answered.

"In support of President Mbasogo," she added.

"That is the consensus."

"I should have known better," she said.

Sherman looked at his watch. Five minutes remained until the next strike. He stood up to find anything to help lift the beam off her leg.

"Why did you leave?" he asked.

"Him," said Charlotte, pointing across the room at a bloody corpse covered by debris.

Sherman looked but didn't recognize the face.

"Who's that?" he asked.

"General Asumu. We had just reached a deal of the lithium when the first bombs detonated."

"That's why you left. To protect the lithium deal?"

Charlotte shrugged. "That's what they pay me for. That's the job, Frank. Make sure America stays on top. We need clean energy to win. We need lithium."

Sherman was not in a position to judge her for following orders. That was the essence of his life.

"I get it," he replied. "The mission matters most."

Charlotte nodded silently in agreement.

"Give me a minute to find something to lift that beam off your leg," said Sherman and continued searching.

"I had it," she said. "We shook on it and everything."

Sherman found a decent two-by-four and jammed it under for leverage.

"I mean it," she continued. "The general agreed to stand by the lithium deal."

"He's dead," said Sherman.

"I know."

"I'm gonna try lifting the beam off your leg," said Sherman. "Try not to scream."

"Why—"

Sherman lifted. Charlotte's eyes widened and her face paled with pain. It took all Sherman's strength to move the beam off her leg and he panted with exertion. A small trickle of blood rolled down from his wound.

Another stitch, he thought.

"I'd say you can rest, but we only have a few minutes before the bombers return."

Charlotte's head wobbled and she might have been seeing stars with all the pain.

"Charlotte," he said and grabbed her hand.

"That fucking hurt," she moaned.

"We need to go, now."

"Bombs, I heard you," she hissed but didn't move.

"Echo Three, Echo One. I have the package, but we need a splint for a broken leg. Over."

"Echo One, no joy. Over."

Sherman glanced around the room for anything and found a fancy wooden chair with spindly arms and a thin back. It cost a year of his salary, but Sherman easily broke it apart with his boot.

"That belonged in a museum," said Charlotte, pointing at the disassembled chair.

"It belongs around your leg," he replied and fashioned a makeshift splint out of the chair and strips of a velvet curtain he cut.

Charlotte managed to stand with Sherman's help, but putting weight on her leg was not an option. She almost fainted after the first try and Sherman didn't want to attempt round two.

With her arm around his neck and his around her waist, they hobbled out of the room and down the hall towards the stairs. Sherman used the flashlight on his rifle so Charlotte could see.

"I don't think this will work," said Charlotte as they stood atop the stairwell.

"I can push you down instead," offered Sherman.

"I don't recall you being such an asshole when we dated," she retorted.

"Age has a way of making one crotchety. Now, hurry up."

Stair by painful stair, they descended. Charlotte winced at the slightest movement and Sherman kept glancing at his watch. Five minutes had passed. The next strike was imminent.

As they reached the bottom of the stairwell, with Charlotte wobbling from the pain and effort, two men stepped out of a nearby room. Sherman swung his rifle at the duo who did the same with their flashlights. Each group stood, illuminated in bright pools of white light.

One of the men reminded Sherman of an oil drum: round, thick, and immovable. The other was thin and sinewy like an old piece of leather. Charlotte tensed and squeezed his shoulder hard. The men were a known commodity and not a good one.

The sinewy guy reached for a pistol strapped to his leg, a reasonable response to seeing an American soldier in the ruins of the Presidential Palace.

Sherman didn't let him clear the holster.

He shot the guy with a burst, center mass. A good grouping considering he held the rifle with one arm.

The man crumpled into a messy heap.

The oil drum didn't move. He stood there like an angry bull steaming from the nostrils but too wise to charge.

"Where is General Asumu?" he demanded.

"Upstairs," said Charlotte. "He's dead."

"You damn Americans!"

"No," retorted Charlotte. "The Nigerians dropped the bombs, not America. They're backing President Mbasogo. We were never your enemy, but I think you know that."

The man glowered but said nothing.

"We're leaving now," said Sherman. "I suggest you do the same but use a different door. If I see you again, you'll end up like him."

"Colonel Nze," said Charlotte in a way that Sherman

knew they'd recently met. "I think it best if you listen to my friend."

The colonel still didn't move. He remained anchored to the floor. Jets roared in the distance and Sherman urged Charlotte out the door.

"Echo Three, Echo One. If a big guy follows us out, put him down. Over."

"Copy that."

The distant rumble rose into an earth-shaking roar as jets screamed overhead. Sherman pulled Charlotte into a dried-out pond in the palace grounds. Her shrieks of pain mixed with the thunder of jet turbines.

Tracers filled the sky in great arcs of orange as the Gendarme shot back.

The explosions arrived seconds later, a delay of gravity and physics and a few thousand feet. Sherman felt them coming like a driver sensing someone would cut them off. There was no sound, but he knew.

He shielded Charlotte with his own body and waited.

A great cataclysmic boom followed. It punched the air from his lungs with a concussive whoomph like a jab to the chest. Sherman's ears popped and rang. They burned at the pressure wave and the decibels.

Fire lit up the sky and, for a moment, he saw sheer terror and childlike amazement etched on Charlotte's face as if illuminated by the sunrise.

Bits of concrete and wood rushed overhead, rolling into the dry pond like clumps of dirt thrown upward by a dog digging for a lost bone.

Basketball-sized pieces of debris sailed past like snowballs and Sherman winced as something sharp grazed his arm. He felt a burning sensation then the warmth of blood flowing freely down his skin.

More bombs landed further out and the ground shook beneath them. For a second, he had another flashback to the stories about his great-grandfather and what he'd endured during the Battle of the Somme almost one hundred years earlier. Sherman shook his head in disbelief at what that man experienced.

"Echo One, Echo Three. Do you copy? Over."

Lopez's voice sounded distant and thin, as if the corporal were talking through a wall.

"Echo One, Echo Three. How copy? Over," repeated Lopez. A sense of urgency threaded through his voice.

"Echo Three, we're still kicking. Out."

"Are you okay?" Sherman asked Charlotte, who still lay on the ground, breathing hard.

"I feel sick to my stomach," she answered.

"It's the adrenaline. It will pass."

She glanced at him and frowned.

"You're bleeding. A lot."

The viscous warmth spread down his arm and Sherman reached for a field dressing in a vest pocket.

"Let me," said Charlotte, who struggled to a sitting position.

He handed her the unwrapped package and she wrapped the bandage around his bicep.

"That looks deep," she said.

"One more scar for the collection," said Sherman, thinking of the dozens of others he'd endured over the years.

Another long burst of machine gun fire rose into the air as another jet roared overhead in the darkness. More explosions thumped in the distance. The sky flashed open in brief bursts of orange light.

Sherman helped Charlotte to her good leg and took most of her weight on his shoulder. They struggled up and out of the empty pond and headed towards the rear gate.

As they neared the thick wrought iron barrier, a single rifle crack rolled across the grounds. Sherman turned to see a barrel-chested silhouette hit the ground.

"I told him to use a different door," he said.

"He was dead either way," said Charlotte. "He backed the wrong horse."

They reached the gate, which Sherman realized Lopez had broken open for their exit. He kicked hard with his boot and the gate budged open enough for them to pass.

Lopez met them on the far side of the street, emerging from wherever he'd hid.

He glanced at Sherman's arm.

"Shrapnel?"

Sherman nodded.

"Bad?" asked Lopez.

"Deep," answered Charlotte.

"Later," said Sherman, knowing they couldn't dawdle downtown. Between the soldiers, the angry mobs, and the bombers, the area buzzed with lethal endings. "We need to find a way of carrying Charlotte."

Even with both supporting her weight, they couldn't move fast enough. They needed a stretcher.

Lopez held up a finger for them to wait and disappeared into a nearby alley. He returned a minute later carrying a long rectangular piece of metal scaffolding and two small pieces of metal that hooked onto the short ends of the scaffolding. Lopez set up the contraption on the pavement.

Charlotte ran her hand skeptically over the hard metal surface but eased herself on top.

Sherman wondered how far he could carry the thing before falling over from exhaustion or bleeding out from the stress it would place on his bicep, but they had no better plan, so off they went.

Chapter Twenty-Seven

Explosions make people jumpy, even professional soldiers and the men outside the US embassy were not at the top of that esteemed totem pole in Raylan Gournsey's opinion. They did not rise above middling. But even a third-rate soldier with a rusted Kalashnikov gets lucky. It's the law of averages. Gournsey knew that much. He'd seen good friends die to kids with ancient Mausers. Unexpected things happen all the time in war. The only consistent part was the suffering. That never changed, nor did the nerves, and the unseen death from above frayed even the steeliest of nerves.

With each successive wave of Nigerian jets, the Gendarme in front of the embassy rose to new heights of agitation. Men shouted. The tank engine whined.

Gournsey watched the welling sea of chaos through his night vision goggles and a narrow slit of open curtains. He'd moved everyone but Jim and Miguel down to the basement for their safety. Moving the injured American wasn't worth the risk. His tenuous hold on life faded with every hour without a doctor.

"What do you see?" asked Miguel.

"A powder keg waiting to explode," answered Gournsey.

"A what?" asked Miguel, clearly missing the vocabulary.

"They're scared out there. Scared people make rash decisions. They shoot first. They don't worry about the consequences."

"You think they're going to start shooting?" asked Miguel.

Gournsey didn't turn to face him but stared out the window. "I know they're gonna start shooting. The question is at what?"

"The embassy," said Miguel.

"Reasonable guess. They surrounded the place and, soon after, bombs started falling. Fair to assume America is the one dropping those bombs."

"Agreed," said Miguel.

"And if they start shooting and no one shoots back, they might think it reasonable to move inside."

"You're worried they might find the tunnel," said Miguel.

"I'm worried about a lot of possibilities right now. The Gendarme finding the tunnel is certainly one of them, along with poorly trained Nigerian pilots and errant bombs. But mostly, I'm worried about what happens when they figure out the embassy is empty. If that was me, I'd tear the neighborhood apart while searching."

"And then they'd come here," added Miguel, taking Gournsey's thought to the logical conclusion.

"And then they come here," Gournsey repeated.

"What happens then?"

"You answer the door," said Gournsey. "And we hope they go away."

"And if they don't?" asked Miguel, sounding uncertain.

"Then I start shooting and we all get blown to bits," said Gournsey.

"This is not a good plan," said Miguel.

"No, it's not, so make sure they go away."

Miguel sighed and headed downstairs. Gournsey didn't blame him. The plan sucked. He needed another.

Gournsey slipped into the next bedroom and checked on Jim. The big American didn't have much life in him. He took shallow, rattling breaths, and Gournsey knew he wasn't long for this world.

"Godspeed," he whispered into Jim's ear before giving the man's arm a squeeze.

Quietly, he moved down into the basement where four faces stared back at him in a faint red glow.

Ambassador Duggan and Edward sat on the floor with a look of grim resignation on their faces. Gournsey couldn't tell whose fate they'd resigned themselves to. Was it their own or Jim's?

Evelyn and Scott stood by the door anxiously waiting for what came next—a good sign as far as Gournsey was concerned. It meant they'd be ready for Plan B or was it Plan C. He'd stopped counting.

"What's the news?" asked Evelyn, her voice straining to sound cheerful.

"The waiting game continues," answered Gournsey with a forced smile. "The Gendarme are still parked outside our doorstep, but they don't seem too keen on anything else. Yet."

"Yet?" asked Edward. "That implies a future change."

"Yes, sir, it does."

"Sergeant, can you enlighten us on what shape this future might take?" asked Ambassador Duggan in a soft voice.

"I'm not in the business of hypotheticals, ma'am," answered Gournsey, not wanting to increase their anxiety levels.

"Give us your highly educated guess," replied the ambassador.

"I'm spitballing here, but I guess they don't know whose bombs are dropping and might be inclined to see them as American, given the circumstances. And having seen downtown go up in flames, they might storm the embassy in retaliation."

"But we're here," said Edward.

"We're not there," corrected Gournsey.

"They'll start searching," said Scott.

"And come here," added Evelyn.

"A likely possibility," said Gournsey.

"And then what happens?" asked the ambassador.

"Miguel answers the front door and y'all go out the back," answered Gournsey. "I'd say we stay down here, but if they search the house, it won't take them long to figure out Miguel doesn't live here."

"You should probably take down the American flag painting hanging in the foyer," said Edward.

Gournsey nodded. He hadn't noticed the picture or the foyer, but those things were not high on his awareness list. "Good idea, Edward. Anything else to increase our chances?" he asked.

"Besides moving the stacked-up chairs and file cabinets?" asked Edward.

"And Jim," added Evelyn.

"I think we all agree that if they come inside, the game is up," said Gournsey.

"Edward," said the ambassador. "There's a boring-looking landscape in the living room. Switch that with the flag so there's not an empty space on the wall."

"Good idea," said Gournsey again.

"And sweep the floor if you can. It's covered with dust, and I've never seen a dusty floor in the country. People take too much pride in that. It would be a giveaway."

Edward stood and headed to his tasks.

"I want the rest of you to grab water, food, and batteries. Start prepping to spend the rest of the night outside."

No one in the room looked happy about spending a night exposed to the mosquitos, but malaria was the least of their concerns and they rose to follow Gournsey's orders.

"Sergeant," hissed Miguel from the first floor.

Gournsey met him by the front window. He needn't ask why Miguel summoned him. The tank's roaring engine and clattering treads told him things were in motion.

"They're going in," said Gournsey.

"It looks that way," said Miguel.

Gournsey turned to the others. "Almost time to go. Finish packing."

Across the street, illuminated by headlights and splays of flashlights, the Gendarme entered the American embassy. The tank broke down the flimsy gate with little effort and blue clad troops surged through the gap. Shouts of anger echoed down the street and the scene thrummed with frenetic energy.

Gournsey watched through the night vision.

Soldiers swarmed the front and back, but those by the front couldn't get past the door. A few angry men fired their rifles in a vain attempt to break the glass, but it held.

"Will they get inside?" asked Miguel.

"There's a giant hole near the back door. Shouldn't take them too long to figure that out," said Gournsey. "Although, they might be confused by the pile of dead Russians in the back parking lot."

Another minute of frantic activity passed before the bullet-ridden front door opened. The siege was short, and the Gendarme moved to secure their newly conquered building.

The celebration was brief. An angry Gendarme officer soon barged through the front doors followed by several soldiers. The officer shouted orders and pointed around the neighborhood.

"Time to go," said Gournsey. "Scott, lead them over the wall. Stay within earshot but get them out of view."

"Understood," said Scott. "Close but hidden."

"Good man," said Gournsey.

The somber group padded out the back door as Scott maneuvered them over the wall and into the concealing thicket of trees.

"What if we just don't answer the door?" asked Miguel.

"You think they'll walk away?" Gournsey countered.

"Honestly, I don't know. Feels like a toss-up."

Gournsey grunted in acknowledgement and keyed his radio. "Echo One, Echo Two. How copy? Over."

"Echo Two, Echo One. Good copy. Over," came Sherman's ragged, out-of-breath reply.

"Echo One, Gendarme units breached and secured the embassy. They started a house-to-house search. I moved our able-bodied guests to the backyard. Over."

"Echo Two, understood. We're thirty minutes out. Over."

"Good luck. Out."

Across the street, like a wave breaking, the Gendarme spread out. They crossed the wide street separating the embassy and descended upon the homes.

All the houses hid behind metal gates and crude concrete walls often topped with broken glass or metal spikes. The clang of rifle stocks hitting metal reverberated down the street. It reminded Gournsey of the lone church bell tolling in his small hometown. With all the existential angst, the sound brought him back to being a teenage boy.

Gournsey backed away from the window, setting up deeper in the house where he could shoot anyone coming through the front door.

Outside, the metal gate to the compound clanged then creaked open. Thin beams of light danced through the curtains.

A knock boomed on the wood door.

"*Open up!*" came the voices on the other side.

Miguel stood nearby but didn't answer.

Another knock arrived, louder than the first. Then another and another.

Miguel opened the front door halfway and stood in the opening, faking an out-of-breath façade and trying to appear welcoming without letting them inside.

"*Good evening,*" he said in Spanish to the three men standing outside.

Two of the men were much younger than Miguel, the third was not. The younger men's eyes had a glazed look to them—an urge for blood that overtook the soul when the end neared, and the end always felt near when bombs fell from the night sky. The older man, who Miguel vaguely recognized, looked worried—not afraid or wild with fear but filled with angst. The look of a family man trying to do his best but knowing things were out of his control and hoping he'd see his kids again.

"*Where are the Americans?*" demanded one of the younger soldiers in Spanish.

Miguel blinked hard as a flashlight cut across his eyes. "*What's going on?*" he asked.

"*Where are the Americans?*" came the reply.

Miguel pointed across the street to what remained of the embassy.

"*No!*" yelled a younger soldier, but the older man stepped in front of him.

"*Have you seen anyone leave the embassy?*" he asked.

Miguel pretended to think for a moment then shook his head. "*I stayed away from the windows once the shooting started.*"

"*So, you didn't see anyone escaping?*"

"*No. I've been hiding in the basement.*"

Worried eyes narrowed and the soldiers' gaze rambled over the interior behind Miguel.

"*This is a nice house,*" said the older man. "*Where's your family?*"

"*Visiting my father near Pico Basile,*" Miguel said, filling his lie with some truth.

"*Lucky timing,*" said the soldier.

Miguel gave a tired shrug. "*I haven't heard from them since the fighting started. Do you know anything from the mountain?*"

The man smiled. "*We have control of the island.*"

"*Oh,*" said Miguel. "*Then they're safe.*"

The experienced man took a step forward and shined his flashlight over Miguel's shoulder and inside. The beam bounded off the newly changed painting, off the wall, and into a narrow strip of living room visible from the front door.

"*Does your wife not clean?*" he asked, shining his light on the still dusty floors.

"*I left the door open the other day,*" Miguel answered with a guilty look. "*She's going to give me hell for it.*"

"*Don't I know you*," said the man, once again shining his flashlight on Miguel's face.

"*I don't—*" began Miguel but was cut off by an urgent cry.

"*Captain!*" yelled a voice from the front gate.

The older soldier turned to look. "*What?*"

"*Come, sir. The women next door heard voices in the forest.*"

The captain looked at Miguel over his shoulder and asked, "*Did you hear voices?*"

Miguel shrugged again. "*I was in the basement*," he reiterated.

The captain hurried towards the front gate and yelled, "*Gather up!*"

The two younger soldiers followed, leaving Miguel alone and suddenly afraid for the Americans hiding in the trees.

"Stay with Jim," said Gournsey from the shadows.

"Of course," said Miguel as he watched the American bound out of the back door and over like an elegant beast of the night.

Chapter Twenty-Eight

Sherman made it to the beach before his arms gave out and his legs turned to jelly. His whole body burned from exertion and exhaustion. Sherman knew his limits and he'd just reached the furthest edge.

They set Charlotte down behind an empty kabob shack.

"See if you can find us a ride," Sherman told Lopez.

The corporal nodded and moved off down the beach road.

"You need to slow down," said Charlotte, awkwardly propping herself up on an elbow.

"This is me slowing down," replied Sherman.

He lay on the ground sucking deeply from what remained of his water supply. No matter how much he drank, he didn't feel hydrated.

"Thanks for coming back," said Charlotte after a long pause. "I know you didn't have to. Langley made it clear that I was on my own."

Sherman wanted to give her a squeeze of acknowledgement but sitting up felt unfathomable.

"You're welcome," he replied. "But tell me next time you need to run off."

Charlotte tried to laugh but winced.

"I will do my very best," she said.

Sherman knew she would and that her best would not overcome the demands of the mission. They both understood that core fact. The mission came first.

"Do you remember that beach in Libya? Our car broke down in the little town nearby and we sat on the beach and ate MREs and drank that terrible shit they called wine."

Sherman did, fondly. "Yes."

"This place has a similar vibe," she added.

"The war is a little closer here."

"That was fun, though."

"It was," said Sherman.

"Do you want to go to the beach with me again?" asked Charlotte. "Assuming we live, and I can still walk."

Sherman chuckled. "Sure, but I think we need to pick a different beach. The one in Libya is covered with landmines now."

"Of course it is," she replied in a mournful tone.

Sherman noticed the metal siding of the kabob shack, which was padlocked shut, had peeled away from the frame.

"Hold on," he said and slid across on his back until he reached the metal.

The tin bent easily despite the little effort he gave.

"What are you doing?" asked Charlotte as Sherman slid through the opening.

He emerged a minute later with an armful of potato chips bags, three bottles of orange Fanta, and a wide grin.

Sherman handed her a bag and a soda.

"This doesn't count as our beach getaway," Charlotte teased.

"No, but I need the calories," said Sherman, greedily munching on the chips.

Charlotte sipped the slightly cool Fanta and gazed towards the fires raging in downtown.

"All this and nothing changes," she said.

"Tell that to the dead," said Sherman.

"You know what I mean. President Mbasogo will stay in power. America will get its clean energy and everyone else will still lose."

"Whose face is printed on the currency doesn't matter to most people," said Sherman. "They almost swapped one dictator for another."

"I know… I tried to facilitate the swap."

"Then you know the people don't have a say in it. This is a democracy in name only. They suffer either way," said Sherman.

"The system wasn't built for everyone to win," she added.

The air was still hot and heavy. Sherman nodded in agreement with Charlotte even if she could only see his silhouette. The snacks served him well and Sherman stood up to watch for Lopez or Gendarme soldiers. A strong sea breeze pushed most of the smoke south. His nostrils happily took in the fresh, salty air.

Further east along the road, a pair of headlights headed their way. Sherman flipped up his goggles and shouldered his rifle. Behind the shack, they were hidden from any vehicle traveling on the road, but he wasn't taking any chances.

"Is that our ride?" asked Charlotte.

"Echo Three, Echo One. Are you driving right now? Over," Sherman radioed.

"Echo One, negative. Over."

"Copy that. I have one vehicle heading west towards our position. Circle back this way. Out."

"Who is it?" whispered Charlotte.

"Not sure," said Sherman, but few people would risk driving on a night like this. They were either soldiers or desperate people. Maybe both.

The headlights bobbed on the rutted road, bathing the empty street in a yellow glow. The lights were round and incandescent, not newer LEDs. Based on the throaty rumble of the engine, Sherman guessed it was a truck. Something big.

"Echo One, I have a line of sight to you. Looks like an old ZIL approaching. Over."

"Get ready. Out."

"Ready for what?" asked Charlotte.

"It's a Gendarme truck."

"Oh," she groaned.

Sherman checked his magazine and steadied himself for contact.

"Echo Three, do you have a headcount? Over."

"Two in the cab, one in the back. Looks like an anti-air mount. ZU-23 or similar. Over."

Sherman did some quick mental math on the odds of being bombed by the Nigerians if they commandeered one of the Gendarme's few anti-aircraft trucks.

Slim, he thought.

"Echo Three, can you take the driver?"

"Affirmative."

"Let it fly as they pass."

"Copy that. Out."

Sherman turned to Charlotte and held out his pistol.

"Things are about to get loud," he said.

"Why are you giving me that?"

"I want you to shoot anyone that comes around the corner here."

Charlotte glanced at the pistol and then at the corner. She took the weapon and press-checked the chamber.

"Okay," she said.

The truck rumbled closer, its engine drowning out the city noises. Sherman edged to the right of the kabob shack and waited.

Through the diesel's growl, Sherman heard glass break. The great engine sputtered and stalled.

A man shouted in Spanish.

Sherman slipped out of his hiding spot and caught sight of the truck. A single hole in the back window led to a blood-splattered front windscreen.

The passenger door opened and a teenager jumped out like a horse bolting from a burning barn. His mouth hung open and his speckled red face brimmed with fear. The uniform he wore fit a much larger man and he was unarmed.

Sherman ignored him.

He turned towards the third occupant manning the two-barreled behemoth anti-aircraft gun. The soldier frantically swiveled the gun back towards Lopez.

Sherman shot the gunner twice in the back without compunction. The man slumped forward in the gun's seat.

The retreating teenager sprinted towards downtown, holding up his oversized pants with both hands. At one point, his grip slipped and he tumbled to the ground with his trousers around his ankles.

Sherman watched the kid go.

"Echo Three, all clear. Out," he radioed.

"Here," said Charlotte and handed back the pistol.

Sherman took the gun then went to open the driver's side door of the truck. What remained of the driver slid out and hit the ground with a wet squish.

He circled to the back and rolled the gunner off the open tailgate. An unceremonious end, but Sherman never stood on ceremony.

Lopez appeared from the shadows at a jog and the two carried the dead soldiers off the road.

They picked up Charlotte, who'd watched the entire affair without saying a word, and placed her makeshift stretcher in the truck bed next to the anti-aircraft gun.

Sherman jumped in the back with her, which was crowded and filled with spent shell casings and boxes of ammo. He handed Lopez a rag from the truck floor.

"You're gonna need that," he said.

"Why?" asked Lopez before looking into the truck's cab. "Oh," he added, seeing the splattered windscreen and dashboard.

"It's a warm night," Sherman said.

"Tire iron?" asked Lopez.

Sherman found one and handed it over. Lopez proceeded to smash the front window and kicked it out in several mangled pieces.

"Better?" asked Sherman.

Lopez wiped down the steering wheel with the cloth and handed back the tire iron.

"Much," he said and flipped down his night vision goggles. "Where to, Cap?"

"Stay on the beach road. I want to circle back to where we came out of the forest. We can finish on foot from there."

"Copy that. Everyone buckled up?" he joked.

Charlotte did not look amused at the possibility of potholes and the truck's stiff suspension.

"Take it slow, Corporal," said Sherman. "Or Charlotte will never forgive us."

Lopez gave a thumbs-up and eased the truck into first gear.

Chapter Twenty-Nine

By the time Sergeant Raylan Gournsey cleared the back wall and landed in the thick grass behind the annex, the shouts of Gendarme soldiers already echoed through the forest. The men in blue streamed in from his left and right. Their voices and flashlights pierced the still air and shadows danced across the tree trunks.

"Scott," hissed Gournsey.

No answer came.

He plowed forward, not worried about making a little noise among the rising throng of voices.

"Scott," he hissed again, this time a little louder.

"Over here," came a faint reply.

Gournsey followed his ears to a clump of dense bushes thirty yards deeper.

Hiding in the thick foliage, Gournsey found four alarmed Americans. He ducked low and wormed his way into the natural concealment.

"What happened?" whispered Scott.

"That doesn't matter," replied Gournsey. "What matters is the next few minutes."

"Okay," said Scott. "Now what?"

"We go to the beach," answered Gournsey, seeing only one way out. "Link arms. Scott, you're in back. I'll lead. No one lets go. No one stops. Understood?"

"Understood," came four quiet replies.

"Evelyn, hold on to my vest, then the Ambassador and Edward. Ready?"

"Yes," they replied.

Gournsey led the way out of their hiding spot and into the deep forest night. None of the others had night vision and the only light came from Gendarme flashlights in the distance.

"Moving," said Gournsey and took the first few tentative steps north toward the beach.

Evelyn moved with relative ease, as he'd expected, but the others expanded and contracted like a slinky tumbling down a set of stairs. One second, they bumped into each other, the next, they strained to hold on.

Picking the path of least resistance proved difficult and whispered winces were heard as they passed through thorny trees and patches of knife-like grass.

All the while, Gournsey watched the long arcs of Gendarme flashlights grow closer. The Americans were not moving fast enough—not nearly.

"We need to hurry," hissed Gournsey.

"We're doing our best," said the ambassador.

Gournsey keyed his radio, which amplified even a whisper and spoke, "Echo One, Echo Two. We are moving north towards the beach. Gendarme units are close behind. What's your location? Over."

"Echo Two, Echo One. Inbound in a commandeered

truck. ETA three minutes. We can support from the beach. Over."

"Echo One, we have a Gendarme squad in pursuit. Recommend a quick withdrawal. Over."

"Echo Two, we'll have you covered. Just get to the beach. Over."

"Copy that. Out."

"Was that Captain Sherman?" hissed Evelyn.

"Yes."

"Are we going to make it?"

The trees around them danced with shadows cast by Gendarme flashlights. Dozens of them. Spanish words slithered through the trees like angry snakes and Gournsey caught snippets.

Footprints. Over here. The beach.

He moved faster, pulling Evelyn behind him the way a toddler might tow a stuffed animal. The line behind grew taut. The voices got louder and closer. Gournsey barreled on, sensing the edge of the forest ahead.

"Wait," hissed Ambassador Duggan.

"*Here!*" shouted the soldiers in Spanish.

"Run!" yelled Gournsey as the night tore open with gunfire.

The forest canopy vibrated with gunshots and staccato bursts of light. Screams and shouts, English and Spanish, all blended into a delirious uproar.

Gournsey saw the edge of the forest with the ocean glistening beyond and flung Evelyn forward like one bricklayer tossing a brick to another. She disappeared through the leaves and down a small berm into the sand.

He didn't see the others.

"Echo Two, Echo One. We have your retreat covered. Over," came Sherman's voice.

Gournsey returned fire at the Gendarme, who seemed to be everywhere.

"Run," came a familiar voice and he saw Scott pushing the ambassador through the gap and down the berm.

Gournsey emptied another magazine and turned to go when he spotted Edward crawling on the ground not twenty feet away. He moved closer as bullets snapped overhead and bits of leaves rained down.

"Edward!" shouted Gournsey, trying to get to the frightened American. "Run!"

In the green glow of his night vision goggles, Edward's head snapped back with cruel force and his body crumpled like a marionette doll whose strings got cut. Gournsey knew he was dead. He'd seen that blank look before.

Normally a sentimental man, Gournsey turned without another look and ran towards the beach. He knew there was nothing he could do to help Edward. That time had come and gone. The dead want for nothing.

Hurling himself through the gap, Gournsey felt the cushion of warm sand and rolled down a berm towards a ribbon of concrete that served as the beach road.

He tumbled head over heels for a few revolutions. When he came to a stop, Gournsey radioed, "All clear!"

The salty night air erupted in a maelstrom of gunfire so thick that Gournsey scarcely understood the situation. Heavy machine gun fire poured in from a nearby Soviet-era truck. For a moment, he thought the Gendarme had surrounded them completely.

This is it, he thought.

But the tracers arced overhead. The thick stream of lead chewed through the forest. Men screamed. Body parts and bark swirled together in a terrible blender of man and nature. Gournsey watched spellbound by the sheer awesome violence of it all.

"Echo Two," came Lopez's voice in his ear. "Move your ass!"

Gournsey snapped out of his reverie and staggered towards the truck pelting out a raging river of suppressive fire. He found Scott and Ambassador Duggan crouched nearby and motioned for them to follow. The machine gun blasts overpowered any words he might yell.

When they reached the truck, Gournsey found Sherman manning a Russian twin-barreled anti-aircraft gun with a look of grim determination on his face. Lying behind the captain, holding her ears with her hands, was Charlotte. A makeshift split wrapped around her leg and her face was scrunched with pain. Evelyn crouched behind the truck with the same covered ears and pained look.

Gournsey helped the ambassador into the truck cab next to Lopez, whose rifle stuck out of the driver's side window. Scott followed into the third seat and Gournsey hoisted Evelyn into the truck bed, her hands still glued to her ears.

He squeezed Sherman on the arm and banged on the roof of the truck cab. Lopez got the message and the heavy vehicle lumbered forward. Sherman kept firing for another minute as 23mm shell casings clanged about, hot and shiny.

The truck clambered down the beach road without headlights as Gournsey's ears adjusted to the relative silence.

Evelyn slowly released her grasp on her head and looked at Gournsey.

"Where's Edward?" she asked, but the pain was already welling in her eyes.

"He's dead," said Gournsey.

Tears streamed down her face.

Sherman slipped out of the gunner's seat and squeezed his shoulder. "Sorry we couldn't get there quicker."

Gournsey sighed and shook his head. "It wasn't you who was too slow."

"Shit happens," said Sherman. "It ain't yours to control."

"You did your best," said Evelyn, then winced at her own words.

Good, bad, or best, it didn't matter. The dead were dead. That was something Gournsey and Sherman had come to accept over the years. Knowing that didn't take the hurt away, but it helped process the grief. Without acceptance, only a terrible spiral of guilt and remorse remained.

"You look like hell," said Charlotte from the floor.

Gournsey smiled, appreciative of her attempt at humor. "And you look like a million bucks."

"Thanks," she replied.

"What happened to you?"

"Damn building collapsed on me," said Charlotte.

"And you?" asked Gournsey, pointing at the new field dressing around Sherman's bicep.

"Shrapnel," said Charlotte, answering.

"I'm fine," said Sherman.

"It's deep," added Charlotte.

"It'll heal," said Sherman.

Gournsey handed Sherman the satellite phone for a call he never wanted to make himself. It was a burden of leadership he did not want to carry.

Sherman took the device with a nod and started dialing. He had to cup his ear to hear over the engine noise.

"Yes, sir," said Sherman. "We evacuated the annex and are mobile for the moment."

He paused as Sanders spoke. Gournsey knew the bad news came next.

"Unfortunately, yes. Edward, the Chief Political Officer, died during the escape."

Sherman covered the phone receiver for a moment and mouthed, "How?"

"Shot in the head," said Gournsey, not willing to mince words or sugarcoat the outcome.

"He was shot during a gunfight with Gendarme forces," repeated Sherman into the phone.

Another pause.

"Things are still fluid. We haven't recovered his body yet. Say again."

Sherman gave a hopeful nod or at least Gournsey thought it was hopeful.

"Understood, sir. I'll relay our position when we hunker down," said Sherman, then added, "And, sir, General Asumu is dead. He was killed in the bombing of the Presidential Palace."

This time, even Gournsey heard the commotion on the other end. Many voices spoke at once.

"Yes, sir. I understand. We'll confirm our final location soon. Out."

"Good news?" asked Charlotte after Sherman ended the call.

Sherman nodded. "State negotiated safe passage for the Marines to land. Wheels down at sunrise."

"That's hours from now," said Charlotte.

"Time to find a nice hotel," said Sherman and produced a brown bottle from his bag and handed it to Gournsey.

The sergeant gazed at the faded label for a moment in

disbelief. A 1955 bottle of Old Rip Van Winkle. No one in his family since Grandpa had tasted that bourbon.

"Where on earth did you find this?"

"Presidential liquor closet," answered Sherman.

Gournsey uncorked the bottle and poured out a few fingers' worth.

"For Edward," he said and then took a swig.

A divine velvety burn trickled down his throat and Kentucky leaped to life in his memory. Trailer parks, cold creeks, Melissa Felter in ninth grade, getting stone-blind drunk under oak trees. It all tumbled out in a glorious blaze of history and nostalgia.

"Still good?" asked Sherman.

"Better," said Gournsey and they passed the bottle around in the back of a Soviet-era truck almost as old as the bourbon.

Chapter Thirty

A bright orange flame jumped out from under the old Soviet truck, slowly burning it down to the frame. Sherman watched from the passenger seat of the stolen Mercedes SUV with Gournsey behind the wheel and everyone else packed in like sardines. Charlotte lay in the back with Evelyn who tried not to bump her leg.

"Can't fault the Russians for lack of functionality," said Gournsey, gazing at the flames.

"They certainly don't make them like that anymore," said Sherman.

"Real shame," added Gournsey.

"Are we talking about the truck or the bourbon?" asked Sherman.

Gournsey held up a half-empty bottle. "You could have grabbed two."

"He only had one," said Sherman. "Unless you want to drink Scotch."

Gournsey sniffed dismissively at the mention of any

other whiskey but bourbon. A true Kentucky boy through and through, but Sherman already knew that.

"Where to now?" asked the sergeant.

Sherman shifted in his seat and checked the magazine in his rifle.

"You're going down the road for another two miles. There's a little hotel on the beach. Fancy resort place. Boutique or so they say. Diego's brother works there."

"Diego? The waiter from our hotel?" asked Gournsey.

"The same."

"Do we have a reservation?"

"Not exactly, but Charlotte has a company credit card."

"And where are you going?"

"To wait with Jim at the annex."

Gournsey nodded. "And Edward?"

"I'll get him too, if I can," said Sherman, knowing of Gournsey's respect for the dead.

"We owe him that much."

"That we do," agreed Sherman.

"Good hunting, Captain."

"Same to you, Sergeant," replied Sherman and then turned to the back row. "Evelyn, come on out. You can take my seat."

"Why do I get your seat?" asked Evelyn.

"The captain is going back for Jim," answered Charlotte, who'd overheard their conversation.

"Oh," said Evelyn.

"Radio if trouble finds you," said Gournsey, then handed over the satellite phone. "You might need that."

Sherman opened the door and jumped out. "See you in the morning," he said and jogged off toward the tree line.

Beyond the towering trees, downtown glowed an eerie scarlet as firelight caught in the smoke like an angry ember next to the sea. Sherman flipped down his night vision and entered the long strip of forest that ran parallel to the beach from one side of the island to the other.

From where they'd burned the truck to the annex was not far as the crow flies. However, trudging through the thick vines and meandering around the gnarled trunks took time. There was no direct path, only many small turns that often looped back on each other.

A centering quiet enveloped Sherman. He enjoyed the night—the totality of its existence, so all-encompassing and complete. Even without night vision, the dark did not frighten him. Long ago, he'd accepted those fears and made them his own. Night was not something to be feared, but a tool and a shield.

Forty minutes later, Sherman came across a scene all too familiar to places where the constraints of morality fray and fracture. Deeper in the trees, Sherman found the terrible aftermath of his actions on the beach. Broken branches, bark, and chunks of tree trunk littered the forest floor as if a hurricane had torn through the area.

Chunks of flesh and bone mingled with the arboreal carnage. Splatters of blood and the occasional arm or leg were all that remained of those dozens of soldiers chasing after Gournsey—all those lives reduced to unrecognizable fragments.

Voices of pain and fear carried through the trees, riding on the sea breeze. Wounded soldiers, dying soldiers, and those witnessing the trauma all spoke their pain into the night—a mournful chorus of grief and loss.

Sherman kept going.

He passed two soldiers dragging a third towards the water. The drawn man only had one leg but those pulling kept going as if he would survive the night. They didn't see Sherman cloaked in the darkness.

Another soldier crawled back towards the embassy, pulling himself with one good arm and little else. The anti-aircraft rounds had shredded every other appendage.

Sherman knew death and suffering. He'd seen his handiwork up close, but even this gave him pause.

As he neared the epicenter of destruction, the true toll revealed itself. A dozen identifiable bodies lay strewn along the ground, then the bits Sherman couldn't decipher—unconnected body parts that, divorced from their homes, seemed bizarrely out of place.

Sherman stepped lightly, avoiding what he could.

A dozen feet from the edge of the forest where Gournsey dove onto the beach, Sherman found Edward's body. The man had come so close to making it out.

Sherman crouched down next to him, and a deep sadness seeped inside. The uselessness of it all bothered Sherman. All the violence… and for what? Same president. Same political order. Maybe someday, something would change, but it wasn't that day.

With a grunt, Sherman heaved Edward's body up onto his shoulders and started the long, sluggish walk back to the annex.

Carrying the dead came with its own burden and Sherman felt the literal and figurative weight. Several times he stopped and considered leaving Edward behind. A profound exhaustion ran through his bones and Sherman knew he was flirting with collapse. Still, he owed it to Edward, even in death. At least, that was what he kept telling himself to motivate his heavy-as-lead legs.

A few Gendarme patrols still prowled the forest, but they were only looking for the dead and dying. Most of the men Sherman saw in the green glow of his goggles twitched at the slightest sound. Fear encompassed their every movement.

Sherman ignored them and kept trudging forward until he reached the annex's back wall. Those eight feet felt impossibly tall, and he set Edward down in the grass, propping him up against the concrete as if the dead cared about posture.

Climbing over the wall took what little energy he had left but Sherman made it to the other side. He approached the back door cautiously, not wanting to alarm Miguel into action.

The back door remained closed and the power out. Sherman knocked three times, not loudly, but with enough force to be heard upstairs.

His watch read 2300 hours—seven-plus hours until sunrise, one hour from when the Marines were originally scheduled to land.

A soft reddish glow filled the interior of the house and Sherman's night vision brightened. He flipped them up and waited just off to the side.

Miguel's face appeared pressed against the French doors, looking anxious and hopeful. Sherman stuck out a hand and flashed a thumbs-up. The door opened a crack.

"Captain Sherman?" came Miguel's voice.

"Good to see you, Miguel."

The door swung open all the way.

"Come inside before they hear us," said Miguel.

Sherman slipped inside and they stepped into the dining room converted into a storage area. Chairs stacked six high covered one wall. Boxes filled the space in between.

"You came back," said Miguel, not asking why.

"I did. How are things?"

Miguel glanced upstairs. "Jim's still breathing. Barely."

"Thank you for staying," said Sherman. "Sergeant Gournsey told me the story."

Miguel pointed up to the ceiling, which reached two stories high. Chunks were missing from where the plaster met the wall. Fist-sized holes let in the night air.

"Was that you?"

Sherman stared at the bullet holes and kicked a piece of sheetrock on the floor.

"We borrowed an anti-air truck from the Gendarme. I may have used it to cover the sergeant's retreat."

"I assume it worked," said Miguel.

"It did."

"And everyone made it out safely?" asked Miguel, anxiously.

"I need your help with Edward," said Sherman by way of answer.

"Is he hurt?"

"He's dead," said Sherman.

"Oh," said Miguel, nodding slowly. "I'm sorry to hear that."

"I appreciate your concern and your actions today. You've gone well beyond anything I had the right to ask."

"Let's call it even," replied Miguel with a half-smile.

"Even if it is," said Sherman.

"I have one more tidbit of information for you," said Miguel.

"I'll bite," said Sherman, wondering what else the night could possibly bring.

"Do you recall what the Russians said back at the SUV?"

Sherman recalled them ordering someone to bring Charlotte to them, but he'd assumed that was the oil drum sized Colonel that Lopez shot. He hadn't given the conversation a second thought since pulling the trigger.

Dead and done, he thought.

"No, I can't say I do," said Sherman.

"They called the person *shark* on the phone."

Sherman shrugged.

"Do you know the Spanish word for shark?"

"Tiburon," said Sherman.

"*Tiburón*," replied Miguel, correcting his pronunciation.

"*Tiburón*," repeated Sherman.

"Not an everyday name," added Miguel.

"If you say so."

"Do you know how many Tiburóns live in Malabo?" asked Miguel.

"I'm guessing you're going to tell me."

"One family, that I know of."

"Could there be more?" asked Sherman.

"I don't think so," answered Miguel with an air of certainty.

"Carry on then."

Miguel motioned for them to sit.

"There is a man named Eduardo Tiburón. A Major General in the Gendarme. The right-hand man of General Asumu. I met him once at some event or another. He lived up to his surname. White teeth flashing like a shark. He's gobbled up chunks of the city. No one cared. Greed comes with the territory."

"A sad but not uncommon story," said Sherman. He'd seen plenty of greedy warlords and bureaucrats over the years.

"He was instrumental in diminishing police power in the city. Took our funding and even some of our buildings."

"Bureaucratic competition," Sherman said blithely.

Miguel smiled an oddly maniacal grin.

"And you're going to do something about it?" asked Sherman.

"Major General Tiburón doesn't live far from here. He didn't move east like all his other rich cronies. Got a nice mansion near the beach on the way to the airport."

Sherman remembered the other fancy compounds near the ambassador's residence and wondered if he'd driven by the place.

"What are you planning?" he asked.

"Given the state of things, I'm going to arrest the shark for treason."

Sherman liked the idea. It spoke to his desire for justice and punishment. However, Miguel had not presented a plan, just a desire to act.

"How?" asked Sherman.

Miguel held up the Makarov pistol and his badge.

"With these," he said.

"You may have the legal authority, but you are lacking the tactical ability. How do you plan on getting to the compound?"

"My feet," replied Miguel, looking determined and unyielding.

"Assuming he is there," said Sherman.

"Cowards like him never go far. He's probably packing up his cash and gold and planning his escape."

"He's not flying out," said Sherman. "Not any time soon. The Nigerians would shoot him down."

"Then he's stuck," added Miguel with a smile.

"Can I offer a suggestion?" asked Sherman.

"Are you going to try to talk me out of it?"

"No," answered Sherman with no intention of trying to stop him.

"Go on," said Miguel.

"A couple areas of your plan could use some attention. Namely, transportation and entry into the compound."

"Both involve my legs," replied Miguel.

"Have you ever heard of a Trojan horse?"

The translation did not process, and Miguel shook his head.

"I'll save you the history lesson, but if you showed up in the Russian SUV, would this guy be more likely to let you in the compound?"

"I see," said Miguel.

"Sergeant Gournsey has the SUV a couple miles west of here. I'll arrange the logistics."

A wide smile crossed Miguel's face. "Thank you."

Sherman walked over to their dwindling stockpile of gear and handed Miguel the last pair of NVGs and a helmet. He still wore the tactical vest from earlier.

"Take this too," he added and gave Miguel a Glock 19 pistol.

"I have this," said Miguel, pointing to the Makarov.

"Only eight rounds," said Sherman. "This has fifteen."

"Will I need fifteen?" asked Miguel.

"I have no idea," answered Sherman. "But if you do and only have eight, you'll be in trouble."

"Wise," said Miguel and took the Glock.

"There's a fancy hotel by the beach, little huts and such, do you know it?"

"I do," said Miguel.

"You'll find Gournsey waiting there."

"And your walk here?" asked Miguel.

"Uneventful," said Sherman, leaving out the tawdry bits. "Stick to the trees and remember you can see them long before they see you."

"Right," replied Miguel and held up the goggles. "How do they work?"

Sherman gave a crash course on night vision use and they stepped outside.

"One last thing," said Sherman. "Help me lift Edward over the wall."

Miguel gave a solitary nod and the duo managed to lift Edward's body up one side and down the other without dropping him. Even if the dead didn't care, Sherman considered dropping a corpse poor form. They carried the body inside and Miguel donned the helmet and night vision.

"It's heavier than I thought," he announced.

"Much in life is heavier than we think," replied Sherman. "Good luck with the shark."

"Thank you, Captain."

"*Adios*, Lieutenant."

Miguel slipped over the wall, leaving Sherman alone with one corpse and one soon-to-be corpse. Out of habit more than hunger, Sherman found a granola bar and sat down to radio Gournsey about Miguel's plan.

Chapter Thirty-One

Miguel knew the sinewy path cutting through those great towering trees well. He'd wandered between their trunks as a boy, running from the beach into town. The thick limbs and rugged roots felt comforting back then, like a silent friend that never left. In the green glow of the night vision goggles, those trunks looked flat and lifeless—more endless barrier than safe harbor.

Even the noises vibrated differently—no trickles of laughter or the crackle of cooking fires, just the buzz of insects, the trill chirps of distant sires, and the occasional scream punctuating the night.

Uncertainty edged into Miguel's thoughts, an unwelcome visitor after so much ardent conviction in his actions. Was he doing the right thing? Tiburon was a traitor, an enemy of the island. Traitors deserved punishment. Wasn't that his job?

The fact that Miguel could not reasonably answer his own questions only heightened his doubts, but he plunged on because he couldn't think of any decent reason to stop.

He passed through the forest and those flickering shadows into the wide expanse of sand. Waves pummeled the beach, churning and turning ancient rocks. Miguel found the endless action an apt metaphor for colonialism—overpowering forces constantly pushing against cultures and people until they'd worn smooth and threatless.

Smooth and threatless described his father and grandfather. The endless pummeling of Spanish rule turned them into collaborators, grains of well-worn sand on a beach of millions of others equally ground down by the system.

What did that make him?

An offspring of collaborators. Perhaps his complacency was not so unexpected.

That changes now, he thought.

A new course needed charting, one that didn't end with thugs or dictators, but real change—not empty promises or internet-controlled mobs.

Palm-thatched huts emerged into the green gloom of his goggles. A brief flash of light caught his attention, followed by another and another. Miguel lifted the goggles to check but saw no visible light. The brightness came from an infrared strobe, as described by Captain Sherman, which meant Sergeant Gournsey was signaling him.

Miguel moved toward the light.

A cool sea breeze washed over his face, salty and refreshing in the early morning hour. Exhaustion rolled through his body and, for a moment, Miguel considered a hotel bed and glass of rum. He shook off the thought.

Sergeant Gournsey emerged from behind a palm tree and extended his massive hand in greeting. Miguel shook it and gave a thin smile.

"Good to see you again," said the sergeant. "The captain informed me of your plan."

Miguel nodded and spotted the SUV nearby. Corporal Lopez sat on the hood.

"Is he coming?" asked Miguel.

"The corporal offered to provide overwatch, if you accept," answered Gournsey.

Having seen Lopez shoot, Miguel didn't hesitate. "I accept," he said.

With a twirl of his wrist, Gournsey spun his pointer in a circle and Lopez climbed into the back seat of the Mercedes.

"Do you need anything?" asked Gournsey. "They've got some decent coffee and mostly stale pastries inside."

"I'm good," said Miguel.

"Best of luck, Lieutenant."

Miguel smiled again, "For the record, Sergeant, I never actually thought you were guilty."

"Good," said Gournsey. "That makes one of us." Then he strode off to the hotel door.

Miguel shook his head in disbelief and walked to the Mercedes. He opened the door and eased himself inside the plush interior smelling of leather and cheap cigarettes.

"Thanks for coming," he told Lopez.

The wiry American nodded but said nothing, his demeanor unphased and unshakable.

"What happens now?" asked Miguel.

"You drive," said Lopez. "Drop me off a half-mile before the compound. No need to stop, just slow way down."

"What about the Gendarme?" asked Miguel.

"They're running for their lives," said Lopez.

"Okay. And if I need your help when I get to the house?"

"I'll be nearby."

The response didn't comfort Miguel, but he hadn't expected company at all, so some help was infinitely better than none.

"The house isn't too far from here," he added.

"Then it's a short drive," replied Lopez.

Miguel couldn't argue with the logic, just the warning bells in his mind that screamed this was a bad idea.

"Okay," he huffed and gently stepped on the accelerator.

The drive was brief and dark. They moved without headlights, less than two miles with no traffic or signs of human habitation, empty roads and dark homes.

Just before a tall concrete wall, Miguel slowed to a crawl.

"This is the edge of his property," he said.

Lopez squeezed his shoulder and jumped out, hitting the ground in stride before disappearing into the trees surrounding the estate.

Tiburón lived in a large complex off the main road only a few houses past the American Ambassador's residence. He'd stolen the property by accusing another crony of corruption and setting the man up in a sting. A surreal incident of the pot calling the kettle black and then stealing the kettle. Without recourse in the courts, the wronged man signed over the deed to Tiburón and fled the country. At least that was the story told in the press. Not the seizure but the flight of a corrupt businessman. Miguel knew the truth and none of that got printed on paper.

The businessman did indeed flee but didn't get past the airport. When Miguel found his body, the only identifiable parts left had sunk to the ocean floor and the Chief of Police wouldn't risk their recovery. Thus, the case disappeared into the archives and Tiburón got a mansion for the cost of a few well-placed bribes and a bag of cement.

As Miguel turned down the long driveway, he spotted lights in the distance. The Major General had a generator and was unafraid of using it despite the risk of Nigerian bombs.

Two uniformed guards stood before a large metal gate at the end of the driveway. Miguel slowed and turned on his running lights. The men raised their rifles and moved to stop the oncoming SUV.

Miguel couldn't stick his head out for fear of ruining the ruse, so he took the opposite tack and honked the horn, playing into the impatient Russian stereotype.

The two guards exchanged a frustrated look of impotence and one of them pushed a button to open the gate.

Miguel could scarcely believe the subterfuge worked but knew slipping inside was better than shooting his way inside.

The gate swung open with a creak and a clang. He drove through as the guards struggled to peer through the SUV's heavy black tint.

Then the gate closed and he was inside the compound.

Beyond lay a level of opulence he'd scarcely imagined. The brazen displays of wealth sickened his stomach and bile caught in his throat.

Expensive cars lined the circular driveway. BMWs, Mercedes, and Ferraris to name a few.

Then came the house itself, a sleek, modern affair with an endless wall of windows revealing an interior oozing with luxury goods. Expensive furniture, large televisions, and massive artworks filled the place. Miguel's disbelief almost got the better of him and he pinched his thigh to snap out of the dream.

He parked facing the glass façade and waited for someone to approach, be it a guard or a butler.

No one came.

Inside, a flurry of activity unfolded as numerous people ran about packing suitcases with all manner of items, few of which were clothing.

The chaos brought a smile to his face.

Eduardo Tiburón deserved whatever strange justice befell him, but Miguel really hoped he'd see a public trial— the kind that shreds a man's credibility and leaves him penniless, begging for mercy and charity.

Visible in the windows, the great surly man paced and gestured. He didn't do any of the packing—that was beneath him—but he did direct the operation with a glass of amber liquid in his hand.

Two men in blue uniforms ran frantically from one room to another, stuffing all manner of valuables into the suitcases. A third, in a suit, helped the haphazard operation. None of them noticed Miguel or the SUV idling outside.

What now?

The Gendarme soldiers were armed, probably the suit and Tiburón too. He needed to split up the operation.

Miguel blasted the horn.

Four heads swirled to attention and Tiburón mouthed several expletives in Spanish. He motioned for one of the soldiers to go and investigate. The burly man huffed with indignation but headed through the front door and towards the Mercedes.

Miguel held the Makarov with his right hand and the door handle with his left.

All or nothing, he thought as the soldier approached the driver side door.

The man rapped his knuckles on the deeply tinted window, which didn't roll down because of the heavy bullet-resistant glass.

Miguel opened the door and the soldier leaned forward to retrieve whatever message the Russians deemed worthy of giving Tiburón.

He found the Makarov's barrel instead.

All or nothing, Miguel repeated, and pulled the trigger. A loud crack thundered in the confined space and Miguel tasted gunpowder.

The soldier staggered back in surprise, glanced down at his chest as if examining a stain, and then collapsed to the ground.

Almost imperceptible amid the ringing in his ears, Miguel heard two successive thuds in the distance—muted sounds that the brain might dismiss as natural phenomena, but which he registered as Lopez firing on the front gate guards.

Inside the house, the reaction was anything but muted. Tiburón gestured wildly toward the fallen soldier. His comrade drew his service pistol and fired at Miguel.

The glass façade of the house shattered and cascaded to the ground. Instinctively, Miguel ducked behind the dashboard, but the windscreen easily absorbed the small-caliber rounds.

Armored, he thought, and closed the driver's door.

Miguel sat up straight and shifted into drive.

The soldier kept firing, panicked by the bullet-resistant glass.

Miguel mashed the accelerator, sending the Mercedes careening into the house.

Tiburón and the suit jumped clear at the first sign of

trouble. The soldier did not. He kept shooting as if the act would change the outcome. It did not.

The Mercedes hit the soldier dead center and kept going, driving through a partition wall and into a kitchen table. He did not survive the encounter.

Stunned by the deceleration and a head knock to the steering wheel, Miguel stared at the shattered body on the hood.

It worked, he thought, almost bewildered.

His moment of triumph ended with another cavalcade of bullets that cratered into the rear window. Miguel shifted into reverse and jammed the accelerator, but the SUV didn't move. The wheels spun, the engine squealed, but Miguel stayed in one place.

"Shit," he muttered as the suit fired another magazine into the rear window.

Panic spread through Miguel's mind. The armor protected him for the moment, but it would quickly turn into a tomb if he couldn't move.

As soon as the impact of the predicament sunk in, the suit's head popped like an overripe watermelon dropped on the floor. All the recognized bits just fragmented in a cloud of pink and red.

"Shit," he muttered again.

Even Tiburón stood there transfixed by the sudden re-configuration of his assistant's facial features.

Miguel seized the moment and stepped out of the SUV. He advanced on Tiburón with the pistol in one hand and his badge in the other.

"Eduardo Tiburón, you are under arrest for treason," shouted Miguel.

The Major General watched him approaching with utter indifference as if Miguel was transparent.

"Who the hell are you?" asked Tiburón, puffing out his chest.

"Lieutenant Miguel Ondo."

Tiburón looked blankly back at Miguel. "Who cares?" he growled.

Miguel pointed at the faceless man on the floor.

"He did."

Tiburón set down his glass and pointed to the bags. "You can pick one," he said. "Take it, get the hell out of here, and I'll forgive what you've done to my house."

Bags brimming with cash lay on the floor. Most had American dollars but there were Euros and British pounds as well.

"I'm not here for the money," Miguel replied, although the offer did tempt him.

"Everyone comes here for the money," retorted Tiburón. "Don't think you're any different."

"I came here because you're working for the Russians and none of you care about this island."

"Ah, an idealist."

"A patriot," said Miguel.

Tiburón scoffed at the word. "There are no patriots because we have no country. An island ruled by fiat from afar is no country. Can't you see that?"

"What I've seen is bloodshed and death because of your greed. You helped start this coup and then played both sides. You're not even loyal to your own cause."

Tiburón shrugged and sat down on a leather couch. "Not everyone can see so clearly in black and white. Most of us see many shades of gray."

Keeping the pistol aimed squarely at the Major General's chest, Miguel moved towards a table piled high with files and documents. His professional curiosity piqued at the sight of legal folders and Polaroid pictures.

Most of what he saw was blackmail material. Politicians doing things no normal human could get away with or even do in the first place. A moral rot in the center of Malabo.

"Now you see," added Tiburón. "I'm not alone in my actions."

"Questionable actions," Miguel retorted.

"No one is clean."

Miguel couldn't argue with that point. No one escaped the overwhelming grind of poverty without a few skeletons in the closet—not even himself.

Towards the bottom of the stack, a picture caught his eye. A recent memory surfaced. Cheap brown tiles and faded paintings on the wall and a dead body on the floor. He knew the crime scene.

Miguel held up the photo with indignation.

"You did this!" he exclaimed.

Tiburón squinted at the photo. "Not me. We did."

"You murdered an innocent woman."

Tiburón flashed a toothy smile. "Innocent is a stretch. The things she did for a hundred dollars…"

An angry fuse blew in Miguel's mind. Rage rose through his body like a rising tide.

"You got the wrong guy," he said.

"What?"

"You arrested the wrong American."

Tiburón finished his drink. "You know a lot for a cop."

"This might surprise you, but I also know the guy you set up to take the fall."

"What?" asked Tiburón.

Miguel wrote on a piece of paper and held it facing towards the front door.

"What are you doing?" asked Tiburón.

The message read: GET GOURNSEY.

"You'll find out soon enough," replied Miguel and poured himself a large glass of expensive rum.

Chapter Thirty-Two

Sergeant Raylan Gournsey walked down the long driveway some forty minutes later. His watch read 0430 hours—ninety minutes until dawn and the Marine's arrival. Night's embrace still clung to the island and the temperature dipped low enough that he wasn't instantly sweating.

At the end of the driveway, splayed out before a large metal gate, lay two Gendarme soldiers. Insects had already descended upon the corpses and Gournsey walked past without another glance. He continued past an assortment of luxury cars and up to what remained of the house's front façade.

Great seas of broken glass covered the interior and exterior. The Mercedes SUV, which Gournsey quite liked, was stuck inside just beyond the living room.

Miguel waved him inside. Next to the cop was a surly man with fancy clothes and flashing white teeth.

"I'm here," said Gournsey, still curious over the unexpected summons.

Miguel waved his pistol at the man.

"This is Major General Tiburón of the Gendarme."

"*Hola*," said Gournsey.

Tiburón gave a fleeting glance in reply and did not look happy to see the burly American.

"I have something to show you," continued Miguel. "It's over there on the table."

Gournsey stepped over and gazed at the Polaroid picture. He knew the location well and the subjects. To the left of the dead woman, he could just make out his naked frame. Pangs of sorrow and remorse caught him by surprise. The woman's death had fallen from his memory with all the recent chaos, but his heart had not forgotten.

"Why does he have this?" asked Gournsey.

"He organized it," said Miguel.

Gournsey moved across the room and took a seat next to Tiburón. Close enough to make the man visibly uncomfortable.

"*This was your doing?*" he asked in Spanish.

"*Not me, but we,*" replied Tiburón.

Gournsey turned to Miguel. "He said 'we', right?"

"He did."

"*Who else?*" asked Gournsey.

"*Many others,*" answered Tiburón.

Gournsey nodded. "*Who else in this room?*"

Tiburón glanced around nervously but said nothing.

"That's what I thought," said Gournsey.

He stood up, walked over to the SUV, and opened what remained of the rear door. He fished around for a moment and returned with a set of jumper cables.

Tiburón sank deeper into his seat, trying to altogether disappear.

"I'm not going to use them," said Gournsey as he slung them over an exposed overhead beam running across the room. He finished tying up the cable into a makeshift loop that hung over the dining room table. "You are."

Tiburón mutely shook his head.

"She was strangled, right?" Gournsey asked Miguel.

The lieutenant nodded. "With a steel wire."

"So, the punishment fits the crime."

Miguel nodded again.

"Would you mind translating this?" asked Gournsey. "I'll never get everything right."

"I guess," said Miguel.

Gournsey turned to Tiburón and spoke while Miguel translated.

"Where I come from is a bit old-fashioned. Folks like Bible quotes and use simple language. We look after our neighbors, go to church on Sunday, and try to forgive those poor souls who fall from grace. Occasionally, things get heated and punches fly. It happens with hardworking folk when there is not enough to go around. But you know what we don't tolerate? Hurting those who ain't done no hurting themselves."

Gournsey stopped and Miguel caught up with his translation. Tiburón squirmed in his seat.

"In the spirit of Kentucky justice, I'm giving you a choice. You can take the easy way out and use those wires over there, or I can slowly cut you to pieces."

Most people would have needed proof of Gournsey's ultimatum, but Tiburón did not. Proof surrounded him. It was splattered on the walls and floors.

He took the easy way out.

Climbing up on the table, Tiburón gave one last look of indignation and stepped off with the jumper cables around his neck.

For a moment, he hung there writhing in pain, kicking

his legs, unable to breathe. Then the knot came undone and Tiburón crashed to the floor with a hefty thump.

Gournsey watched the affair with disinterest. He hadn't expected the cable to hold Tiburón's weight, not even for a moment. He turned to Miguel, who did appear surprised.

"Now you can arrest him," said Gournsey.

Miguel did a quick double-take and then, as if realizing the true depth of Gournsey's malice, smiled.

"Eduardo Tiburón, you are under arrest for treason and murder."

Tiburón spluttered on the floor, trying to catch his breath, red with humiliation.

"You can bring him to the hotel for safekeeping," Gournsey offered.

"I'll wait 'til dawn and drive him in," said Miguel, pointing to the numerous cars in the driveway.

Gournsey glanced over the table of blackmail and added, "Suit yourself."

He turned to leave but stopped. A small file had snagged his attention but he couldn't say why. The papers crinkled at the edges and had yellowed with time. Gournsey picked up the contents and flipped through the pages. The hairs on his neck stood on end.

"Shit," he muttered.

"What is it?" asked Miguel.

"This is the file for the annex across the street from the embassy. It even has the blueprints for the tunnel."

"Captain Sherman is still there," said Miguel.

Gournsey whirled on Tiburón like a darkening storm ready to split open.

"Do the Russians know?" he demanded.

Miguel translated.

A tiny smirk creased the corner of Tiburón's mouth.

The slight was all it took for Gournsey to snap the man's collarbone like a twig.

No longer smirking but shrieking, Tiburón nodded.

"They wanted everything I had," he moaned.

Gournsey keyed his radio. "Echo One, Echo Two. How copy? Over."

Nothing.

Gournsey reached for the button again when his earpiece buzzed to life.

"Echo Two, Echo One. You ruined my nap. Over."

"Echo One, the Russians know about the annex. Over."

"Echo Two, so they do. Out."

"I'm gonna need those keys, now!" Gournsey yelled.

Miguel tossed him a fob with the BMW logo. Gournsey clicked the unlock button and ran toward the flashing lights, hoping he wasn't too late.

Chapter Thirty-Three

Even with the trees blocking most of his view, Sherman sensed movement outside the front gate. A faint flicker of green dancing between the otherwise still leaves.

So much for a nap, he thought.

He left Jim's room and the barely breathing man, heading downstairs towards the last of their supplies. Sherman didn't like last stands as they lacked imagination. Hopeless situations were only hopeless if you couldn't come up with another option and, in Sherman's mind, another option always existed.

What supplies remained in the dining room consisted mostly of pistol ammunition, glow sticks, and snack food. After some digging, Sherman found two claymore mines and a detonator. He grabbed them and another granola bar. If he was going to die, it wouldn't be hungry.

The claymore, like most shaped explosives, channeled the blast outward. Combined with some steel balls, you had a very deadly shotgun effect.

Sherman placed one mine between two boxes near the

front door and pulled the wire up the stairs. He repeated the process again, this time, pointing a mine toward the back door. Sherman hid that claymore in a pile of books.

The wide-open dining room rose up two stories in height. The stairs connected to one side of the room. Looking down upon this space was the walkway leading to the bedrooms. He angled a mirror in the dining room so he could see part of the front door from the second story, which also had a direct line of sight to the back door. Both entrances, one hiding spot.

He connected the wires to the detonator and unwrapped the granola bar for the wait.

His watch read 0445 hours. Less than two hours until the Marines landed.

Sherman keyed his radio but found only static.

Clever, he thought. *Jammed by the Russians*.

Given the body count thus far, Sherman reasoned there couldn't be too many attackers left. Getting more than a dozen operators in country without raising alarms was difficult. A handful—at best—remained.

Sherman was right, but also very wrong.

When the front door burst open in a spray of splinters, at least six bodies surging forward could be seen in the sliver of mirror. Most wore Gendarme uniforms, one did not.

Sherman hit the detonator.

Concussive force shook the house and a great boom echoed around like a pinball careening between the walls.

The back door shattered apart moments later as more men in blue burst into the fray. Only, they were no longer confident and swaggering but confused by the sudden chaos into which they emerged.

Sherman hit the second switch and, once again, the house shook.

Men screamed as metal tore through flesh.

Then a strange silence descended and Sherman heard only the explosion ringing in his ears. Darkness returned, and in the fuzzy green of his goggles, Sherman saw the truly grisly aftermath of his actions. But the burden and weight of that outcome did not rest solely on his shoulders. War cannot be blamed on a single individual and Sherman did not feel remorse for his actions. His was a world of death, kill or be killed, and he held no shame for playing to win.

For five long minutes, Sherman didn't move even as those still breathing stopped doing so. Patience was an art honed by years of practice. His instinct said wait, so he waited.

Soon enough, he heard the faintest thump of boots on a hard surface. A lone figure or two moving carefully inside with quiet diligent steps. The mirror had fallen over in the blasts and Sherman could no longer see the front door.

He heard the intruders sweep through the bottom floor with methodical precision. Sherman tracked their movements in his mind—each room, each angle, until they moved towards the stairs next to the dining room. It was the only way up to the second story, a set of exposed steps that he alone controlled. Of course, anyone with plans to the house knew such information, which meant the Russians knew the layout.

Sherman tensed at the thought.

Before he could move, the floor beneath him shattered with bullets fired from below. Splinters and bits of carpet filled the thrumming air around him.

Sherman retreated into Jim's room as the firing stopped. The clack and clank of reloads reached his ears. Sherman pulled out a flashbang and waited. The lights remained off and he didn't see any flashlight beams, so he knew they had night vision too.

The attackers also had patience. They didn't wantonly push out into the open.

Sherman heard their muffled steps and breathy whispers.

Timing in such moments was the hill on which you lived or died. As with patience, timing was an art not a science. A thing learned as well as intuited.

Sherman pulled the pin on the flashbang and scooted gingerly forward to the railing.

Ever so carefully, he extended his hand between the railing's wooden balusters. He let go and turned away, closing his eyes tight.

A blinding flash seared the room in white-hot light.

Sherman bounded down the stairs until he saw two men stumbling into the boxes and stacked chairs. Their hands frantically rubbed their eyes, hoping to regain some semblance of vision.

One of the men shot wildly upward towards the stairs but missed Sherman by a dozen feet.

Sherman didn't miss.

He hit the Russian three times just above the vest at the base of his neck, instantly killing the man.

The second attacker, sensing the danger, dove for hard cover but found only a stack of file boxes.

Sherman fired what remained of his magazine through the boxes, hitting the target as well as fifty years of government records.

After a quick reload, Sherman edged around to get an angle on the second attacker still concealed behind the boxes. Sherman knew he'd hit flesh. Blood splattered on the floor said as much, but an injured threat was not a neutralized threat and Sherman wanted certainty.

What finally came into view wasn't much of a person anymore, but a leaking corpse.

Sherman walked through the wreckage nudging bodies with the toe of his boot, seeing if anyone might have survived. A few of the Gendarme soldiers showed signs of life and Sherman kicked away any weapons within reach.

Gournsey's voice crackled over the radio, "Echo One, Echo Two. Where do you want me? Over."

"Echo Two, all clear. Come on in. Out."

Gournsey arrived a minute later through what remained of the front door, which wasn't much. He stopped short of the carnage and gingerly stepped over the dead.

"I'm guessing they didn't knock," he said.

"No, they came in hard. Thanks for the warning."

"Any time," said Gournsey.

"How'd you know?" asked Sherman.

"That guy Miguel arrested... he worked for the Russians and had an old file with blueprints and everything. After some convincing, he admitted giving it to them."

"Lucky me," said Sherman.

"Unlucky them," added Gournsey.

"All of the above," added Sherman.

"Guess what else Miguel found?"

Sherman shrugged, unable to imagine anything else unfolding.

"That guy, Tiburón, was the one who set me up and killed the woman I was with."

"Did you repay the favor?" asked Sherman.

"Not directly," said Gournsey with a grin. "But I may have messed with his mind a bit. Oh, and I broke his collarbone."

In Sherman's mind, the sergeant had shown restraint. Under other circumstances, the Major General would have ended up in some bushes with a hole in his head.

"Mighty generous of you," said Sherman.

"I get the sense that Miguel won't let him walk away from this."

"That was my impression as well," said Sherman.

"I can stay with Jim," Gournsey offered.

"No, I'll stay. Go back to the hotel and prep everyone for our exit."

Gournsey looked at his watch. "Wheels down in sixty minutes."

"I don't think anyone else is coming through those doors in the meantime."

"They'd be crazy to try," said Gournsey.

"Let's hope so, but it's been a crazy night."

"One for the books."

"And nothing changes," said Sherman.

Gournsey tilted his head in thought. "All this chaos lit a fire in Miguel. Maybe others like him can make something new."

Sherman appreciated the sergeant's optimism. "Fingers crossed."

"Are you sure you don't want to switch?" asked Gournsey.

"If Jim is going to die, it'll be on my watch."

"Alright, see you soon," said Gournsey and disappeared into the night.

Sherman placed the mirror back into position and resumed his watch at the top of the stairs. Time slid past. Outside, the edges of night blurred and the birds sang to the coming morning.

Chapter Thirty-Four

Sunrise arrived in a fiery hurry of heat and illumination. Sherman set down his night vision as the light revealed a gory scene in vivid color.

Too damn vivid, he thought.

Punctual as ever, the sound of Marine vehicles rumbled in the distance. Sherman stood and stretched, cracking his back and knees.

Jim lay still in the corner of the room. Hesitantly, Sherman leaned close to check if he was still breathing. Amazingly, his chest rose and fell.

"You're a tough bastard," Sherman said.

"Captain Sherman?" came a gruff voice from down below.

"Up here," he replied.

A thick, tan soldier emerged into view. He was in his early forties with blue eyes and a crooked nose broken many times over.

"Captain, I'm Colonel Abbot. Sorry for the delay."

Sherman gave a nod of appreciation as other Marines

swarmed into the house. Splattered with mud and blood, bandages and stitches, he was a sight to behold. Some of the younger Marines gawked when they saw him and the scene inside the house—not the colonel, though.

"What do I need to know?" asked Abbot.

"One critical upstairs, one KIA over there," said Sherman and pointed to Edward's body.

"And them?" asked Abbot, sweeping his arm towards the dead Gendarme and Russians.

"Not ours," said Sherman.

The colonel nodded and barked orders to his men. A man in disheveled fatigues and a stethoscope around his neck ascended the stairs and attended to Jim. He spent a few minutes in quiet concentration examining the injured man as a medic hovered nearby.

"Start an IV and push as much blood as we have," he ordered and turned to Sherman. "Did you stitch him up?"

"No, an ex-Air Force nurse."

"They should go back to nursing. That's the finest work I've seen in the field in decades. No doubt saved his life."

"Make sure you tell her that," said Sherman.

"I will," said the doctor and gave Sherman a long glance. "And how are you?"

"I can wait until we're airborne," said Sherman.

The doctor gave him an incredulous look but returned to Jim's side.

Ten minutes later, everyone and everything of value was loaded into the Marine vehicles. Sherman slid into the back seat behind Abbot and gave a silent nod of gratitude to the embassy and annex, glad to still be alive.

"Care to tell me what happened here, Captain?" asked Abbot. "My boys tell there's a bunch of dead soldiers laid out like a cord of wood in the embassy parking lot."

"Started as a coup," answered Sherman. "Ended in greed."

"Which is another way of saying greed through and through," added Abbot.

"Yes, sir," said Sherman.

"Ain't no sirs here," said Abbot. "You ever need another ride out, just call. We'll come even if the whole damn Nigerian Air Force is in the air."

"I appreciate the offer, Colonel. I may take you up on it one day."

"I look forward to it," said Abbot, and Sherman could see the man meant every word.

On the drive to the hotel, the night's chaos emerged. Gendarme trucks smoldered near abandoned roadblocks and giant craters replaced sections of pavement. The Nigerian assault was far wider spread than Sherman realized. Smoke blew across the island like cottonwood in early summer, drifting and accumulating as it went.

As ordered, Gournsey had everyone ready to go when the Marines arrived. Sherman stepped out and hugged first Gournsey then Lopez.

"Did Jim make it?" asked Evelyn, her voice small and straining to retain hope.

"The doctor said you saved his life," answered Sherman.

Evelyn smiled and blinked back tears. "Thanks for all you did."

Sherman pointed to his bandaged side. "No, thank you."

Two medics passed carrying Charlotte, who was hooked up to an IV.

"Frank," she said and motioned him over.

Sherman walked with them to the back of a repurposed Humvee.

"It's good to see you," said Charlotte with a loopy smile. "We should do this more often."

"That's the morphine talking."

"Maybe," she said and winked.

"I'll see you on the plane," added Sherman and headed back to Abbot's vehicle.

"We ready?" asked the colonel.

"As ever," said Sherman.

The convoy moved away from the hotel and towards the airport at speed, not stopping for anything or anyone. The vehicles drove directly into the KC-130 cargo planes waiting on the still intact tarmac.

"How long is our window on the ground?" asked Sherman.

"Before the Nigerians arrive?" replied Abbot.

"Yeah."

"We've got twenty minutes left before their troops land here."

"Best not waste any time," said Sherman.

"Best not," Abbot agreed and started barking orders again.

The turboprop engines powered up in a tremendous growl and Sherman sat down next to Gournsey and Lopez. At the other end, Edward's body lay in a black plastic bag— a morbid reminder of the last twenty-four hours.

Abbot appeared briefly before takeoff and shouted to a nearby Marine.

"Corporal, what are you waiting for? Get these men a beer."

The Marine obliged and handed out cold cans from a cooler. Sherman took a long swig as the plane lifted off into the thick morning air. Great pillars of black smoke rose above downtown. He watched the island recede through the small circular window and felt a deep sense of remorse.

"You think they'll ever just be?" he asked Gournsey.

"One can hope."

Two weeks later, Sherman was enjoying another cold beer in vastly different circumstances. He sat on a lounge chair under the shade of an umbrella overlooking a rocky beach in Massachusetts.

"This isn't the beach I had in mind," said Charlotte.

"Have you seen my salary?" joked Sherman. "Besides, you can't even get in the water."

Charlotte lowered her sunglasses and looked at the cast around her leg. "That doesn't mean I can't enjoy the sand."

"What's a beach without water?" asked Sherman.

"It's a start," said Charlotte. "What's next for you?"

"Medical leave for a few weeks," said Sherman.

"Nothing is wrong with you."

"I got shot," he said.

"Fine. Where are you going?"

"Visiting a friend out west."

"You don't have any friends," she said and gave him a coy smile.

"Not many," said Sherman and then changed the subject. "Any news from Malabo?"

"Do you want the bad news or the bad news?"

Sherman opened another beer and said, "The bad news."

"The Nigerian army controls the streets and President Mbasogo installed his son as the governor of the island to keep a close eye on things."

"Sounds like marshal law."

"There's been a significant crackdown on dissent."

"Any word on Miguel?" asked Sherman.

"I had a local asset check out the Major General's house to see if Miguel was still there. No sign of him, but I've heard rumors of someone stirring up trouble in the country-side. They say he's well-financed with bags of foreign currency. You wouldn't happen to know anything about that?"

Sherman smiled and shook his head. "Nope. No idea."

Next in the Frank Sherman Thrillers series

vinci-books.com/franksherman7

A letter from the past. A town steeped in secrets.

A battle for survival.

When Frank Sherman arrives in Hilt Bay to investigate a
mysterious letter from his father's old Marine Corps spotter, he
finds a town shrouded in secrets. As a storm brews and isolates the
town, Sherman's friend suddenly disappears. Uncovering clues
that link the disappearance to a deadly grudge from the past,
Sherman realizes that the town's secrets threaten everyone's safety.

Turn the page for a free preview...

A Long Violent History: Chapter One

Mali, West Africa

The envelope arrived on Captain Frank Sherman's bunk late in the afternoon when the heat pushed everyone inside. A staff sergeant dropped it off with little fanfare, as if getting mail in the badlands of Mali was an ordinary occurrence. Perhaps that was true for most soldiers, but Sherman had no family besides his mother, and she couldn't recall the year let alone write to her son.

Sherman picked up the envelope and turned the rectangle over in his calloused hands. A half-dozen markings decorated the weathered paper—forwarding stamps from one army base to another as the letter followed Sherman around the world.

The original address read Camp Lejeune, where Sherman lived as a teenager decades earlier, back when they followed his father from posting to posting.

He squinted at the return address, which had no street number—Hilt Bay, Oregon.

Where the hell is that? he wondered.

Sherman sat down on the army-issued cot, which was more home than he'd ever known, and slowly opened the envelope.

He removed a single sheet of stiff notecard stock and unfolded the letter. The handwriting slanted across the page in all caps. What began with clean and precise letters took on a hurried edge as if the writer ran out of time.

FRANKY, it began.

No one called Sherman that—at least not in recent memory. Not his mother or teachers, and certainly not anyone in his unit. He hadn't heard the name since childhood, so many years before.

The letter continued:

I'VE BEEN MEANING TO WRITE THIS LETTER SINCE YOUR FATHER DIED, BUT I WAS NEVER MUCH FOR WORDS. THEN AGAIN, NEITHER WAS YOUR FATHER. TWO BRUTES WE WERE. ANYWAY, I'M GETTING OLD, AND THE OLDER I GET, THE MORE I DWELL IN THE PAST, AND THE MORE I DWELL IN THE PAST, THE MORE I... WELL, I'M NOT SURE WHAT. I DO KNOW I NEED TO SPEAK WITH YOU IN PERSON BECAUSE THEY'RE ALWAYS LISTENING. IT'S ABOUT A 'YOU KNOW WHAT' WITH YOUR FATHER.
BEST,
UNCLE HAL

Stunned by the sudden echo of the past, Sherman placed the letter down on his bunk and leaned back against the plywood wall. The air-conditioner crudely attached to the wall buzzed with concerted effort. Voices carried down the hall.

Uncle Hal was Sergeant Hal Cooper, his father's old Marine Corps spotter. A man he hadn't seen since they put his dad in the ground ten years earlier. Sherman recalled a brief handshake and some platitudes, but little else of the exchange at the funeral.

As a child, Sherman hadn't known much about Uncle Hal. The man appeared at family barbeques and drank longnecks with his dad late into the night, but he wasn't a fixture in Sherman's life. He remembered a thin, ramrod straight man with sinewy muscles and thick hands. His brown eyes were so dark, they edged towards black. Scary as most strange adults can seem to small children, but Hal was not unkind. He played catch with Sherman on the front lawn, which was more than his father did.

No one talked openly about what Hal and his father did. They never mentioned specifics. Their missions were, for the most part, state secrets. Sherman only heard scraps here and there. A few boasts by Uncle Hal about how his father was the best sniper, but he'd never be in a record book. *Ten-thousand five-hundred and sixty feet* they'd murmur in hushed voices after one too many beers.

As a child, Sherman didn't understand what that meant. Now, as a Special Forces captain, he knew exactly what Uncle Hal meant about unwritten records. Some stories could not be told, not by anyone, and secrets they would remain.

This thought brought his attention to the last few lines, where the writing started to tilt and lunge across the page. After all those years, what could Uncle Hal possibly have to share about 'you know what', which Sherman assumed meant missions.

He couldn't imagine Uncle Hal breaking his code of silence to tell old ghost stories from Vietnam or the Cold War. The world was a different place back then.

Why bother dredging up the past now?

Even with his security clearance, Sherman wasn't sure he wanted to know about the carnage Hal and his father wrought.

"Captain, a word," said a gravelly voice.

Sherman looked up to find Major Sanders, his commanding officer, hulking in the doorway.

"We just received word that the U.S. Army is *persona non grata* in Mali. Command ordered us to pack up and torch the place on our way out. We don't want to leave anything for the Russians or Chinese."

Sherman glanced around his plywood room and army-issued cot. The base wasn't much to look at, but the CIA had spent millions of tax dollars building a counterterrorism launchpad in the Sahel. Losing the base would set back security in the region for decades to come.

"How long do we have?" asked Sherman.

"Twenty-four hours," answered Sanders. "After that, we're headed stateside. Your men are free for the next two weeks or so until we get our next rotation sorted out."

"Understood, sir."

"Take the essentials, burn the rest," said Sanders.

Sherman nodded and picked up the letter. "Major, one more thing. Have you ever heard of Hilt Bay, Oregon?"

Sanders stopped his exit and stepped into the room. Sherman handed him the letter and the major cast his eyes across the page. He was a decade older than Sherman and much too young to overlap with Uncle Hal, but Sanders was a wise and connected man with many sources inside and outside the government.

The major looked up from the letter and asked, "Who is Uncle Hal?"

"My father's spotter," said Sherman. He didn't need to relate his father's past glory as a sniper. The legend was still alive and well.

Sanders nodded. "Some stories are best left buried."

"Like my father," agreed Sherman. "Do you know the place?"

Sanders handed back the letter. "Not personally, but it's the kind of place you go when you don't want to be found."

Sherman glanced down at the paper. He wanted clarification, but Sanders had already left. Placing the letter in his bag, he focused on the task at hand. But no matter how much he packed away, a question nagged in the back of his mind, stuck like an acacia thorn.

What will I find in Hilt Bay?

A Long Violent History: Chapter Two

Portland, Oregon

Terrance Wilder hated airports—the traffic, noise, crowds, and, perhaps most importantly, the cameras. They clung to every wall and protruded from every pole, constantly surveilling everyone coming and going. No privacy or anonymity. A perfectly constructed police state rammed down travelers' throats for no reason—at least none he could fathom. Terrorists weren't blowing up planes anymore. No one really needed to take off their shoes. The litany of conspiracies orchestrated by the U.S. Government could fill a book... if Terrance ever got around to writing one. Maybe two volumes with the state of the broken world.

Bah, he thought as he watched people pass his parked car. *You're all sheep walking to the slaughter*.

He'd parked in the passenger pick-up lane of Portland Airport not five minutes before, and the local traffic cop was already giving him the evil glare of authority. Terrance always got the same glare wherever he went as if cops shared photos of those needing intimidation.

Terrance wanted to stare back and give that entitled ass a piece of his mind, but instead, he pulled his hat down and looked away. His was not a joyride. He wasn't picking up family or friends who would understand his animosity to authority.

This pick-up came at the behest of his father, Tom Wilder, during their weekly chat through the plexiglass at Oregon State Penitentiary. Tom caught a bad case of racketeering and was three years in on a ten-year stint. None of the inconveniences of incarceration had stopped Tom from overseeing the family business, but the execution fell to Terrance, and he did not want to disappoint his father. Rage was a family pastime.

The cop's glare burrowed through Terrance's hat, and he felt that all-familiar surge of anger. He was about to circle around to cool off when someone knocked hard on the passenger window.

A rather plain-looking man stood on the other side of the glass. Terrance rolled it down.

"Are you Mr. Wilder?" asked the man.

A wide-brimmed hat that looked almost quaint shaded his face and Terrance couldn't make out his features.

"Who's asking?" Terrance blurted out, forgetting where he was for a moment.

"You're my ride," replied the man. He spoke slowly and evenly, like a schoolteacher explaining the properties of a rectangle to a dense student.

Terrance hated school for his entire life. Book learning never clicked in the way other kids took to it. The only math he excelled at was counting cash.

"Well, then, don't dawdle. Get on in."

The man opened the back door and slid inside, pushing a wave of detritus off the seat. Terrance hadn't cleaned the backseat because he was no taxi and friends sat in the front.

"You can sit up here," said Terrance.

"This is fine," replied the man in his measured tone.

Terrance took an instant dislike to the stranger in his backseat.

"Well… what should I call you?" he asked.

"You can refer to me as Stanton," said the man, who still wore the wide-brimmed hat.

Terrance glanced in the rearview mirror and thought the man a priest or undertaker all dressed in black with that damn Quaker hat.

"Stanton," he muttered to himself. Even the name came out stodgy.

Merging into traffic, Terrance headed back towards home—the only place he felt himself, but even that small joy cooled under the stranger's shadow.

Only when they were well out of Portland and on the coastal highway heading south did Stanton remove his hat. A long glance in the mirror found an early-forties man with hard angular cheeks and blue eyes so pale they seemed to wash away with the overcast light. Where Terrance had an unruly mane of black hair under his baseball cap, Stanton kept his speckled gray hair cropped close.

"It's not polite to stare," said Stanton.

Terrance almost swerved trying to shift his gaze away from the mirror and onto the road. The sudden influx of conversation and the edge to those words sent his pulse rising. He felt like a middle schooler caught daydreaming in class.

"Sorry," he muttered.

"How old are you, Mr. Wilder?"

Terrance hazarded a glance back at those blue eyes. "Twenty-two," he replied.

"Your father assured me you could handle all the details of my visit."

Terrance didn't appreciate the snide remarks about his competence or his age, but his usual rage did not rise, quelled by the quietly imposing figure in the back.

"I can handle anything. I've been handling all the family business for the last three years since Dad got sent to—"

Stanton cut him off. "That's good to know, Mr. Wilder."

"Call me Terrance or Terry. Everyone does. Mr. Wilder is my dad."

Stanton rolled the name around his tongue as if searching for a bad taste. "I prefer to keep things formal, Mr. Wilder," he replied.

Terrance frowned. "Suit yourself, Stanton," he said, drawing out the stranger's name.

They drove south in uneasy silence for another hour as the clouds overhead thickened into a dark gray collage of thunderheads. Wind tore across the road and the air smelled of salt.

Terrance cast another glance at the backseat as they exited the highway where the road cut inland to avoid the undeniable geographic difficulties of the coastline.

The road home crept west through a smattering of roadside businesses that Terrance never visited and homes of families that he considered townies because they were not facing the sea. Finally, they came to a three-way stop and a green roadside sign announcing the possible destinations.

To the left and backward, the sign informed drivers of ways back to the highway. A loop of sorts that skirted sections of the coast, passing through thick strands of ever-greens that only hinted at the churning sea beyond.

Straight ahead was closed according to an orange rectangle affixed to the green sign. Once a temporary affair from a spate of construction, locals had welded the addition years before, and the black letters had faded with time and brine. To further the point, a yellow diamond declared *NO OUTLET.*

Terrance eased the car forward on the narrow strip of asphalt that disappeared into a bank of fog. They rose up a hill into the swirling mass of white. A sense of safety washed over him.

"Welcome to Hilt Bay," Terrance said with a little snig-ger, hoping to see Stanton's expression change.

The stranger's face remained stoically blank.

Grab your copy...
vinci-books.com/franksherman7